Praise for *Maya's L...*

"A charming, funny, and unique twist on challenging the laws and traditions that shape us."
  —Abby Jimenez, *New York Times* bestselling author of *Yours Truly*

"Just as sweet as the romance that blossoms between Maya and Sarfaraz is the satisfaction of watching Maya learn to prioritize her own desires. Figuring out what she really wants in life is tricky enough; throw in familial expectations, a possible curse, and the right man at the wrong time, and you've got a delicious recipe for an engaging, relatable, and rewarding read."
  —Sarah Hogle, author of *You Deserve Each Other*

"Fans of the romantic slow burn will fall for *Maya's Laws of Love*. The international setting provides the perfect backdrop for an emotional plot worthy of a K-drama, and readers will cheer Maya on through her many adventures (and misadventures!)."
  —Lily Chu, author of *The Comeback*

"*Maya's Laws of Love* is the perfect enemies-to-lovers read, with a dreamy cinnamon roll hero at the center. Loved this!"
  —Erin La Rosa, author of *Plot Twist*

"Funny, vulnerable, and heartwarming. A beautiful story for the people who are still figuring life out."
  —Hannah Grace, *New York Times* bestselling author of *Wildfire*

"*Maya's Laws of Love* is a whirlwind debut you won't want to miss. Khawaja marvelously crafts a hilarious, sweet romance with nuanced, fleshed-out characters and excellent tension. A true joy, this is the type of comfort book you read again and again."
  —Aamna Qureshi, award-winning author of *The Lady or the Lion*

"Khawaja understands yearning well as this couple navigates attraction and tension through their delightful journey. Her story reminds us that we must get out of our own way to make our own luck." —Charish Reid, author of *Mickey Chambers Shakes It Up*

MAYA'S
LAWS
OF *Love*

ALINA KHAWAJA

mira

mira™

Recycling programs
for this product may
not exist in your area.

ISBN-13: 978-0-7783-0524-8

Maya's Laws of Love

Mira
22 Adelaide St. West, 41st Floor
Toronto, Ontario M5H 4E3, Canada
BookClubbish.com

Printed in U.S.A.

To my parents, for always supporting my dreams,
and for never telling me to stop buying books, even when
I had to resort to stacking them on top of each other on my shelves.

Dearest reader,

This book is for the women who don't have it all figured out.

Specifically, for the brown Muslim women. For the women who don't feel like adults. Who go straight from their parents' house to their husband's house. Who find it hard to make friends in adulthood. Who long for companionship but are worried it won't happen for them. Who had to grow up too soon. Who don't have a sense of their own identity.

But it's also for the brown Muslim women who love shalwar kameez. Whose hearts come alive watching Pakistani dramas, and who long for their rom-com moment. Women who whisper prayers in their daily life and think in more than one language. Women who deserve their big, grand love stories without having to compromise who they are.

Maya's Laws of Love came from a lot of different places, but mostly it arose out of my desire to see more faces like mine in books. To show Pakistani Muslim women that they're worthy of whirlwind, heart-fluttering romances just as much as anyone else. With that being said, please keep in mind that this is just one experience. There are 1.9 billion Muslims in the world, all from different countries and cultures; it'd be wild to expect this book—or any book, for that matter—to completely encompass the experience of every Muslim. I know the phrase "my Muslim experience" may seem like a bandage that people slap on to cover any imperfections in their portrayals of Muslim characters, but that's just it: there will always be imperfections. The Perfect Muslim doesn't exist. Our backgrounds (given that Islam is a religion and cannot be associated with specific races or cultures) inform so much about how we practice. My experience will be different from yours, and it will be different from the next book you pick up, and the next book, and the next. We are all trying the best we can, and everything else is between a person and Allah (SWT).

That being said, this book is about life, love, pain and the happiness that comes from being our truest selves.

So, grab your ticket, your suitcase and your mind, and prepare to lose them all on Maya's journey to finding her truest self.

And never forget: no matter what, you deserve the world.

All my love,

Alina

1

Maya's Law #1:
Anything that can go wrong will go wrong.

"Dr. Khan, you know how desi families are when it comes to weddings." I lift my head from the back of the loveseat I'm lounging on. "Everything is an emergency. I feel like I spent all my breaks during the school year planning for this wedding. Once this whole fanfare is over, I'll be able to focus on me for a change."

My therapist's office is very Zen, which I suppose all therapist's offices should be. Three pale blue walls, with the last wall behind her desk being white. The desk, which she rarely sits behind during sessions, is long and gray. There's some clutter: stray pens, a file stuffed with papers, a coffee cup that's half-empty and looks like it's been sitting there for a while. Hanging on the white wall are three white canvases with gorgeous Arabic calligraphy in shades of cerulean and gold. The only thing that seems out of place is the bright orange love-seat; it's such a strange color for an office scheme, but according to my therapist, Dr. Zaara Khan, it was a gift from her uncle who leases the place, so she couldn't refuse it. I hated the color when I first started coming here, but it's grown on me so much I would defend it to anyone.

"Well, you know how much I love it when you take 'me time,'" Dr. Khan says. She pushes her dark brown hair over her shoulder, and the fading sunlight streaming in through the window gives it a golden glow. "You need to be more aggressive about it."

"Dr. Khan, I'm the daughter of a Pakistani," I say, disbelief underlining my words. "I was raised to be a people pleaser."

Dr. Khan winces, but she can't contradict me. Her understanding of how Pakistani Muslim families work is exactly why I picked her over the other therapists my family doctor recommended. Dr. Khan knows what our culture is like, so she knows not to recommend certain things, and she also knows how to navigate situations when I barge into her office frantic about whatever my mom did this week to push my buttons. She straightens up. "And how are you feeling about the wedding?"

I bite my lip. "I'm excited."

She flashes me a look of disapproval. "Maya, every time I ask you how you feel about your wedding—or about the details of your relationship—you brush it off." She taps her pen against her notebook. "Now, as your therapist, I can't push you to talk about it before you're ready to, but we've been seeing each other for three months now and nothing."

"That's because there's nothing really to tell," I insist. I sit up straighter in my seat. "Imtiaz and I met at university. We were in the same sociology class because we both needed a social science credit, and we were friendly to each other for the whole semester. But we weren't great friends or anything; we sat next to each other and occasionally texted to ask for notes. He went on to med school, I went to teacher's college, and then two years later when I wanted to teach abroad in South Korea, Ammi wouldn't let me unless I got engaged first. And by a wild coincidence, Imtiaz was the first suitor my mom found. We remembered each other from school, and we remembered getting along well enough, so we went for it. It's not exactly a fairy-tale romance, but it's good enough for me."

"And why isn't it a fairy-tale romance?" Dr. Khan wonders, setting her chin on top of her fist. "By your own admission, you and Imtiaz met at a time in your lives when you were trying to figure out who you were as people and then went in two different directions, and then he ends up being the *first* rishta your mom finds for you." She tilts her head. "Doesn't that sound like fate to you?"

I squirm in place. "I guess," I allow. "That doesn't matter now anyway. Imtiaz is great. He's kind, funny, and he's going to be a surgeon, so job security."

"I'm sure the security must make you feel really good," Dr. Khan says. "I know how committed you are to having a plan for everything."

"Of course." I square my chin. "When you're cursed like me, you have to think of every disaster scenario first."

Dr. Khan's sigh fills the office. "Maya, what did we talk about?"

I bite the inside of my cheek, but at her incessant stare, I give in. "It's not the power of the curse, it's the power you *give* the curse," I recite.

Dr. Khan grins. "Exactly. You can think your bad-luck curse is real, but it all depends on how much you allow it to control you."

I barely refrain from an eye roll. At least Dr. Khan didn't try to dissuade me from my personal affirmation that I was cursed. My older sister, Hibba, thinks it's all in my head, but I've grown up with the worst luck anyone could ever have.

Especially when it comes to romance. I'm twenty-eight, and I've never been in a real relationship. Okay, that's also because dating is technically haram in Islam, so any time I even *tried* thinking about a boyfriend when I was a teen, Ammi would shut me down. Then, somehow, she was confused when I entered my twenties and couldn't make conversation with boys.

"That's what I have my laws for," I remind Dr. Khan.

My laws—which all started with Murphy's Law, the idea that anything that *can* go wrong *will* go wrong—are the only things that kept me sane while growing up. When I was a kid, it was mostly a joke; it was the only way I could make sense of all the bad stuff that happened to me. But eventually as I got older and bad things kept happening—especially in my love life—they were all I had.

"Why don't we change the subject?" she suggests in a polite tone. "Tell me about Imtiaz. He must be excited to see you."

"He only left a few days ago," I start. "I'll see him in a couple of days. My flight leaves on Sunday, so I'll be in Pakistan by Monday."

My therapist quirks a brow. "And are you ready to get married?"

I wrinkle my nose. "Of course I am. I wouldn't be getting married if I weren't. I thought that was obvious."

"I'm being serious, Maya," Dr. Khan says with a deep frown. "In the few months we've been together, you've rarely mentioned Imtiaz. You only talk about him when I bring him up. Don't you wonder why that is?"

"It's because I'm happy and comfortable about that area of

my life," I respond. "Why shouldn't I be? If I had a problem with it, I'd talk about it."

"And you don't have a problem with it?"

"No!" I swallow back my frustration. "After spending my whole life wanting love but thinking I'm cursed to be alone forever, I found this great guy who, for some reason, wants to be with me."

"Why is it *for some reason*?" Dr. Khan questions. "Usually, that reason is because he loves you. Does Imtiaz not love you?"

"He…does," I say, though I don't know how true that statement is. He's said it to me, but sometimes it feels like it's more out of obligation than anything, or else it feels platonic. "Plus, love isn't always necessary in brown marriages. My mom always told me she fell in love after she got married." I set my jaw. "Not that it did her any favors when Dad left."

"Your dad may have left, but from what you've told me, it seems like she managed just fine raising two daughters," Dr. Khan points out.

A smile graces my face. "Oh, yeah, she did a great job. My mom worked two jobs to keep the lights on and keep us fed. And even despite working all the time, she *still* found time to come to school events and spend time with Hibba Baji and me. She had to put providing for us first, yes, but she also prioritized being present in our lives. It must've really worried her to think that I was going to end up alone as I got older and had no success in finding a husband."

Dr. Khan tilts her head. "And what's so wrong with being alone?"

I snort. "You're kidding me, right?"

When she stares at me in an I'm-not-kidding way, I gnash my teeth. "Dr. Khan, in the desi community, if you don't get married, there's something *wrong* with you."

"What could possibly be wrong with someone not wanting to be married?" she asks.

"It reflects badly on you *and* your parents. My mom already doesn't have the greatest track record in our community thanks to the whole spousal-abandonment thing. Do you know the kind of rumors people spread about her?" Heat rushes to my face. "That my mom was a cheater, that she was so annoying she drove him away, that there was something *wrong* with her for a man to have left her alone with two young daughters."

I clench my hands into fists, my nails biting into the soft skin of my palm. "All of that aside, I just don't want to be alone." I sink back into the cushiony couch. "As much as I hate when she's right, Hibba Baji mentioned once that Ammi isn't going to be around forever, and I can't stick to my sister's side. She has her own family, and I want one, too, someday. And I don't want to do it alone."

Dr. Khan clicks her pen. "I think before you start worrying about other people loving you, you should consider loving yourself."

"What do you mean?" I ask. "I love myself."

She gives me a dubious look. "When was the last time you did something for *yourself*?"

"I gave my mom a head massage yesterday."

"And how was that something for *you*?"

"It meant I had a couple hours of quiet while she napped on the couch."

I expect Dr. Khan to be upset with me because I am very obviously dodging her question, so I'm surprised to see her curl her lips inward while her breath hitches, like she's trying hard to keep a laugh in. After a beat, she's back to being professional. "Don't think I don't see what you're doing. Be serious, please."

I set my jaw. "I'm doing absolutely *fine*. I'm going to Pakistan in a couple of days. I'm having a destination wedding. I'm getting married. I'm the happiest I could ever be."

Dr. Khan leans back in her seat. "Who are you trying to convince? Me or you?"

I open my mouth, but no sound comes out. Just as a stutter bursts from my throat, the timer on Dr. Khan's phone goes off, signaling the end of our session. Dr. Khan sighs, but she presses Stop on the alarm.

I get to my feet before she can speak. "I'll book another appointment when I get back from Pakistan." I don't make eye contact as I gather my things. "But I'll be so wrapped up in postmarital joy that I don't know when I'll be able to see you again."

"That's fine," she assures me. "I hope all goes well with the wedding."

"Thanks," I mumble in her direction. I grab my purse and head for the exit.

Dr. Khan's voice stops me at the door. "But remember this, Maya," she says. I steel myself, then look over at her.

She offers me a kind look, her fingers laced together. "No one is incapable of love, but we all have the ability to sabotage our own happiness, even if we don't realize it."

2

Maya's Law # 2:
Always hide how you really feel.

There's truly no sound worse than a six-year-old crying.

It's like your neighbor's lawnmower going off at 9 a.m. after you stayed up all night doing an assignment. It's like closing your fridge door and hearing something fall inside. It's like driving over something and hearing your tire pop.

I try my best to calm Mohinder, the little boy who, earlier today, abruptly paused the creation of his Play-Doh horse to look me in the eye and say, "When you die, you go to God, and you don't come back."

That caused Zack, another boy in our class, to yell, "That's not true because God isn't real!"

Mohinder promptly burst into tears, and I've been consoling him for the better part of an hour. Luckily, school ended not long after the incident and Zack's mom took him home, so at least Mohinder had stopped yelling about how God *is* real.

"It's okay, sweetie. You can believe whatever you want." I pat Mohinder lightly on the back.

"How can he say that?" He sniffles. "My mama says that people who don't believe in God aren't good people."

Did she *actually* say that to him? Maybe he misinterpreted her. Either way, it's a strange thing for a kid to say.

"People put their faith in different things," I tread carefully, because the last thing I want to do is tell this kid one thing and then have his mom upset with me. "Some people put their faith in God, some people put their faith in family, or in science. The point is that *you* believe in God, and you believe that He always makes things right for you." I twist my mouth, the words heavier on my tongue than I expected. "Even if you sometimes forget that."

A hiccup erupts out of Mohinder's throat. "I don't know…"

Against my own personal rule, I check my watch. The school day ended fifteen minutes ago. Mrs. Singh is running late. I was hoping that all my kids would go home early today, especially because it's the last day of school. My plan was to clean up the classroom as fast as I could. I still have to finish packing.

Mohinder stares up at me with wide red eyes. "But, Miss Mirza, what if he's right? What if there *is* no God?"

I pause. Then I say, "That's a conversation for your mommy and daddy."

He sniffles, and I give him another tissue before patting his back again. Luckily, Mohinder is the last student to be picked up today. Anaïs Bordier, my support worker, has already gotten a head start on cleaning the classroom. She's currently fetching the giant plastic bins that we put the toys in for the summer from storage.

The bell to our classroom rings. We have an official entrance for the front of the school, but the side classroom door is where parents drop off and pick up their kids. I stand too quickly, and my chair tips backward. "Oh, Mohinder, that must be your mommy!" I gesture to the door. "Come on! Time to go home."

Mohinder pushes himself away from his desk. He shuffles behind me as we head for the cubby area. I open the door while he grabs his backpack. His mother steps inside, a gift bag in the crook of her arm. "Hi, Miss Mirza!" she greets.

"Mama!" Mohinder cries. He launches himself at his mom's legs.

Mrs. Singh makes an *oomph* noise, but she grins down at her son. "Hi, baby!" She bends down to his level and drops a kiss to his cheek. She gives the bag to Mohinder. "You want to give Miss Mirza the bag?"

Mohinder looks up at me, suddenly shy, as if he hasn't spent the better part of an hour crying in my lap. He holds the bag out to me. "This is for you, Miss Mirza."

My heart swells. As much as this job can drive me nuts, the kids are too cute for me to ever hate working here. I take the bag from Mohinder. "Thank you, Mohinder," I say, then turn to Mrs. Singh. "Thank you so much for this—it's really not necessary."

"Of course it is," Mrs. Singh says. "It's the last day of school, and you're getting married this summer!"

My gut twists, and I peek down at the engagement ring sitting on my finger. The diamond stone catches the light streaming in from the window and glitters brilliantly. Everyone told me I'd get used to the weight on my finger eventually, but every time I slip it on in the morning, I can't help but feel it's weighing me down like a thick winter coat. I curl my fingers into a fist. "Well, thank you again."

She smiles at me, then takes Mohinder's hand. "Time for us to go home, then."

"Oh, wait, before you go." I step forward and lower my voice. "There was an incident earlier. It's nothing too major, but Mohinder got into an…argument, for lack of a better word, with another kid. It was about the existence of God."

Mrs. Singh frowns. "What?"

I nod sympathetically. "Yeah, I have no idea where it came from, either. But you should probably talk about it with him. I didn't want to say anything because I'm not sure what your family believes."

"Thank you, that was very considerate," she says. She checks on Mohinder, who's now stomping his feet in an attempt to get his Skechers to light up. Looking at him now, you'd have no idea he was crying less than five minutes ago. His face is dry and his nose snot-free. "I'll talk to him tonight." She heads for the exit. "You have a good summer, yeah? And good luck with your wedding!"

I wave as she steps out of the building. "You have a good summer, too!"

I watch them make their way to the parking lot, and then move to shut the door, but just before it closes, a leg pops into the doorway. "If you break my leg, it's a lawsuit!" Anaïs calls out.

I refrain from an eye roll but push the door open wider to give her more room. She stumbles in, three large storage bins in her arms and clearly in danger of toppling over. She peeks over her shoulder. "Mohinder's gone?"

"Yeah." I take one of the bins from her so she can see better.

"Thank God," she huffs. She sets the bins down on the tiny brown activity table. "I thought he was going to go on for *hours*." She points in the direction of the door. "*That* is exactly why I'm never having kids."

I set my bin down next to hers, then head over to my desk to put the gift bag next to the ones that a few other parents gave me. I give her a strange look. "Anaïs, you literally work with children."

"I said I don't want them, not that I hate them, Maya," she corrects. She wraps her burnt orange hair into a bun at the base of her neck. "But these kinds of questions, sitting there for hours when they cry, having to drop everything for them..." She clicks her tongue. "Not for me."

I'm not sure what I'm supposed to say next, so I get back to work. Having conversations that go beyond the surface-level is awkward with Anaïs because I don't know her very well. We're coworkers, yes, but I don't know if I'd call us *friends*. I haven't had much success keeping friends in the past, so it's just easier not to get too close to anyone—that way, I won't be upset when they inevitably leave.

I head over to the student tables and start picking up stray crayons and neglected papers.

We both work quietly for a while before Anaïs lets out a long, dramatic sigh. I stop and look up at her from my spot by the bookshelves. "Care to share, Anaïs?"

She smirks at my use of the phrase that we say to the kids. "Oh, nothing... I'm just thinking about how when you come back from Pakistan, I'll have to refer to you as *Mrs. Porter.*" She smirks. "Miss Mirza rolls off the tongue so naturally. Plus, the name sounds better."

I stiffen, then continue rearranging the bookshelves, putting my back to Anaïs. "Well, who says I'm changing my last name? Religiously, I'm entitled to keeping it."

"I'm honestly surprised you're even still going through with the wedding," she blurts, and at my offended expression, she quickly backtracks. "Oh, no offense, it's just...you guys have been engaged for a long time, is all."

"Two years isn't that long," I argue, though even by Western standards, it *is* quite a while. If it were up to the desi parents, engagements would only last as long as it takes to plan the wedding. "I think it's time I put the guy out of his misery."

"At least he's cute," Anaïs points out. "The last four dates I've been on have all been duds."

"Maybe that's because your only goal is to go home with any woman who'll have you," I tease as I pass her on my way to the crafts closet.

She snorts. "You don't have to call me out like that." She picks up the plastic toy box from the floor. She's going to take it to the kitchen area in the school, where we can properly wash the toys before we put them away until the fall. "I'm super jealous you're having a destination wedding. Pakistan sounds *beautiful*."

"It really is," I breathe dreamily. I haven't been back in a long time, so I'm excited to breathe in the sweet air of my motherland. "And it makes sense for the wedding to be in Pakistan. When my family came to Canada, it was only my parents. All my extended family is in Karachi. It wouldn't make sense to have everyone come here when it's much easier for a few of us to go there."

Anaïs clicks her tongue. "Still, if I ever got married, I don't think I could afford to have it anywhere but city hall."

"With our salaries, I wouldn't blame you," I agree. "I'm lucky Imtiaz's family is…" I pause, thinking of the right word.

Anaïs smirks. "Loaded?"

I chuckle. "Not how I'd put it, but yes."

"I'm not sure how you managed to land someone who's hot *and* rich. With all the stuff you've told me about your love life, it seems almost impossible."

I open my mouth to protest but stop. "Yeah, fair enough.

I'm happy to have found someone. Imtiaz is kind, he's smart and funny." I press my lips into a thin line. "He's great."

Anaïs whistles low. "Except you don't seem happy like a bride *should* be a week out from her wedding."

Yikes. I flex my fingers for a second, sneaking a look at the ring on my finger. Then, I go over to Anaïs and take the box from her. "I'll sanitize the toys," I say. "And let's be quick about this." I brush past her, heading for the door. "I still have some important things to do."

3

Maya's Law #3:
Trying to be stress-free only
stresses you out more.

The house is too quiet without the trill of Ammi's constant chattering on the phone, or the whistling of the kettle, or the anger-tinted voices of ARY News blasting on the TV. I drop my keys into the bowl beside the front door, my stomach clenching at the reminder that this could very well be the last time I do this while this place is still considered my home. When I come back from Pakistan, it'll be my mother's home.

I guess it's always been my mother's house, though. She picked out the royal blue couches that sit in the living room. She chose the muted gray paint that coats the interior. She decided on the decorations, from the forest painting hanging above the television to the crystalized ornaments that line the shelves attached to the walls. It's just been me and her in this house since I was twenty, when Hibba Baji got married at twenty-six. Anything that's truly mine is up in my room. Or, at least, it *was*. I already moved almost all my belongings into the apartment I'll be sharing with Imtiaz. When we get back, I'll take whatever's left here, and that'll be it.

I ignore the thought and head upstairs so I can change and pray Dhuhr and Asr together, the two prayers I usually miss while I'm at work. Once I'm done, I traipse into the kitchen. I twist my hair into a bun. I struggle for a second with the long brown strands that swing against my back, but once I secure the tie, I peek into the fridge. Bare shelves stare back at me. At first I'm confused, and then I remember that because I'm leaving for another country, I haven't been grocery shopping. Ammi would be so mad if she knew I wasn't cooking and instead ordering takeout, but she's not here to berate me for it. I shut the door at the same time as I pull out my phone to place an order with Uber Eats.

Just as I'm about to set my phone down, it rings.

I bite the inside of my cheek when I realize it's a video call from Imtiaz. I inhale deeply through my nose and answer the call. "Hey!"

Imtiaz's handsome—there's no denying that. His striking green irises are the first thing anyone notices about him; they pop against his light brown skin. His bushy brows are surprisingly lighter than his hair, but that's because he dyes his hair darker. When I found out about it in university, he swore me to secrecy because he didn't want it to affect how he picked up girls. What a wild turn of events that I ended up being the one engaged to him.

He smiles, though the bags under his eyes betray how tired he is. It's like 8 a.m. in Karachi, so he must have just woken up. "Hey," he yawns.

I smirk. "Yeah, that's exactly how you should greet your fiancée the eve before your wedding."

Imtiaz snorts. "Technically our wedding isn't for another week or so," he reminds me. "So it's not really the *eve*."

"True." I pad over to the stairs. "Why are you awake so early?"

"My mom wants me to go looking for some clothes." He rubs his cheeks. "She said that since I arrived early to Pakistan, they might as well take advantage of it and host some dholkis. I need more outfits for them. Can't be caught wearing the same thing twice, after all."

Imtiaz is in his third year of his general surgery residency, with the eventual goal of specializing in pediatrics, but that won't happen for another three years, at least. He went early to help finalize some last-minute details, and then the plan is to fly to Cancun the day after the wedding to spend five days there for our honeymoon. It's not ideal to go right after the wedding—I'm worried we'll be too tired from all the festivities to actually enjoy the trip—but it was either that or wait months for our honeymoon, and I didn't want to do that. "That sounds like…fun."

He gives me a look. "There's no way you believe that."

I snort. "Yeah, I don't. Sorry."

I reach my room, and another pang hits my chest at how bare the place is. My room has always reflected whatever obsession I had at the time—from *Twilight* posters covering my walls to my own artsy paintings to photos with childhood friends—but now, the only things staring back at me are the bare lavender walls. My three bookshelves are empty; I packed away the books I wanted to take with me and then donated the rest because I don't have room for them in the new apartment. My drawers are bare, as is my closet. I've been mostly living out of a suitcase these past couple of weeks, and today I'll drop off the rest of my stuff at the apartment.

I swallow back my emotions and sit down on my bed. I zoned out before, but I tune back into the conversation as Imtiaz says, "In a few weeks, we'll be at our own house and settling into our new life."

My stomach churns. "Yeah!" I say, a bit too enthusiastically. "It'll all be great. We'll be able to make our own choices. I can decide what I want to have for dinner without having to get my mother's input." I lean back against the headboard. "I'll cook all your favorite meals. Aloo gosht, daal, chicken pulao. You can call me Gordon Ramsay, except I promise I won't curse at you."

Imtiaz's smirk falters, and I scrunch my face. "What? What is it?"

"Nothing, it's just…" He awkwardly clears his throat. "I don't really like those dishes, especially daal."

"Oh." These are dishes I like. I assumed he liked them, too. "But didn't you have, like, two servings of daal at my house when you came over for the Baat Pakki?"

"Yeah, I only ate it to be polite," he says. "And I did tell you that later, because you mentioned how green I looked afterward."

"Right," I murmur. I clear my throat to dispel the tension. "I'll have plenty of time to learn your favorite meals when we go on the honeymoon. I know I was pretty disappointed when you said you didn't want to go to Switzerland, but now that I've gotten used to the idea, I'm warming up to Cancun, especially because it's nice this time of year—"

As I speak, Imtiaz's face contorts, hesitation creasing his forehead. I stop. "What?"

"I thought we talked about the honeymoon."

Dread twists my gut. "What do you mean?"

"You know Dr. Sun?" he starts. "The doctor who I was getting to cover me while I'm in Pakistan?"

I nod, already not liking where this is going.

"Well, she got an offer to attend a medical conference with her mentor and now she can't cover me anymore," he explains. Regret lines his mouth. "I thought I told you. I guess with all the chaos, it slipped my mind." He rubs his ragged face. "I'm sorry, Maya. We'll have to postpone it."

I nod again, not trusting myself to make a noise that isn't squeaking. Disappointment wraps itself around my throat. I shake it off. "Okay," I begin, proud of the way my voice doesn't break. "When do you think we'll be able to go?"

"Maybe later in the year?"

The lines in my forehead deepen. "How am I going to do that? I have work. I can't take two weeks off during the school year."

"We can reschedule to the winter break," Imtiaz suggests.

"You mean during the holiday season?" I splutter. "When it's incredibly expensive to travel to hot climates? We're renting a space in Toronto, not to mention my pay as a teacher is terrible and you're still paying off student loans."

I can tell by the way Imtiaz opens and closes his mouth and runs his palms along his pants that he's panicking. I don't get worked up very often, but when it *does* happen, all he can do is stammer until I calm myself down. I close my eyes and inhale deeply three times, a strategy Dr. Khan and I came up with for when I feel myself starting to spiral. When I open them again, my chest is much looser. "It's okay," I tell him. "We can figure it out later."

Imtiaz's shoulders deflate. "Yeah, cool, that sounds like a good idea." He scratches the back of his neck. "Oh, hey, there's something else I wanted to talk to you about."

I hate the way alarm immediately rises in my throat at

those words. They're the same ones Ammi said right before she told us Baba left in the middle of the night and wasn't coming back. I squish the rising fear and struggle to keep my composure. "What's up?"

"There's someone I invited to the wedding," he begins, his tone casual, but with the way his fingers fidget I know he's nervous. "I didn't mention who it was earlier, but now that you're on your way I think I should—"

A bell echoes up the stairs and in through my open door. When the bell rings again, I stand up. "Oh, hey, that's my dinner," I say. I look back over to Imtiaz, who still looks pretty nervous. I decide to let him off the hook, because I don't care who he's invited last minute; that's an issue he'll have to take up with our mothers. "Listen, I have to eat and finish packing. Whoever you invited to the wedding is fine with me. It's your wedding, too; it's all good."

"Really?" Imtiaz blows air out of his lips. "Because—"

My screen abruptly goes dark, the white circle flickering in the middle of my screen before shutting down completely. I try to turn my phone back on, but a battery-bar icon appears with red at the end, signaling that I need to charge it.

I groan but plug my phone in. I set it down on the side table and leave to grab my meal from the front door. When I come back after a few minutes, my phone is back on and charging. I debate calling Imtiaz back, but I'm hungry, and I really do have a lot of work to do before I get on my plane tomorrow. He's gotten my blessing to add his last-minute guest to the list; he doesn't need anything else from me.

So, I sit on my bed and dig in.

"You are *not* going to believe what Asma Mami did," Hibba Baji says the moment I answer her video call later that night. It's 1 a.m. here, which means it's 10 a.m. in Karachi, so everyone is up and bustling about. She's still feeding breakfast to her six-year-old daughter, my niece, Iqra.

I balance my phone on my side table, then return to packing. "Tell me. I'm sure it's riveting."

She ignores the sarcasm in my tone. "She told Ammi last night that her daughters were *not* wearing the clothes you picked out for them."

I stop for a second. "I picked out clothes for our cousins to wear?"

Hibba Baji pauses. "Didn't you?"

"I'm sure Ammi picked them out for me. Or I don't remember." I shrug. "There's been so much stuff happening for the wedding, and I feel like I'm not even planning most of it myself."

"Don't feel too special," she says. She stuffs another piece of egg into Iqra's mouth, then nods at her when she asks to be excused. "Ammi took over most of my wedding planning when I got married, too."

"I'm not surprised," I retort. I fold a kameez and stuff it into my suitcase. "Mom is the most control-freaky person I've met."

"True." She shakes her head. "Anyway, back to what Asma Mami said. So, she doesn't want her daughters wearing the suits you picked because she thinks Ammi was intentionally trying to make them look bad to make us look better. Then Ammi went and talked to Rashid Mamu, and then—"

She keeps going, but I drown her out as I flit around the room. All the stuff I personally need for the wedding, like jewelry and clothes, is already in Pakistan. Ammi took it with her when she went at the end of May. All I'm packing now are some things just in case of an emergency—spare clothes, toiletries, chargers, and an adapter for my phone. I grab my backpack from the floor. It holds my iPad, my travel documents, and a few other things I'll need for the fourteen-hour plane ride. I only have to bring myself to Pakistan, and even *that* was a struggle to achieve. I'm a teacher, and my area manager refused to give me vacation days for my own damn wedding.

I check and double-check and triple-check to make sure I have everything I need from the list I made.

"Maya!" Hibba Baji's voice screeches me to a stop.

I look over to the phone, irritation thinning my mouth. "What?"

Her annoyed face fills up the entire screen. "Have you even been listening to me?"

"Nope," I admit cheerily. At her annoyed nostril flare, I roll my eyes. "I don't care about petty family drama. Tell Asma Mami to let her kids wear whatever they want. I don't care. I'm too busy trying to sort things out on my end before I leave tomorrow." I hold up a finger. "In fact, you shouldn't even be telling me any of this stuff because as the bride, I deserve to be as stress-free as possible."

"That's not how it works," she retorts.

I give her a confused look. "Those are literally the words you said to me when *you* got married nine years ago."

Hibba Baji avoids my gaze. "That's what I thought," I tease. I duck out into the hall, grab my hairbrush from the bathroom, then step back into my bedroom, which I still cannot get used to seeing so bare. We briefly talked about finding a place to live after the wedding, and when Imtiaz mentioned living with his parents, I flat-out refused. Don't get me wrong, my in-laws are as great as they come, but I'm not sure I could ever have sex in a house where my father-in-law might be in the next room. Plus, after spending my whole life living under my mother's roof, I knew I wouldn't be able to continue living somewhere I couldn't fully be myself. Thankfully, Imtiaz agreed, and he secured us a place close to the hospital where he was doing his residency.

I return my attention to the call. "I'm just excited to start the next phase of my life and get Ammi off my back."

"Maya," Hibba Baji lightly chastises. "You shouldn't talk about Ammi like that. You know she only worries about you being single because she doesn't want you to be on your own."

My fingers pause on the zipper of my suitcase. I frown at my sister. "Baji, I'm twenty-eight. I went and lived on my own halfway around the world for two years, remember?" I zip my luggage closed. "It's insulting that Ammi thinks I can't take care of myself. You know how much convincing it took to get her to leave for Pakistan without me?"

"It's just how our culture is," Hibba Baji reminds me, her tone gentle.

"What, that unmarried women are infantile?" I grumble.

"No." She pauses, then winces. "Okay, maybe. But it's also the burden of being the younger child. Ammi's bound to continue to smother you, especially because you still live at home."

Unfortunately, that's the truth. In Pakistani culture, young women never leave their parents' house before they're married. If they do, they're gossiped about; people say she had an argument with her parents, she was kicked out, or she ran away.

"This whole mentality is a bunch of crap," I start. "Forget if a woman wants to start her adult life away from her parents but without a husband. Forget if she wants a shred of independence that she isn't going to get if she continues to live under her parents' roof. Forget that there's a *reason* most people leave their homes at eighteen—the older you get, the more you butt heads with your parents. If you leave your home, but it's not to move into your husband's house, then there's something wrong with you."

Hibba Baji stares at me. "You're really that desperate to leave Ammi? After all she did for us?"

Annoyance rises to my face. "Ammi is the reason I didn't

leave home for uni," I tell her. As much as I hated the "log kya kahenge" mentality, I couldn't bring any more ridicule to Ammi's name by doing something that would bring her shame in our community, not after she spent so much of our lives being the butt of every joke because Dad left. "I know she worked herself to the bone so we could have nothing but the best. The least I could do was stay with her as long as I could, but now I want to live my life how I want. Why is that always too much for a brown girl to ask?"

Hibba Baji looks away, and in the ensuing silence, I pick my suitcase up off the bed and set it by the bedroom door. "I texted you my flight information," I start, changing the subject. "Make sure you send it to Huzaifa Bhai. I don't want him to be late picking me up."

"Don't worry, he'll be there on time," she assures me, her tone much lighter now that we're on a safer topic. "Make sure you're as early as possible for your flight so you don't miss it by accident. The last thing we need is the bride late for her own wedding."

I glare at her. "I've never been late to anything!"

Hibba Baji raises a hand. "My thirtieth birthday dinner—" she puts a finger down "—Ammi's fifty-fourth birthday—" she puts another down "—*your own teacher's college graduation*—"

"Okay, okay, fine!" I relent. "But it isn't my fault. I have bad luck because of my curse."

Hibba Baji let out a long groan. "Please don't start with the *curse* thing."

"It's true!" I sit down on the edge of my bed. "Someone put their nazar on me as a kid, and because of that, nothing has ever gone right for me, *especially* in the relationship department."

Hibba Baji, who has been trying but failing since we were teens to convince me my curse isn't real, clicks her tongue.

"Then think about this time as the beginning to your fresh start. It looks like your curse is finally going to be broken. You're getting *married*, Maya. You're going to be so happy."

"I hope so." I check the time on my phone. "I should go to bed. My flight is at eleven a.m."

"I should go, too," Hibba Baji says. "I'll see you soon, Inshallah. Khuda hafiz!"

"Khuda hafiz." I hang up. I set my phone beside me, then flop back on the bed. I stare up at the ceiling, thinking about how this is the last time I'll be in this bed by myself. Tomorrow, everything changes.

"Tomorrow's going to be a long day," I mutter to myself. "But at least I'll be one step closer to being free."

4

Maya's Law #4:
When you think you're lucky, think again.

I stir restlessly, nestling deeper into my bed, wrapping my sheets around my body like a burrito. I struggle with insomnia so even on a good day, I get only three or four hours of good sleep. Last night, though, I guess the exhaustion caught up with me, and I slept uninterrupted for a couple of hours. I stretch my arms out, seeking my phone on the side table. I hold it to my face, and my eyes fly open when the time registers.

9:36 a.m.

I bolt up, throwing my blanket off and trying to jump out of bed at the same time. My feet get tangled in the sheets, and I crash onto my knees. Bursts of pain shoot through my body, but I brush it off as I scramble to stand up.

I don't have time to take a shower, so I hastily brush my

teeth and wash my face before throwing on a simple outfit: a T-shirt and flowy floral-printed pants. Thank God I packed all my stuff last night, because all I have to do is grab my purse and my suitcase. I run down the stairs as I call an Uber on my phone at the same time.

I calm down once I'm in the car. I rest my elbow on the door. Setting my chin on my hand, I let the soothing scent of the mehendi adorning my skin calm me down. Ever since I was a young girl, the earthy, sharp smell of the sweet paste was enough to bring my soul peace, and it's exactly what I need to keep myself from losing my mind.

My phone buzzes, and I lift it from my lap to see a WhatsApp message from Ammi. It's a photo of her with Imtiaz's mother—my future Saas—in front of a huge pile of clothes. Last minute your cousins decided to change their clothes. This is what they've picked. Which one do you like?

I survey the colorful stacks of heavy shalwar kameez in plastic wrap. I assume they didn't open any of them because they plan to return whichever ones they decide not to wear, but the grainy picture makes it hard to see the details. In the end I text back, Whichever ones they like. They have to wear them!

Ok. It's your wedding photos.

I refrain from an eye roll. Like I said to Hibba Baji, it doesn't matter to me what my cousins from Pakistan wear. I'm not close with them, having been born and raised in Canada with only a few monthlong trips to Karachi as a child, but I like them enough to let them pick what they want to wear. As long as they stick to the color scheme of green and gold, I don't care what their designs look like.

Soon enough, the car comes to a stop, and I jump out with a hasty wave to the driver. He eyes the mehendi design that stops above my elbow, but he offers me a salute. I catch a glimpse of the back seat as I shut the door, wincing at the tiny flakes left behind, and mentally add a note to increase his tip. My younger cousin Fizza would have to go over my mehendi again, and I'm already dreading the hours-long process. It was hard enough to sit there the first time, unable to move or eat or go to the bathroom without assistance, while the warmth slowly drained out of my limbs.

I take my suitcase out of the trunk, swing my backpack on, and then dash through the doors. After checking through security and leaving my luggage at baggage claim, I pull out my folder of travel documents and find the one with my gate information. Just as I look down at the papers, a shoulder collides with mine.

I gasp, stumbling to the side. The papers fly out of my hands. "Crap!" I grumble.

The guy who bumped into me, wearing a red sweater and dark wash jeans, barely looks back as he continues on his way. His surprisingly deep dark brown eyes (seriously, they're almost black) briefly meet my own, but he quickly faces forward again as he glides between slower couples in front of him.

"Yeah, no need to say sorry or anything, jerk!" I call after him. A second later, I wince at the dirty looks people flash me, especially from the mother who glares at me and tugs her son closer to her as she walks past me. I'm not even sure if the guy heard my insult, but it feels good to say it despite the public shaming.

A whimper slips from my chest as I hastily pick my papers up, scrambling to put them in order. I check my watch, only to pause. The big and little hand are in the same spot as they were the last time I checked it in the Uber—which I arrived in at least twenty minutes ago. I tap the glass a few times, but the hands refuse to budge. I pull my phone out of my pocket. 10:45 a.m. stares back at me.

10:45? But boarding started at 10:15! And according to my boarding pass, the gate's *all the way at the end of the airport.*

With a barely concealed shriek, I shove the remaining documents in my backpack. I push myself to my feet and take off, zigzagging desperately around people walking way too slow for a busy place like an airport. I bump into a few people, but unlike The Jerk, I toss a quick apology in their general direction as I keep going.

Lungs burning, I make it to my gate. It's empty, with most of the passengers already boarded, but the door's still open as I stumble to a stop in front of the flight attendant. "Are you alright?" she asks in a concerned tone.

"Fine," I wheeze. "I'm not too late, am I?"

"No, but you almost were! I was about to close the gate."

I grin even though my chest is on fire. "Thank God." I pluck my passport and boarding pass out of my bag and give both to her.

After a quick ID check, she gestures to the doorway. "Go right ahead."

I take back my documents and walk down the path. I can't afford to walk too slow, though, because I'm not sure when the doors to the plane will close, so my legs still hurt as I get to the entrance of the plane. One of the air hostesses greets me. "Assalaam-o-alaikum, and welcome to Jinnah International Airlines! Please find your seat."

I make my way toward the back. I have to pause a few times, waiting for mothers to snatch their children out of the aisle and for people to put their luggage in the overhead compartment, but I make it to my seat. Unfortunately, I got saddled with the middle seat, but I won't let it drag me down.

A young girl sits at the window, staring out at the tarmac. She pulls the shutter up and down and giggles at her own antics. A woman wearing a beige hijab is trying to fit a suitcase into the overhead bin. I assume she's the girl's mother, because she notices what the girl is doing and says, "Khadijah, baaz ajo!" in a dismissive tone. Khadijah slumps back into her seat, her lips pulled downward.

I clear my throat. She looks over at me, and I offer my best "teacher" smile. "Sorry, but I need to get to my seat," I tell her in Urdu.

She perks up. "Oh, you're the passenger in the middle seat?"

"Yeeesss. Is there a problem?"

"Oh, my husband," the woman explains. "He had a work trip that got canceled last second, so when he bought his ticket, he couldn't get a seat close to our family." She points to someone behind me, and I look over to see an older man wearing a white topi sitting a few aisles away. He stares at us, anticipation wrinkling his face.

When I look back at the woman, she continues. "I hoped you wouldn't mind changing seats with him so our family could sit together?"

I contemplate saying no, but one look at the woman's hopeful face and Khadijah trying to peek over the seat in front of her to look at her dad makes me cave. "Sure, I'll change seats. I don't mind."

"Oh, really?" She beams. "Shukriya, beta! May Allah reward your kindness." She beckons her husband over, and he gets up to make his way down the aisle. He gives me a grateful nod as we pass each other, and I return it. I briefly pause in the aisle and watch as he reaches his family. Khadijah stumbles as she tries to get to her father, but he catches her before she can face-plant and they share a laugh.

I look away from their exchange and continue on to my new seat. An older man sits at the window, and the middle seat has a bag on it, so either it belongs to the guy at the window, or someone else occupies the middle seat.

I suppress the grin fighting to take over my face. I get the aisle seat! I don't have to shuffle past someone to get to the bathroom, which is infinitely worse than having someone shuffle past *me* to get there.

The laptop case is covering half of my seat, but I don't want to move something that's not mine. I wave at the man in the window seat to get his attention. "Excuse me," I say in Urdu, and he looks over at me. I point to the bag. "Is this yours?"

"Nehin," he answers. "There was a man here before, but he went to the bathroom. I'm sure he'll be back soon."

I edge the bag over to the middle seat. I sit down and place my backpack at my feet, then close my eyes, leaning my head back against the rest.

Against all odds, I made it onto the flight. Despite being hours late to the airport, despite someone bumping into me, and despite a seat change, I'm here, on the plane, and ready to take off. I'm going to take that as a win.

"Excuse me?" I hear. "Could you move your legs? I need to get to my seat."

I open my eyes, and they meet a pair that are so dark brown they're almost black.

Hai Allah. The Jerk is my new seat partner.

5

Maya's Law #5:
The person you like the least will be
the person you meet the most.

I hate that my first thought is, *Wow, he's cute*.

I may hate it, but I'm also not wrong. He's tall—so tall his head brushes the top of the airplane—and for a second, I wonder how the hell he's going to fold himself up enough to sleep on this flight. His dark hair is shorter on the sides and at the back, but longer on the top. His skin, shades lighter than even the fairest Kashmiri, throws me off, too.

My next thought is, *What's a white guy doing on a plane to Pakistan?* It's not like we're going to Paris or something, where it would make sense to have a blend of people on the flight. Most of the time, the only people going to and from Pakistan are actual Pakistanis.

"Oh," I say, the word coming out before I can stop myself. "You're the—"

"The Jerk," he finishes, an unimpressed look on his face.

So he *did* hear me. At least the dirty looks were worth it now. I lift my chin. "Well, you did bump into me."

"And?" He shrugs. "I was in a hurry to catch my flight."

And, of course, it had to be *my* flight he was trying to catch. "I was in a hurry, too. You made me drop all my things, and you didn't even bother to help me pick them up." I stare up at him. "Are you going to apologize?"

"No," he replies, his tone almost bored.

I open my mouth to retort, but I pause when I notice people are craning their heads to see what the fuss is about. I grit my teeth and stand up so he can get to his seat.

The Jerk sidesteps past me, and his broad back briefly slides against my chest. I catch a whiff of his scent—strong coffee and fresh pine. I unconsciously inhale deeper, trying to catch more of his smell, but when he sits down the spell breaks. My face flushes, but I sit down, as well. I sigh deeply, flopping my head back against the rest.

He grabs the stuff off his seat and settles in next to me. Once he's seated, he peels his red sweater off. I move out of the way, shaking my head, before he can accidentally hit me. He could at least try to avoid me. He reaches into the case at his feet and pulls his laptop out.

I look away from him, swallowing back my annoyance. I don't want to put my headphones in until takeoff in case the flight attendants say something important, so I look around the plane and people-watch. An elderly man helps an equally elderly woman into her seat in the cluster beside us. A man passes by, guiding a young boy who looks like he's going to pee his pants to the bathroom. Down the aisle, a teenager helps her mother wrangle two young kids into their seats and gives them their iPads so they'll settle down before the flight starts.

The plane is mostly filled with families; flights from Canada to Pakistan generally are. Because it's so expensive to travel to Pakistan (even on an airline like Jinnah, which is the cheapest of the cheap), people take their whole families when they go. And they tend to go for at least a couple of months. But we take the time, and we pay the price, because no matter how much it costs or whether you were born there or not, Pakistan is still our homeland.

But strangely, this guy seems to be traveling by himself. Judging by the earlier comments from the man sitting in the window seat, I assume they're not together. I mean, I'm also traveling alone, I guess, but I had no choice.

The longer I stare at him, the more he seems…restless. His foot taps lightly against the floor, like his legs are poised for takeoff. Every few seconds he looks out the window, though I'm not sure what he's staring at; it's just the tarmac out there. When he's not looking outside, he checks the watch on his wrist, tugging at the leather strap. It's like he's trying his best to focus on the work in front of him, but he can't. His fingers twitch as he types on his computer. I don't think he realizes he's doing it, either. It's like something he's doing on a subconscious level.

I stare at him for a beat too long, because when he looks over at me I barely have the time to look away and fumble with my phone in my lap. I pretend to answer a very important text, but I don't know if he's buying it. After a second, I feel his stare leave my cheek.

I lower my phone back into my lap. I don't need to know why he's traveling alone, or why he seems so fidgety. It's not my business. I cross my arms over my chest.

My phone buzzes in my lap. We technically haven't taken

off yet, so I haven't switched my phone to airplane mode. I hit Talk when I see it's Ammi calling. "Assalaam-o-alaikum," I greet.

"Walaykum salam. Are you on the plane yet?"

"Yes," I respond in English. I sneak a peek at The Jerk, then switch to Urdu as I add, "Some rude white guy bumped into me on my way to the plane. I almost missed it because of him. Now he's sitting next to me. I don't know how I'm going to survive a fourteen-hour plane ride with him. I hope he doesn't try to talk to me or anything. Strangers talking to you on a plane is the worst."

"I know," Ammi agrees. "On my flight here, there was a woman who was traveling alone sitting next to me. She talked my ear off. Eventually I had to pretend to sleep so she would stop."

As much as I feel bad that my mother was annoyed on her flight, I can't help but sympathize with the woman who was next to her. Sometimes, traveling alone sucks. You have to remember everything yourself, take responsibility if you're late, and sit by yourself while people around you happily engage with family or friends.

I risk a glance at The Jerk. He's still not paying attention to me. Even if he were paying attention, he doesn't know what I'm saying. "I sincerely hope he doesn't ask for alcohol on this flight. I don't want to have to be the one to calm down the offended flight attendant."

"Some people have no class," Ammi says, clicking her tongue. She gets right back to business, though. "Be sure to read the dua'a before traveling, okay? And call me when you land."

"Yes, Ammi," I say. I'm reciting a script I've said to her so many times. If my life had a song, its chorus would be "Yes, Ammi." We chat for another minute or two, but when a flight attendant shows up near the front, I say, "Oh, it looks like we might be taking off soon."

"Okay, beta. I love you and I'll see you soon!"

"I love you, too," I say, and I hang up the phone, switching it to airplane mode and then tucking it in the compartment in front of me.

The Jerk has been silent this entire time. Suddenly, he opens his mouth. "You know, it's not polite to talk about people in another language," he says in completely flawless Urdu.

My stomach sinks. Urdu? Did he just speak Urdu? Slowly, I look at him. "I'm sorry?" I say in English.

"Just because I appear white doesn't mean I don't know what you're saying," he goes on. He doesn't even break his focus from his screen; he continues to type away. "You assumed I didn't know how to speak Urdu, so you said whatever you wanted about me. You also *assumed* I'm not Muslim or Pakistani, but I am." He drags his attention away from his screen long enough to flash me a look of disapproval. "I'm half-Pakistani, and you shouldn't judge people based on their outward appearance."

My face reddens. I don't know what else to say, but thankfully my teacher instincts kick in and the words come out reflexively. "Oh, sorry," I mumble.

He narrows his eyes at me, then looks back to his screen at the same time as I face the seat in front of me. Silence creeps around us.

Great, just what I needed. Awkward tension between me and the person I have to sit beside for the next fourteen hours.

The Jerk balances his laptop on his knees. He unlocks the screen to some sort of document, and I catch a glimpse of a name at the top. I can only see his first name, though; another window covers up the rest. *Sarfaraz.*

The Jerk—Sarfaraz—pauses, and the lines in his forehead crease as he stares at me. "Can I help you?"

I quickly look away. I hear him huff next to me, but I don't dare move my head. In fact, I'd live very happily if I never saw this guy ever again. Dr. Khan is going to be really annoyed when she ends up having to give me yet another lecture about how awkward interactions with strangers don't define my life.

I buckle myself in properly, then tap my fingers against my knees while the flight attendant instructs us on what to do in case of an emergency and the captain's voice comes through the overhead speakers.

Sarfaraz watches my finger-tapping and huffs loudly, shaking his head. He stops, reaches into his pocket, and produces a pair of AirPods. He sticks one in each ear and resumes his work.

"Okay, passengers," the captain declares. "Please prepare for takeoff."

Sarfaraz's fingers freeze on the keyboard. His breath hitches, and he slowly closes the lid of his laptop. He squeezes his eyes shut, his hands holding tightly onto his computer. His shoulders noticeably tense, the muscles going taut under his shirt. He clenches his teeth, causing the sharp line of his jaw to become more prominent.

I frown at his reaction, but I look away, reaching for my phone. I searched up the dua'a for flying and copied it to my notes app last night so I'd have it ready. I open the app and recite the prayer under my breath. I peek at Sarfaraz out of the corner of my eye, and he's still tense.

Without thinking, I lean forward—not enough for him to notice—and blow the remnants of my prayer on him. It's a thing you can do when praying for yourself; lightly breathing your prayer on someone else, especially someone in distress, can help them, too. I usually don't do it for regular people, but he's a fellow Muslim and he's clearly anxious and…he's alone.

Still, I cross my arms over my chest and lean as far away from him as I can. The plane slowly begins to lurch forward, and with every movement, Sarfaraz flinches beside me.

After some time, the plane glides through the air, and the seat belt light flickers off. I keep my belt on, though. I feel more secure with it.

Next to me, Sarfaraz lets out a long breath, wiping at the sheen of sweat on his forehead. My chest prickles. I want to open my mouth, offer words of comfort, but it'd be weird if I did that for a stranger. I tell myself it's my teacher instinct and it has nothing to do with how scared his annoyingly cute face looks.

Unfortunately, Jinnah International isn't the type of airline to have in-flight entertainment, so I had to bring my own. I pull out my iPad, where I loaded up some movies and TV shows on Netflix last night. I plug my headphones in, select *Humsafar*, and settle in.

6

Maya's Law #6:
Trips are never smooth sailing.

After the opening credits, it becomes clear it's going to be in-credibly difficult to focus on the series, and it's because of my seat neighbor.

For one, Sarfaraz types very obnoxiously on his computer. It's like the pitter-patter of rainfall, which is normally very calming, but he goes at warp speed, his fingers dancing across the keyboard like he's trying to break some sort of world re-cord. I check to see if it's bothering the guy on the other side of Sarfaraz, but he has his eye mask on and appears totally dead to the world. At least, I hope he just *appears* dead.

Another thing: he's taking up most of the armrest. I know there isn't exactly a rule about who gets the armrest when you have to share with someone, but he has more of his arm on it. It brushes against mine every now and then, and I pull my arm away while fixing him with an annoyed stare. And every time, he offers me a confused look before going back to his annoying typing.

After a while, Fawad Khan's antics loses my attention, so I shut the iPad off. I thumb through the book I brought along, but I don't feel like reading, either. Finally, I cave, reach into my backpack and produce an eye mask. I don't know if I'll be able to sleep, but I can at least pretend to so no one bothers me. I stick my earphones in, play some soft, classical pieces on my phone, pull my mask on, and rest my head against the seat.

I don't know how long I stay like that; all I know is I don't sleep. I always have a hard time sleeping, but on a plane it's virtually impossible. I try anyway, in some vain attempt to be proven wrong, but nothing happens.

I groan and sit up, pulling the mask off my face and stashing it back in the backpack at my feet. I place my elbow on the left armrest and prop my chin on top of my fist. I look around at the others on the plane. Most people are asleep, others chat with the travelers around them. Watching the people around me converse so easily strikes a pang in my chest. I'm not on a plane with my mother, or my sister, or even a friend. I'm here by myself, with only my thoughts to keep me occupied.

A familiar feeling of loneliness crawls through my veins, creeps into my chest, and settles there. My throat dries. Okay, I need to do something. I need to talk to someone before I start crying on this plane. I survey the area around me, but the person in the aisle seat nearest to me is asleep, and I can't try to talk to the people in front of me—I feel more secure while wearing my belt for the whole flight, and I'd have to take it off to scoot close enough to be able to talk to them. I peek around the side of my seat to see who's sitting behind me, but it's a row of aunties discussing Pakistani politics, and that's a conversation I *know* I don't want any part of.

I sit back in my seat, trying to conceal a grumble. With twisted lips, I force myself to look at the man next to me. His position's remained unchanged. This time, though, he has an iPad on his lap. I have no idea how he's focusing so well on a plane filled with crying kids and chattering adults, especially after seeming so tense at takeoff. But he seems better now.

I can't believe I'm this desperate, but I swallow my pride and open my mouth. "What's your name?"

Sarfaraz doesn't hear me at first, or he pretends not to. It's not until I stare at him for a while that he finally gives in. "Are you talking to me?"

"No, I'm talking to the comatose guy at the window." I lean forward. "I hope he's actually just asleep."

Sarfaraz checks on him. "His chest is moving. He must have taken some killer sleeping pills."

Sleeping pills. Dr. Khan and I considered it once, but I was too afraid of becoming dependent on them. I focus on Sarfaraz again. "So. Your name?" I already know it, of course, but I couldn't think of another good conversation starter.

He stares at me for a few moments before ducking his head back down to his papers. "Sarfaraz."

I tap my fingers against my knees. After a couple of silent seconds, I say, "This would be the part where you ask *my* name."

"Yes, it would be," he agrees. He crosses a line through the word he's written. "If I cared to know your name."

Ouch. "I'm only trying to be friendly."

"That's funny." He looks to me, smiling without humor. "I thought you told your mom you were worried about *me* making small talk with *you*."

"I'm sorry. It's a long flight, I'm traveling by myself, which

I haven't done in a while and…" I trail off when he looks back to his work. "You don't care, do you?"

"Not really."

I know I'm being annoying, but, with eight hours to go, I don't know what else to do. I shift my weight so my arm takes up more of the rest. Sarfaraz jerks away. I ignore his irked face and look down at his iPad. "What are you doing? Work?"

He tries to intimidate me with an extended bothered stare, but he relents when he realizes I'm not going to let up. "You have excellent deduction skills, Miss…"

"Mirza," I fill in. "Maya Mirza. See, you would have gotten that information earlier had you done the polite thing and asked me my name when I asked you yours." I shrug. "Just a suggestion for the next time a stranger tries to make small talk."

I twist my lips into a friendly smile. "So…what are you working on? I'm surprised you can focus enough to work on a plane."

"If I answer, will you leave me alone?"

"Yes."

He breathes heavily through his nose but responds in a neutral tone, "I'm a family lawyer. I'm finishing up some paperwork so I don't have to worry about it on my trip."

"That's ironic," I say, and when he fixes me with a questioning look, I add, "I'm on my way to my wedding."

"I figured."

I tilt my head to the side. "How?"

He gestures to my mehendi-coated palms. "The design is way too detailed for you not to be the bride. That, plus the engagement ring on your finger, but the lack of a wedding band."

Huh. He's been paying more attention than I thought.

Sarfaraz's voice breaks me out of my thoughts. "Congratulations," he says. "Was it love or arranged?"

I clear my throat. "Arranged."

"You know, statistically, fifty percent of marriages end in divorce."

My jaw drops. "Why would you say that to me?"

"Just making small talk," he says with a shrug. Despite his nonchalant attitude, his next words carry a hint of sadness to them. "I know all too well that sometimes things don't work out the way you hope they will."

As much as his words annoy me, I can see how he thinks that. He's a family lawyer; if there's anything he knows, it's that there can be a lot of issues in personal relationships. Still, there's something else there. Something that lingers in his tone, like melancholy. I want to ask more, but I promised I'd leave him alone, so I do. I hear nothing beside me for a moment, but after it becomes clear I'm not going to ask him anything else, Sarfaraz goes back to work.

Somehow, I feel even worse than I did before. There's nothing *wrong* with arranged marriages. My parents had one, and while that didn't exactly end well, Hibba Baji also had one, and she's very happy with her husband and their daughter. Arranged marriages aren't what Western people think they are. It's not the girl being like, twenty-one, while the guy is a forty-year-old man. It's not her being sold to the highest bidder or forced to marry a man against her will. I'm sure it's like that in some places, and that's devastating, but most of the time arranged marriages are…suggestions. Like the parents of one of the parties will send a proposal, referred to as a rishta, to the other person. If the two people happen to like each other, they can court for a few weeks, or months, before getting formally engaged. Then they get married and from there, it's like any other relationship; you have to work hard for it. And, if you work hard enough, you can sometimes find love *after* the marriage—so I've heard.

I reach for my eye mask again, eager to escape the anxiety bubbling in my chest. But as I unzip my bag on the floor, the plane lurches to the side. I gasp, but I manage to steady myself.

I press myself into the back of my seat. I wait for a few seconds to see if the plane will teeter again, but when it doesn't, my muscles relax. I pull my backpack onto my lap, but before I can pull my mask out, the plane jerks again, harder this time. The force is so abrupt I instinctively drop my bag.

Sarfaraz freezes in place, his face paling. He's already white, but he somehow goes *whiter* than white. The plane bumps again, and he drops his pen to clutch the armrest between us. This pushes my arm off the rest, but I don't complain because I don't have the chance.

I push myself up, though it's a bit of a struggle because of how hard the plane is shaking. I grit my teeth and try to take in slow and steady breaths. The cups and drinks on the flight attendant's cart rattle, a few of them fall to the side despite her desperate attempts to keep them from toppling over.

"Passengers," a voice crackles over the intercom. "This is your captain speaking. We're experiencing some turbulence as we approach—" he pauses as if searching for a word that won't induce more panic "—an unsteady storm. I have switched on the fasten–seat belt sign. Please, if you're standing, return to your seat as quickly as possible. I ask that you please remain calm."

No. No, no, no, no, *no*. I can't believe my bad-luck curse has gotten so bad I'm now endangering other lives.

The seat belt sign flickers above us. I breathe a small sigh of relief when I remember I never took my belt off. My pulse skyrockets once more when the plane takes a hard dive to the left.

That throws the crowd into another panic. A few people hastily buckle themselves into their seats, while others grab onto the nearest thing to keep them balanced. The plane steadies itself again and the passengers—with the exception of a few crying kids who are clearly terrified—stay quiet while we wait to see if the situation stabilizes.

Just as I start to relax, the front of the plane dips into a nosedive. The drop feels similar to the adrenaline rush I get when I'm on a roller coaster, but the feeling coursing through me is completely different. Instead of electricity racing through my body and leaving me pleasantly buzzed, terror seizes my veins and fills my lungs, threatening to drown me. The sensation is so consuming I can't even scream; all I can do is sit there and let fear tie me down to this seat.

The plane levels out, tossing everyone in their seats. The lights flicker, briefly launching the plane into darkness. This elicits a couple of low screams from the crowd, but they stop when the lights turn back on. The overhead bins burst open, and everyone instinctively reaches to cover their heads as displaced pieces of luggage barrel toward them. I shrink low in my seat, but I look up long enough to assess the damage around me.

The plane has erupted into chaos. The body dips again, this time much lower than before, causing more screams to burst from the crowd—this time louder and from more people. Panic hangs in the air and fills our throats like thick smoke. The front of the plane plummets, and the top half of my body falls forward. I barely manage to catch myself on the seat in front of me, my fingers clutching the hard material.

"Ladies and gentlemen," the captain's voice echoes across the cabin. "Due to the severity of the storm, we will be making an emergency landing in Switzerland. Please continue to remain calm."

I don't think anyone else heard those last words, because at the mention of an emergency landing, the trills of the panicked passengers get louder.

"Oh, God," Sarfaraz groans, and I flinch at the sound of his voice. For a second, I had completely forgotten he was even there. His face has shifted from white to green, and his palm covers his mouth. Tiny beads of sweat stain his temple, and his Adam's apple visibly bobs. His dark eyes are wide open, and they shine so bright it looks like he's trying really hard not to cry.

Without thinking, I reach over and take his hand. Sarfaraz jerks away instinctively, but I hold on tighter. "It's okay," I say.

I brace my feet on the floor, and Sarfaraz's face becomes even more sweaty, if that's possible. "It's going to be okay," I assure him.

He doesn't get the chance to respond because the plane jerks hard to the right. He clutches me as he bends his head forward, desperately trying to keep his breaths even.

I awkwardly pat his shoulder. He doesn't respond to my touch, so I face forward. I take in deep, calming breaths.

After a while, the plane starts to slow. I peek out the window to see the concrete of the landing area. It's incredibly dark outside, but I can hear the slamming of intense rainfall against the plane.

"Ladies and gentlemen," the captain announces. "Welcome to Zurich, Switzerland."

7

Maya's Law #7:
Something that "almost never happens" will always happen to you.

I lean back, but I pause when I notice Comatose Guy is *still* knocked out. Did he sleep through the whole commotion?

I'm about to poke him when he suddenly jerks awake. He lifts his mask off his face and blearily looks around. "Have we made it?" he asks groggily in Urdu.

Before I can say anything, Sarfaraz lets out a guttural groan. He seems to be doing a lot better now that we're no longer in the air, but his face still has a greenish tint to it. "Are you okay?" I ask.

He inhales and exhales deeply through his mouth a few times, but he nods. "Yeah. I'm okay." A hint of gratitude peeks through his guarded mask. "Thanks."

"You're welcome."

That's when I realize we're still holding hands. I peer down at our entwined fingers, and after briefly casting my eyes back up to his, we both let go at the same time. He flexes his fingers, and I wipe mine on my pants. I continue to avoid eye contact with him until the seat belt light switches off, which is when I unbuckle my belt and stand up.

I wait awkwardly for the people in front of me to grab their bags from the overhead compartment (the few that managed *not* to fall all over the plane) before I step into the aisle. The only bag I have is my backpack, because my suitcase was too big to be a carry-on. I follow behind the slow-moving line, crossing my arms over my chest.

Once we're off the plane and in the actual airport, I look out the window to see the clouds closer to the ground are a lot darker. The sky is a deep purple, and every now and then a bolt of lightning flickers in the darkness. I flinch at the first rumble of thunder, then check my phone and see that it's 7 p.m. If it's 7 p.m. Zurich time, then it's almost 1 p.m. in Toronto. Exhaustion unexpectedly hits me so fast that I lower my head, my chin brushing my chest as I struggle to keep moving and brush it off.

The best thing to do is find my luggage. I don't know how long we're going to be stuck at this airport; hopefully it's not for long, but in case it is, I want to change my clothes.

I go over to the carousel area and wait. Eventually, suitcases begin popping out of the conveyor belt, but even after standing there for a while, I can't find mine. I do one more circle around the area, then head toward an employee working behind the desk. I squint at his name tag: STEFAN. I offer him a kind smile. "Hi, I was wondering if I could get some help?"

Stefan tears his attention away from the computer. "Of course, miss," he says, his Swiss-German accent strong. "What can I help you with?"

I point to the conveyor belt. "Could you find out where

my luggage is? I've been waiting around for a while and I'm getting concerned." I tilt my head to the side. "Or are we not getting our luggage at all? Will it stay on the plane?"

"Let me check for you." He types something into the computer. After a moment, Stefan gives me an apologetic look. "I'm sorry, miss," he begins. "But it appears your luggage is still in Canada."

I freeze. "Excuse me?"

"It seems like your luggage got lost somehow," Stefan continues. "I don't know when you will be able to reach it, but I will call the airport and make sure it is on the next flight to your original destination. Where are you going?"

"Islamabad," I say weakly. I give him the rest of my flight information, which he scribbles down onto a piece of paper.

"Alright, I'll look into it right away," Stefan promises. "I'm sorry this happened. Really, there's only a one percent chance of your luggage getting left behind at the airport."

I groan, dropping my head onto the counter. "Of course there is," I grumble.

Frustration lines my throat, making it harder to suck in breaths that aren't tainted by anger. I want to snap at Stefan, yell at him. But I continue to breathe deeply. It's not Stefan's fault the pilot had to ground the plane. It's not his fault my luggage got left behind. And it's not his fault I was born with the worst luck in the world. "Thank you for all of your help, anyways."

"Of course, miss."

I stumble over to the waiting area and collapse into a chair. I pull my cell phone out of my pocket and turn it back on. The screen blinks back at me—*1:36 a.m.* My eyes feel heavy, but I unlock the screen. I'm glad I ignored Ammi's advice and paid for the travel plan, because now I can call her and give her an update about what's going on.

I call her Pakistan phone number. To avoid having to pay for a travel plan, whenever Ammi comes to Pakistan, she has my uncle buy her a temporary SIM card. It's technically 4:36 a.m. over there, but with all the wedding prep, she might be awake. I listen to the phone ring a couple of times before she picks up. "Maya?" she asks. "What's wrong? Why are you calling me?"

"There's been a slight problem," I say. I explain the situation, and she screeches on the other line.

"We'll send someone to come get you from Zurich," she insists.

"It's fine. I don't think we'll be waiting long," I say, my tone insistent. "It would probably take longer for someone else to get here to pick me up."

"I can't leave you there on your own."

"Ammi, I'm fine," I assure her through clenched teeth. "I'll wait here at the airport until it's time to leave again. I'll be back on another flight before you know it." I check the status of my battery. "Listen, I should go before my battery dies. I'll talk to you soon, okay?"

I hang up quickly, ignoring her protests as I do so. I sink back into the seat, hanging my head over the back.

"That bad, huh?"

I straighten up when I see Sarfaraz looming over me. He looks so much better now that we're off the plane. The color has returned to his face, and he no longer slouches. I sit up. "What's that bad?"

"Whatever your call was about," he answers. He takes the unoccupied seat next to me.

I ignore his comment. I don't feel like talking about my problems with my mom with a stranger. "Do you have any idea how long we're supposed to be grounded in Switzerland?"

Sarfaraz grimaces. "Unfortunately." He reaches into his pocket and produces his phone. "I asked one of the employees earlier. There's a freak storm rolling in, and we got caught in the beginning of it. Apparently, the airline can't afford another lawsuit, so they decided the best course of action was to land the plane and wait it out…but we're going to be waiting for a while."

"Crap," I mutter. I should have expected something like this to happen; the ticket was alarmingly cheap. I knew Jinnah International was a shady airline, but I didn't have the budget for anything else. A teacher's salary does not cover direct flights on secure airlines. In fact, since I also couldn't afford the connecting flight, I had purchased tickets for the much cheaper seventeen-hour bus ride for the final leg of my journey from Islamabad to Karachi. "What are we supposed to do now?"

"Well, it looks like the storm's going to be in Zurich for at least a few days," Sarfaraz explains. "The airline can only afford to put us all up in a hotel for one day, but after that we have to figure it out on our own. They're anticipating the storm will end by Wednesday."

My jaw drops. *But it's only Monday!* "Wednesday?" I splutter. This can't be happening. "I'm getting *married*! I still have so much to do when I get to Pakistan. This throws off all my plans."

Sarfaraz shrugs as he scrolls through his phone. "That sucks."

I'm slightly irritated by his lack of empathy, but I huff out a worried breath. "Okay, I guess I should figure out my next move."

"That's probably a good idea," he says. He gestures to the phone in my lap. "You should check your inbox. The passengers on the flight were supposed to get an email with information about a hotel room for the night."

I lift my phone and swipe it open to see I do, indeed, have an email from Jinnah International. They say sorry for the in-

convenience, which is a funny way of apologizing for us almost dying on their crappy flight, but there's a hotel next to
the airport where they've booked me a room for the night.
They make sure to mention that they don't know how long
the storm is supposed to last and that they're fulfilling con-
tractual obligations to lodge us for one night. After tonight,
I'll have to arrange my own place to stay.

I pocket my phone and pull on my backpack. Just as I stand
up, Sarfaraz looks up from his phone. "Hey, wait a second."
His fingers brush against my own, but at the last second, he
jerks his hand back and stuffs it into his pocket.

Confusion scrunches my nose, but I pause. "Yeah?"

His expression is guarded. "What happened on the plane..."
Sarfaraz clears this throat. "If it wasn't obvious, I get nervous
on planes. It can get pretty bad, especially with long flights.
I was super anxious about it and it made my temper short. I
behaved badly to you, but you were still nice to me and tried
to help." His eyes tentatively meet mine. "So, thanks."

My heart stutters, but I crush the feeling as I say, "Well...
helping a stranger is the best thing you can do."

This time, he lifts a brow. "And why is that?"

"Because it's a selfless good deed," I explain. "The kind
where you don't expect to be helped in return, because you'll
likely never see that person again. But that person will always
remember the stranger who helped them when they needed it."

Sarfaraz mulls over my words, ducking his head and pulling at a loose string hanging from the seam of his laptop bag.
"I guess," he mumbles. He abruptly stands. "Okay. I hope you
make it to your wedding."

He moves to walk away and I blurt, "Do you want to stick
together?"

He pauses. "What?"

I barely stop myself from clapping my hand over my mouth.

Instead, I cover my reddening ears with my hair. "If we're going to be here for a few days, we could stick together. Might not be as daunting being in a foreign country if you're with someone you know." I pause, and add, "Even if you only know them a little bit."

Sarfaraz considers it for a second, then says, "Thanks for the offer, but I think I'm good."

"Oh," I say, and disappointment pinches my side. "That's cool. Good luck with the rest of your trip."

"You, too," he responds, and with one last wave, he walks away.

Great. I'm alone again.

I guess I should call Ammi and tell her it looks like I won't be reaching Karachi for a few days, but honestly, I don't want to deal with her freaking out. I'm trying not to panic myself; the last thing I need is for her shrill voice to be screaming in my ear about how I can't be left alone in a foreign country. Besides, I keep saying I can take care of myself. So, let's take care of myself.

With renewed confidence, I walk toward the exit. It may be the summer, but it's pretty chilly outside, and it's still raining. I scan the area, looking for a cab. I eventually locate one, and on the way to the hotel, I scroll through my phone for other places to stay. There aren't a lot of hotels available, and the ones that are have crazy high prices. It's a touristy area, after all.

I change course and look for hostels instead. I don't want to spend the next few days sitting at this airport, waiting for the storm to pass. I don't need anything fancy—just a place to sleep at night. When I lived in Seoul, some of my coworkers and I visited Japan, and we stayed in hostels each night before moving on to the next city. It saved us a lot of money, and it got me used to sleeping around strangers. Not that my mother knew; it was a coed trip, and I don't know how she would've reacted had she known I was staying with boys. It's incredibly taboo in our culture, *especially* because I was engaged at the time. Of course, I was with friends then so it was technically safer than if I were alone, but whatever.

If I do this, I might be able to sightsee, too. Parts of my favorite Korean drama, *Crash Landing on You*, were filmed in Switzerland. A quick search confirms the weather in the cities where they filmed—Iseltwald and Sigriswil—will be a lot better than the weather in Zurich. I can explore and still make it back in time for the flight to Islamabad. Tonight, I'll stay in a hotel, and then tomorrow I'll explore Zurich. In the evening, I'll make my way to Interlaken.

I need to look on the bright side. Yeah, okay, this stop was unexpected, but I'm in Switzerland! I wanted to come here for my honeymoon, and when Imtiaz said he didn't want to, I was more crushed than I let on. So now that I'm here, I'm going to take advantage of it.

With that plan in mind, I find a hostel in Interlaken. They don't take reservations, so I'll have to hope they have a place for me when I get there. God may have thrown my plans off course once again, but I'm going to take the location as a good sign.

Except…maybe it's not a good idea to leave Zurich. Knowing my luck, I could very well miss my flight or maybe the hostels won't have room for me to stay. I imagine wandering the streets for hours in the rain, trying desperately to find a hostel with enough room to take me but ending up with nothing. It's safer to stay here rather than explore the areas where they shot *Crash Landing on You*, and it'd probably be easier to find a place to stay.

It's okay, I rationalize to myself. Inshallah, one day I'll come back to Switzerland, and I'll be able to thoroughly explore. For now, I'll stick around Zurich and ignore the pit in my stomach that longs for more than I'm willing to risk. Unfortunately, my body hasn't caught up to the fact that my luck sucks. Missing my flight isn't a risk I want to take. I'll make peace with it.

Someday, Inshallah.

8

**Maya's Law #8:
You'll never be as cool as you think you are.**

The hotel room is kind of crappy, with the space only big enough for a single bed and a congested bathroom, but it's better than sleeping on the floor. I don't have any clothes because my luggage isn't here, so I just get into bed with my plane clothes on. I crawl between the sheets and wait for sleep to come.

I manage to squeeze in a couple of hours, and in the morning, I take a shower and change back into the same clothes. One of my stops today definitely has to be a clothing store.

One peek out the window confirms the storm is still on. It doesn't look as bad as it did yesterday, though; instead of the loud and rough slamming of raindrops against the window, it's more of a soft but steady flow of water from the sky. The clouds shifted at some point in the night from the darker indigo tones of a thunderstorm to lighter hues of blue, but I guess the airline still didn't want to risk a potential lawsuit. From how Sarfaraz spoke yesterday, it seems like they've had more than their fair share of legal troubles and aren't looking for any more, even if their caution causes inconvenience.

I drop the blinds and grab my backpack off the floor. After I check out, I stop at the gift shop. I buy an umbrella and at the last second, I grab another one. Knowing my luck, something bad will happen and I'll end up needing a backup.

A quick online search before bed last night led me to a Zurich City Bus Tour package. It wasn't too expensive, either, so I figured it would be good enough for one day. After I'm done at the gift shop, I take a cab over to the bus station terminal.

I get there just as the bus is pulling into the terminal. It's big enough to seat sixty people on each level. Sleek black windows shape the top half while red paints the bottom. The words *Classic Trolly* cover the middle of the bus against a black banner, and beside that are the flags of countries whose languages the company offers a recorded version of the tour in.

I claim a seat in the middle of the bus, which is generally a safe spot. As a teacher, I always have to sit at the front when I go on field trips with the kids, and for some reason it's still ingrained in my mind that the back of the bus is reserved for the "cool kids"—a group that I, a brown Muslim daughter of immigrants, never belonged to—so the middle is my sweet spot.

I settle in my seat while the rest of the bus slowly fills up. I wish I'd had more than a coffee and a croissant from the hotel for breakfast this morning, but I had to hurry out the door so I wouldn't miss this bus. I tap my fingers against my lap, then lean my head against the window. I end up taking my phone out so I can shoot someone a text, but my fingers pause on the screen. My mother wasn't happy when I informed her of my new plans to stay in Switzerland for a while, but there wasn't exactly anything she could do. I scroll through some unanswered text messages to her and my sister. Everyone is probably too busy preparing for the wedding, including Hibba Baji. I contemplate messaging Imtiaz, but sometimes awkward conversations with him can weigh on me for the rest of the day, and I don't want to dampen my tour before it's even started. I lock my phone and lower it in my lap. Without Ammi or Hibba Baji, there isn't anyone to text.

"Hi!"

I fumble with my phone to keep it from slipping out of my fingers. I catch it right before it can hit the ground, and I look up to see a blonde woman smiling kindly at me. She looks around Hibba Baji's age, but if the wrinkles in her face are any indication, she's older. Two small blond children stand behind her in the aisle; the taller one is a boy, who seems to be twelve or so, and judging by his bored expression, he already wishes he were anywhere else. The shorter child is a girl around six years old. She traces some kind of nonsensical pattern on the fabric of the seat in front of her.

The woman, who I assume to be their mother, gestures to the seat next to me. "Do you mind if I sit here?" she asks, a soft German accent lacing her words.

I gesture to the empty seat. "No, go ahead."

She places her bag in the chair. She goes back to her children and situates them in the seats next to ours. The girl begs her mother for the window seat, but her mother makes her sit in the aisle seat so she's within her reach. The boy sits down at the window and pulls a video game console out of the backpack he carries.

Once both children are settled, the woman collapses into her seat. Her elbow bumps mine, and when I pull away, she offers me an apologetic look. "Sorry about that," she says, and I can hear the exhaustion in her voice.

"It's fine, really," I assure her. I peer over at her kids. "I can't imagine it's easy traveling with children."

"Oh, it's a real challenge," she groans. "One has to go to the bathroom all the time, while the other is hungry all the time. But at least I'm not doing it completely alone. My husband is here for a conference, so we thought we'd make it a family vacation. He's in his meetings right now, so I offered to take the kids on a tour so they're not stuck inside the hotel room all day while we're waiting for him to be done." The woman pauses. "I'm sorry, I'm telling you all of this, but I didn't even introduce myself." She holds out a hand. "I'm Kelly."

I accept her shake. "Maya. Nice to meet you."

"Nice to meet you, too. My son's name is Felix, and my daughter's name is Emma."

"Those are lovely names. They seem like good kids."

"Yeah, that's because you don't know them. Just wait until they're hungry—they become completely different people." Kelly chuckles. I smile politely back, but I guess she interprets it as something else because her face twists with worry. "Oh my God. I'm bothering you, aren't I?"

My mouth forms an O shape. "Oh, no! You're not, I promise."

"I'm sorry," she says anyway. She gestures to her kids, who are now both occupied with devices. "It's lonely traveling by myself with only young kids to talk to. Don't get me wrong—they're my kids and I love them, and I love being around them, but sometimes it's nice to talk to someone about something other than video games." She lifts a shoulder. "I guess I got so carried away I forgot I was talking to a stranger."

"I get it," I say. It's exactly what I did with Sarfaraz on the plane, after all. "Sometimes it's easier talking to strangers." I peer over her back, but thankfully her kids are still engrossed in their games. "I really hope they didn't overhear that."

We both have a laugh, then the tour guide appears and lets us know we're about to get started. He passes out earbuds for us to plug into the headphone jack above us so we can listen to the commentary.

"So," Kelly begins, "what brings you to Switzerland?"

"I'm exploring the country before I leave for my wedding," I answer. It's a much easier response than explaining everything that led me here.

"You're getting married? Congratulations! You must be so excited."

"I…am," I respond, my words hesitant, but I quickly mask the uneasiness with a reassured look.

Kelly clears her throat before saying, "You're smart. I wish I thought about taking a vacation by myself before getting married. I mean, my bachelorette party was in Mexico with my friends, but that wasn't the same as taking a trip alone." She secures the headphone jack into the port. "Where did you go with your friends for your bachelorette?"

"I didn't have one," I explain. I elaborate at her questioning stare. "It's not something I was comfortable with. That, plus… I don't have a lot of close friends I could have celebrated with."

"Oh," she says, in a confused-slash-pitying tone.

The words fumble out of my mouth before I can stop them. "It's not like I didn't try to make friends," I continue. "I fell out with a lot of my high school friends after we graduated; they were the kind of people who I realized were only my friends because we saw each other every day, you know?"

"Oh, yes," Kelly sympathizes. "I definitely had a few of those."

"Then in university I was painfully shy, so I only became close friends with two girls," I continue, like I'm physically unable to hold my words in. I've never spoken any of these feelings aloud, but now that I've started, I can't seem to stop.

"I lost touch with them once I entered teacher's college. Then I befriended one guy, who, at the end of our degree, told me he couldn't be friends with me anymore because it made his girlfriend uncomfortable."

"Yikes. That doesn't sound like a healthy situation."

"It really wasn't, but what was I supposed to say? We ended up finding each other on Instagram a year or so later, and I learned he'd left her shortly after we stopped being friends because the relationship had become too stifling. We stayed in casual contact after that, but we aren't close. But he *is* the one who told me about the great opportunities people find teaching English abroad. He was teaching in South Korea, and he came home for a visit. We had dinner, which is when he convinced me to consider joining him in teaching over there. He had nothing but positive things to say, and since I'd been feeling like I was stuck in a rut, I agreed."

"South Korea?" Kelly grins. "That sounds so exciting! You up and left for a whole other country, just like that?"

My smile falters. "I had to convince my mom, but eventually I went and stayed there for about two years."

"Wow. Now I'm even more jealous of you. You're living life how you want. You should enjoy that independence while it lasts, because after you get married, everything changes. Your priorities shift. You can't decide to go somewhere by yourself, because you have someone waiting for you at home. Take this time to have some fun. I promise you'll regret it if you don't."

I know that's what my situation looks like on the outside, to a stranger. Young woman about to get married having the time of her life by herself in Switzerland.

And I kind of *like* the image of myself Kelly has in her head. Like I could be that young jet-setter who has it all: a handsome fiancé, two years of living in a foreign country under her belt, and the kind of self-confidence that only comes from being comfortable living with yourself. Someone who is absolutely fine traveling on her own and doesn't feel like she needs to talk to the stranger sitting beside her on a plane to keep from feeling like she's falling apart.

Maybe…maybe I *should* go to Interlaken. Yes, it's risky to leave the city where my flight leaves from, because a dozen things could go wrong in my attempts to return. But Kelly's admiration of me makes me want to fully encompass the image she has of me. Besides, if *Crash Landing on You* has taught me anything, it's that even if I end up on the wrong train (or plane in my case), I'll still end up at the right destination. So why shouldn't I take the risk? Why shouldn't I try to break a few rules before I get married and my life changes forever?

This is me taking control of something, and I know it's going to work out.

"I definitely will."

9

Maya's Law #9:
Right when you think you've got it figured out, the world will humble you.

The first stop on the tour is Lake Zurich. The tour guide speaks primarily in German, so I pay more attention to the prerecorded information the bus itself provides. Kelly and I chat lightly while we listen to the tour, and she even interprets some of the tour guide's commentary for me.

I forgot how fun it can be to hang out with strangers. When I went to South Korea, I told myself I wasn't going to make the same mistakes as I did before when it came to being in a new environment. I'd be outgoing, and make friends, and have the time of my life. I was only going to be there for two years, and when I got home, I'd be back in the real world, one where I was going to be married. I was not going to waste the incredible life experiences I was offered.

And for a while, it worked. I was open and engaging and made a bunch of friends within the program. When those friends made plans to travel around the rest of Korea and Japan, I took charge of the planning so I could be as involved as possible. While the rest of them got drunk, I was always the friend you could rely on to get you home safely. I was the everyman, with a toe in lots of different groups.

But the problem with pretending to be someone else? It's not sustainable in the long run. After the first year, I returned to my old ways. I didn't want to go out. I preferred to stay in and mark assignments. The farthest I went from home was the restaurant around the corner from my apartment. The problem with being in lots of different groups is you don't quite belong in any of them. There were times I missed inside jokes. Times I wasn't able to make it to one group's outing because I was desperately trying to mend a hole in another group. I got to a point where I naturally drifted right out, so I stopped trying to find friends in strangers.

But hanging around Kelly is effortless. Maybe it's because she's a mom, and my closest friend is my mom. Maybe it's because she's funny. Or maybe it's because we know that at the end of the two hours, we'll go our separate ways and never see each other again. Maybe that's the beauty in friends you meet on vacation: you can be whoever you want to be, but at the end of the day, you go back to being yourself.

"It's so beautiful, isn't it?" Kelly says as we stand at the lakeside and stare out at Hafen Enge. She moves her eyes every couple of minutes to check on her kids, but she remains engaged with me, making great use of that multitasking talent moms have.

"It sure is. The pictures don't do it justice."

"They never do," Kelly points out. "Sure, it'll look like the place, but there's a certain…magic missing."

Standing here, staring out at Lake Zurich, watching the way the light makes the reflection on the water glitter, it's hard to believe I won't live in this moment forever. I'll have to get back on that bus. I'll have to get back on that plane. I'll have to keep going.

"Maya, do you think you could take some photos of me and the kids?" Kelly's voice breaks my reverie. She holds her phone out to me.

"Of course."

When we get back to Zurich, Kelly and I exchange Instagram handles. "If you ever find yourself in Germany, be sure to look me up," she insists.

"I will."

We say our goodbyes, and then Kelly and her children get into a cab and drive off.

I check my phone and realize it's almost lunchtime. My stomach growls, and I remember I didn't have much for breakfast. I find a restaurant with good reviews online, then take a cab there. The menu is in German, so the waiter has to explain to me in broken English what the meals are. I eventually settle on an oyster pasta.

After lunch, I decide I can't keep wearing this outfit until Wednesday, so I go shopping. The prices in the stores make my stomach clench, but I have no choice. I buy one dress, a couple of shirts and pairs of pants, and some underwear. I also add a large duffel bag to my purchase; it's way too expensive, but at least I'll have something to put all these extra clothes in apart from my backpack.

I spend the rest of the day walking around Zurich and taking photos. The rain started to pick up again after lunch, so I open my umbrella and hold it over my head as I stroll the streets. I play one of the songs from the *Crash Landing on You* soundtrack on my phone. If I block out the noise of the busy street and focus on the soft tunes in my ears and the pitter-patter of the rain against my umbrella, I can pretend I *am* that jet-setter Kelly thinks I am. Here I am, in Switzerland, after a disastrous flight forced me to stay, unplanned, in a foreign country. The panic I felt earlier fades with each wet step against the concrete. The worry disappears with every earthy breath I take. The loneliness that hung over my head slips off. It dissolves slower than the other feelings, but all that matters is it *does* go away.

See, Maya? I think triumphantly to myself as I expertly avoid an old man approaching me. *You can roll with the punches. Maybe this is the end of your bad luck.*

My stomach gurgles, and I falter in my step. My hand flies to my midsection, and I wait for the churning to stop. It fades for only a second before another wave of pain bubbles in my gut. This one hurts, and I tighten my grip around the handle of my umbrella. I swallow thickly. I take in deep breaths through my nose, hoping it'll soothe the growing discomfort.

It helps somewhat. It still feels like my stomach is flip-flopping, but I can tolerate it. Maybe I need to use the bathroom and then rest. I check the time on my phone, and it's almost 8 p.m. It's a reasonable time to end the day. I haven't had dinner yet, but with the way my stomach is griping, I can't fathom eating. I think back to the last thing I ate. Oyster pasta...

My stomach rolls for a second before it settles again. I grit my teeth. *Damn it. It was definitely the oyster pasta.*

I take a cab to the hostel, and during the ride over, my pain picks back up...but worse. Instead of the light ache, it's a deep one. It crawls up my throat and thickens my tongue. I open the window despite the rain and try to suck in the cool air, but all it does is make me aware of the growing sheen of sweat on my forehead.

By the time the cab makes it to the hostel, I have to breathe deeply in through my mouth because it's the only thing keeping my stomach calm. I hurry over to the pastel purple door of the building and get inside as fast as I can.

Thankfully there's no line at the small front desk. The boy sitting behind the desk looks up from his computer screen when he hears the door open. "Hi," he says when I stop in front of him. "Can I help you?"

"I'd like to book a bed, please," I say through clenched teeth.

He frowns at my strangled voice but starts typing on the computer. After a few seconds, he asks, "How long do you plan on staying?"

"Until Wednesday."

"Then I have a bed available for you." He writes something down on a pad and looks up at me. "How would you like to pay?"

Another ache spreads through my stomach, and I wrap my arm around my middle as I give him my credit card. "Visa, please."

He takes the card and swipes it. "Sorry, it looks like your card's been declined."

"What?" I stammer. *Declined?* That can't be possible; I haven't spent anywhere near my limit this month, and I called to let them know I would be traveling abroad so they shouldn't worry about any strange transactions. "Could you try it again?"

He does, but it's still rejected. "Sorry, nothing." He holds the card out to me. "Do you have another method of payment? Like Swiss francs?"

Of course I don't. I didn't plan on making a long pit stop in Switzerland, so I don't have any of their money. I take the card back from him. "No," I grumble, pocketing my useless card. "Thanks anyway."

The man waves, though his eyebrows thin with concern. "If there's anything else I can help with…"

I head for the front door. "No, I can handle this. Thanks." I could have asked to use their bathroom, but I really, *really* don't want to throw up, so I'd rather track down some medicine to settle my stomach. I pause at the door when another surge of nausea rises in my throat. I swallow, hard, before glancing over at the front-desk worker. "Actually, do you happen to know if there's a pharmacy anywhere nearby?"

"Yeah," he answers uneasily. "Once you walk out of here, go left, and keep going all the way down the street. Then turn left again. There's a place on that corner."

"Thank you," I manage to get out, and I step outside. I don't even bother to reach for my umbrella just in case me pressing on my stomach is what's keeping me from hurling. I let the rain soak my skin and blur my vision as I walk as fast as I can down the street.

When I stumble into the pharmacy, I get a lot of weirded-out looks from the few patrons inside. I can understand why: I'm dripping wet, my hair is frazzled, and I'm sure my face is greener than an avocado. I keep my head down and beeline for the aisles.

I wipe the water out of my eyes as I go through each row, trying to find where anti-nausea medicine is. I blink hard a few times as I try to focus on the products in front of me. Frustratingly, the labels are in German, so I have no idea what I'm reading. The churning in my gut pulses through my body with every heartbeat. At this point, the nausea is so bad I feel like if someone even *touches* me—

"Maya?" I hear at the same time as a hand lightly touches my back.

I turn around, and my jaw drops. "Sarfaraz?" I rasp, my mouth filling with saliva.

The lines in Sarfaraz's forehead deepen. "Are you okay? You don't look so good."

"I'm fine," I instinctively say.

"Are you sure?"

"Yes," I grit. "I can take care of my—"

A spew of vomit surges up my throat, and before I can choke it back down, it sprays out of my mouth. To my horror, it hits Sarfaraz square in the chest, splattering his front. My hand flies to my mouth as if that's going to stop the puking, but it just leaks out between my fingers.

I expect Sarfaraz to spring away from me, but he just wrinkles his nose before reaching for my shopping bag, which I must've dropped at some point. He grabs it blindly and opens it up to catch my flow of vomit. "Don't—!" I start, but I'm cut off by another wave of bile spewing from my throat. Despair wracks my chest as I watch my own puke ruin the clothes I bought today.

Finally, my gut seems to calm, but pain still plagues my stomach. My body aches all over. Exhaustion overwhelms me all at once, crashing against my skull.

Sarfaraz lowers the bag warily from my face. "Are you okay?"

"For now," I respond. I wipe my mouth, but all that does is spread the vomit around. A clerk kindly steps forward with a roll of paper towel and a bottle of hand sanitizer. I give her an apologetic look as I accept both gratefully from her. It's not going to be fun cleaning my puke off the floor. I try my best to clean my face and my hair, but the stink lingers.

The clerk also gives Sarfaraz a paper towel roll and sanitizer so he can clean his shirt. Guilt and mortification spread through my chest as he dabs at the stain on his shirt.

"I'm sorry about that," I say.

"No…worries," he replies, though the way he pinches his lips together tells me he's trying hard to hold back a snarky comment. "It was my fault for pushing you. It set you off."

Once we're done, I find a garbage bin to throw the used paper towels away, and I clean my hands with the sanitizer. When I return to the aisle, Sarfaraz holds out a small bottle to me. "Here. This is what you need."

I wrinkle my nose. "You can read German?"

"No, but the pharmacist can, and he can speak some English," he explains. "Plus, I think it's pretty obvious to everyone you need anti-nausea medication."

"Asking the pharmacist." I bite the inside of my cheek. "I probably should have thought of that."

"Well, to be fair, you had other things taking priority," Sarfaraz points out. "Like trying to hold your stomach acid in."

I snort, but the action irritates my middle. I take the medicine from Sarfaraz. "Thanks," I tell him, and I start to head toward the cashier when I remember one crucial detail: I don't have any money. "Damn it," I hiss under my breath.

"Something wrong?" Sarfaraz asks, and I jump, whipping my head to look back at him. For some reason, I'd assumed when I started for the cashier that he left.

"Uh, yeah," I answer. I breathe heavily through my nose. "My credit card got cut off, and I don't have any Swiss francs, so I can't pay for this."

"Didn't you call your bank and let them know you'd be stranded for a few days so they wouldn't be alarmed by any charges coming from Switzerland?" he wonders.

"I did—" I feel the remaining color leave my face "—but not for Switzerland. I told them I'd be going to Pakistan but forgot to tell them I was stranded in another country. So much has happened in the last twenty-four hours I could only focus on what needed my immediate attention." I rub my temples. "This is such a mess."

Sarfaraz hesitates for a moment before taking the bottle back from me. "I got it."

"What?" I blurt. "No, I can't ask you to do that."

"Then it's a good thing I'm offering." He continues on to the cashier without another word. I can only stare after him for a moment before I brush it off and grab my vomit-filled bag from the floor. I should probably toss it, but those clothes were expensive. If I can find a laundromat or a dry cleaner nearby, maybe I can salvage them.

After Sarfaraz pays, he gives me the medicine and gestures toward the exit. I have no choice but to follow him. I feel slightly better when the cool breeze touches my face and slips down my sweat-laced neck.

"Where's your hotel?" Sarfaraz asks, bringing my attention back to him. "I'll take you back there."

"I don't have a hotel," I explain. A small twinge hits my stomach again, and I cross my arms over my abdomen. "I was planning on staying in a hostel tonight."

"A *hostel*?" he splutters. "You mean a great spot to get robbed in your sleep? Not to mention they're incredibly unhygienic."

I don't bother pointing out we're both wearing my vomit as I say, "I'm sure they clean the place up. It's not like it's rat-infested. As for the robbing…" I shrug. "I barely sleep. I'm always alert."

"Hostel guests practically sleep on top of each other," Sarfaraz retorts. "It's the perfect place for disease to hop between hosts."

A laugh unexpectedly bursts from my chest. "What do you have against hostels?"

"Nothing," he admits. "I just like having my own space."

"Yeah, well, I'd prefer that, too," I grumble. "But the hostel's the only place I can afford." I give him a once-over. "Not all of us are rich lawyers, you know."

His teasing face quickly morphs back into the sullen one I've become so accustomed to. "Yeah, of course."

I'm treading on uneven ground right now, so I change the subject. "I've been sightseeing since we got here, so I just need a place to sleep. I didn't need a whole hotel room for only one night. I'm going to Interlaken tomorrow."

"Interlaken?" he repeats. "Why?"

Pink blooms in my face. "There's a show I love called *Crash Landing on You*, and they filmed some of the scenes here. I wanted to check out the locations after exploring Zurich. Interlaken is close to the two cities where they filmed most of the scenes, so I was going to stay there and take the train."

Sarfaraz looks like he's trying hard not to judge me. "I mean… I guess that's an effective way to spend your time," he says, his voice even. He avoids my gaze as he says, "If you want, I managed to get a hotel room. You could sleep there. It's a two-bed room."

My jaw slackens. "I thought you didn't want to hang out with me."

He exhales deeply through his nose. "It's not that I didn't want to hang out with you," he begins. "I'm used to being on my own. But after what happened, it wouldn't feel right leaving you by yourself." He gestures to my purse. "Plus, didn't you say your cards are frozen? You can't pay for a place, anyway."

"I can call my bank right now and explain the situation." I check my phone. "They should be open."

"It might still take them a while to complete the process." He looks at me, but I swear he keeps his focus on my forehead. "Look, you're sick, you're stranded, and you need help. Let me help."

I pause for a moment, looking him up and down. I don't know him well, but he seems sincere. "Really?"

His face flushes. "I know you didn't have the best first impression of me, but I'm not that much of a jerk. And I'm just offering you a bed. We don't have to interact with each other."

I hum. On the one hand, if anyone in Pakistan finds out I stayed in a hotel room with some random man, my izzat—and by extension, my family's—would be stained so fast it would win a world record. But on the other, it's late, I'm exhausted, I smell like vomit, and I'm scared about what to do next, and this random stranger is offering to help when he could have left me and gone on his way.

Eventually, I nod slowly. "Yeah. That'd be good."

10

Maya's Law #10:
Your wardrobe is always going to be lacking.

Sarfaraz calls a cab to take us to the hotel. We sit in silence for the whole ride with the windows down to combat the smell of puke. I discreetly look over at Sarfaraz. Exhaustion lines his forehead, but he seems alert as he stares out the window. Every now and then, the light from the streetlamps flickers over his face, and I catch a glimpse of something like apprehension in his expression; but the flash is always so brief I can never tell.

The cab screeches to a stop in front of the hotel. Sarfaraz gets out first, and just as I unbuckle my belt, the door opens on its own. I look up, blinking against the darkness.

Sarfaraz stands there, holding the door open. He jerks his head to the side. "Come on."

I smile my thanks and climb out of the car. Exhaustion

weighs me down as I step out. The events of the day have caught up with me, and all I want to do is sleep.

It's still raining, and tiny droplets pelt my face. I press the sides of my fingers to my brow bone so I can see without the rain blinding me. He closes the car door behind me, and we head to the entrance.

The place is quaint. More like an inn than anything. The lobby is small, with a receptionist's desk set up against the wall. There's a sitting area on the left, with one red couch and two tan chairs surrounding a coffee table. Tall potted plants are set up near the front doors, and they bristle from the wind blowing in when we open the door.

The lobby is empty, with only a bored-looking receptionist sitting behind the desk. Sarfaraz leads me down the hall to where I assume his room is. We walk there in silence, the only sound being the echoes of our footsteps.

I can't believe I'm staying in a room with a *stranger*. Yeah, okay, I've stayed with strangers before; technically when I taught in Seoul, I didn't know my roommates, but I had time to become friends with them, and we all had background checks before we were permitted to room with other people. I know absolutely nothing about this guy, other than his name. I don't even know how old he is.

Maybe that's one thing I can cross off. We stop in front of the door. "How old are you?" I ask.

He gives me a strange look. "That's a weird question."

"Are you going to answer it?"

Sarfaraz presses the card against the lock. When it flashes green, he twists the doorknob. "Thirty-four."

Damn—that's six years older than me. He certainly doesn't look like it, though. Maybe it's the short stubble, which ironically should make him look older, but it frames his square jaw in just the right way. Maybe it's his hair, swept back and longer in the front but shorter in the back, with a few strands that curl over his brow. Or maybe it's the way his broad shoulders fill out his tight-fitting shirt. Not that I've been looking.

He switches on the light but lets me in first, and I breathe a sigh of relief when I realize there are in fact two beds. There's also a TV set up on a stand in front of the beds, and a small table with two chairs. Two lamps hang off the wall in between the beds, and underneath them is a long side table. I go over and turn both lights on.

I want to sit down on the bed closest to the window, but I'm too afraid to get it wet. I look down at my clothes, and my ears redden as I make a crucial realization.

"Something wrong?" Sarfaraz asks. He heads over to the closet and slides the door open. I watch him pull his suitcase out. He lifts it and places it on the bed closer to the door.

I curl a clumped section of hair over my ear. "I have no clothes."

He pauses, his fingers on the zipper of his suitcase. "What?"

"Somehow, the airline didn't get my luggage onto the flight." Biting back an annoyed groan, I hold up the bag that contains my new—and puke-stained—clothes. "The new clothes I bought today were in this bag, but you used it to catch my vomit."

Guilt contorts Sarfaraz's face. "I'm sorry. Why didn't you tell me?"

"I tried to warn you, but I was interrupted by the bile coming out of my mouth." I lower the bag. "So, I have nothing to wear."

He snorts, and when I glare at him, he waves an apologetic hand. "Sorry, it's just… It's really not your night, huh?"

Yeah, except "it's not your night" is also "it's not your day" and it repeats in a vicious cycle. "I guess I'll…sleep in the tub?"

"Don't be ridiculous."

"I'm not. There's no point in sleeping in a dry bed if I'm going to make the sheets wet and smell like vomit."

He flips his suitcase open, rummages around for a second, then pulls out a huge Beatles T-shirt. He holds it out to me. "Here."

My pulse spikes. "What?"

He waves the shirt in my direction. "You need something to wear."

Cautiously, I take it from him. "But what about pants?"

Sarfaraz's eyes linger on my legs, and the urge to cover myself up races through me. "I sincerely doubt my pants are going to fit you," he says. He pulls out a pair of pajamas for himself. "Wear the shirt. It'll be long enough on you."

I choke out a noise of disbelief. "I can't have my legs bare around you."

"I promise I won't be looking at your legs, if that's what you're worried about."

I bite my tongue and look down at my legs. The rain made the material stick to them so you can see their shape. I guess it's good that he's promising not to stare at my bare skin. "Okay," I relent.

He gestures toward the bathroom. "You can shower first if you'd like. I think you need it more than I do."

Despite the fact that I should feel grateful he's helping me, a rush of annoyance floods my chest. "Thanks," I drawl, but I head over to the bathroom anyway. I leave the clothes bag beside the door, but thankfully, the underwear I bought is enclosed in a plastic package, so I take that out of the bag before stepping into the bathroom. Once I'm inside, I place the pharmacy bag and underwear on the counter and face the mirror. My bangs cling to my forehead in clumps, soaked from rainwater, and my hair looks scraggly. There's a stickiness to it, probably from the vomit. Yellow tints the area around my mouth, and I resist the urge to gag at the memory of throwing up all over Sarfaraz and myself. Red rims my irises, and bile sours my tongue. I can't believe I was around Sarfaraz in this state.

I shrug before moving toward the shower. It's not like it matters.

I peel my clothes off, wincing at the stiffness of the material. I step into the shower and twist the faucet. The hot water against my aching muscles feels so good I have to swallow back a moan of relief. I use the shampoo and body wash bottles the hotel provides and wash the events of the day down the drain. When I'm done, I towel myself off. I put the underwear on and pull the T-shirt over my head. Concern courses through my body when I realize it stops around my knees. It's fine, but it still feels like too much skin exposed in a room with a man who is *not* my fiancé. Even Imtiaz has never seen this much of me before.

I reach into the pharmacy bag for the medicine, but I pause when my fingers wrap around something distinctly *not* bottle-shaped. I pull out a brand-new toothbrush still in its packaging. I don't remember grabbing one; Sarfaraz must've slipped it in there when I wasn't looking.

My grip tightens around it slightly, before I set it on the counter and reach for the medicine instead. Thankfully, the bottle comes with a cup to measure the dose, so I pour some of the syrup in and chug it down. The bitterness puckers my lips, but it doesn't last for long. After a moment's hesitation, I open the toothbrush and brush my teeth. Minty freshness replaces the unpleasant taste in my mouth.

When I'm done, I gather my clothes from the floor and fold them before tiptoeing over to the door. I poke my head through, keeping my body hidden. Sarfaraz is still in his clothes—he must have been waiting for me to finish in the bathroom. I clear my throat, and he looks up at me. "Could you close your eyes?" I ask.

Thankfully, he does it without question. I step out of the bathroom and move to drop my clothes next to the shopping bag, but I pause when I realize it's not there. "What happened to my clothes?"

"While you were in the shower, I asked the housekeepers if they could wash your clothes," he explains, keeping his eyes closed. "It cost me extra, but they'll have them ready for you by tomorrow morning."

My chest warms. "Thanks," I say, before clearing my throat. "Just let me know much that costs tomorrow."

"Sure."

I plug my phone into the wall to charge, then dive for the bed and get in between the sheets. Once I'm situated and sure I'm totally covered, I say, "Okay, I'm good."

Sarfaraz opens his eyes. "Lovely." He turns back around, grabs his clothes, and heads for the bathroom. After a few seconds, I hear the shower running.

I slump into the mattress, fatigue overwhelming me now that I'm in a soft bed. German medicine must be made from the elixir of life or something because the nausea is already starting to flush out of my system. While I will my breathing to even, I stare up at the ceiling.

Okay. I'm in a hotel room with a strange man, who seems decent enough but will blurt something insulting right after being nice. It's not that I'm worried; if I didn't trust Sarfaraz, I wouldn't be here. And sure, I might be trusting him too quickly, but while he's annoying, there's something so…familiar about him. It's enough to make me lower my guard sooner than I usually would around a man. I groan and bring the sheets up over my head, though all that does is make the smell of Sarfaraz's shirt more overwhelming. I was expecting it to smell like pine and coffee, but I'm pleasantly surprised that it smells faintly of lemons and fresh laundry.

It's…it's *weird*. I've never been in a hotel room with a man who isn't related to me. I have memories of staying in hotels when my dad was still around, but it was so long ago that time has blurred the edges. After he left, we rarely went on vacation, and if we did, it was only Ammi, Hibba Baji, and me. No boys anywhere. I've never even shared a hotel room with Imtiaz before; even though we're engaged, that would be way too scandalous in our community.

It may seem strange for an engaged couple, but trust me, I've seen weirder stuff when it comes to intimacy between a guy and girl in the desi community. Once, my cousin got in trouble for dancing too close to a guy at a party. The guy was her husband, and the party was their wedding. They literally got in trouble for being too close to each other during their first dance as a *married couple*.

It's stuff like that, so instilled in us, that makes us uncomfortable when it comes time to get close to a member of the opposite sex. So, while I'm…attracted to Imtiaz, I've never been intimate with him in any sort of way. I'm not sure what it's supposed to feel like. What does kissing the grown-up way feel like?

Ya Allah, the *grown-up* way? I'm going to be so screwed on my wedding night.

I pull the sheets back down when I hear the bathroom door open, but I tuck the blanket under my chin. Sarfaraz comes out in a well-worn green T-shirt and plaid pajama bottoms. He puts his suitcase down on the ground, then turns the room light off. It's not completely dark, though, because of the two lamps beside the beds. He pauses when he notices me staring. "Do you need something?"

My face flushes. "Why are you doing this?" I ask, bewilderment pursing my lips. "Why are you bending over backward to be so nice? I don't know you, and you don't know me."

He's quiet, and for a second, I think he's not going to answer me, but then he says, "Someone once told me helping a stranger is the best thing you can do."

"And why is that?"

Even in the almost-darkness, I can see a hint of a smile. "Because more likely than not, that person will always remember the stranger who helped them when they needed it. And just maybe, that stranger will be able to return the favor somehow."

I didn't say that last part to him, but something soft touches my chest at his addition. "She sounds like a wise person."

He pulls the sheets back. "How'd you know it was a woman?"

"Because women tend to be smart like that."

Sarfaraz chuckles but doesn't say anything else. He settles himself in bed, then reaches for his lamp.

"Wait," I say, lifting my head. His fingers pause on the switch, and he looks over to me. I take it as a cue to continue. "Thank you," I say, trying to throw all my gratitude and sincerity behind my words. "Seriously. All of this is… It's very kind of you."

Sarfaraz's throat bobs, but he says, "You're welcome," before he flicks the lamp off. Then he places his back to me. Within seconds, his breathing settles, and he even starts snoring.

Really? I drop my head back against my pillow. Not even a good-night? Also, how does he fall asleep that fast? I know my sleeping habits aren't exactly normal, but what human being falls asleep that quickly?

I huff but turn my own lamp off. I roll over to the other side, putting slightly more distance between us. My options now are, one, attempt to sleep, or two, be alone with my own thoughts. I honestly don't know which is worse.

I groan and bury my face in the pillow.

I need a third option.

11

**Maya's Law #11:
If you're "too nice," it'll come back to bite you.**

I manage to fall asleep at some point, though it's fitful. I throw my blanket off when it gets too hot, but then I paw the bed for it again when a cold flash hits my bare legs. How do people sleep without pants on? I feel too vulnerable. It's the same kind of rushing panic that hits you when you stick one foot out of the blanket, only to realize it's the perfect bait for whatever demon is definitely lingering under your bed.

File that thought under "what to tell Dr. Khan next time I see her."

After what feels like forever, I peel my lids open. It's still dark in the room, but my eyes burn anyway. It's the unsatisfactory feeling I get whenever I desperately need sleep but can't get any. I wait for a wave of nausea to hit my gut, but to my intense relief, my stomach is pain free. Maybe the elixir of life really *is* in that medicine.

I roll to the other side of the bed. I check my phone for the time—*7:56 a.m.*

I want to groan, but judging by the sound of soft breathing, Sarfaraz is still asleep. His hair is tousled from bed head, his face calm and free of the lines I was beginning to think were a permanent feature on his face. He wrinkles his nose before he readjusts his body, throwing an arm over his forehead. He looks less like a man and more like a boy: innocent and vulnerable.

I have to admit, he looks kind of cute. But maybe it's because he's not talking.

I get out of bed, watching Sarfaraz in case he decides to wake up. I peek out the window, only to see the outside world is nearly as dark as it was last night. Heavy rain patters against the glass and glimpses of lightning flash sporadically in the sky. The storm must've gotten worse overnight.

A soft knock at the door draws my attention. I look at Sarfaraz to see if he heard it, but when he doesn't wake up, I tiptoe over to answer it myself.

When I open it, a woman stands on the other side. "Good morning." She holds out a bag. "I was told to bring this to your room."

"Oh," I say, accepting the bag from her. A quick peek inside confirms it to be the clothes I bought last night, now clean and vomit-free. "Thank you."

I shut the door and step back into the room. I pull out a top and a pair of pants, then go into the bathroom. I take a shower, then slip on a short-sleeved sunshine-yellow top and shimmy into the light brown pants. Even though I feel a lot better, I take another dose of medicine for good measure before brushing my teeth. When I'm done, I fold Sarfaraz's T-shirt and leave it on the counter.

I step out of the bathroom, only to see Sarfaraz still asleep. I move quietly about the room, grabbing my phone from the side table, then step outside into the hall. Toronto's time zone is six hours behind Switzerland's, but luckily my bank has a 24-hour helpline. I explain the situation to them, and they agree to unfreeze my credit card right away. After that's done, I pull up search results for hotels in Interlaken. I manage to snag a single room for one night at a halfway-decent price, and thankfully, the weather doesn't seem to be as bad in the places I want to go. It might still be raining, but the reports say it'll be gentle, if at all. Not the best weather to be exploring Switzerland in, but I didn't exactly plan this trip. Maybe this will be one of the few times Allah feels bad for all the bad luck He gives me and says, "Here, have a good day, as a treat!"

I sneak back into the room but stagger to a stop in front of Sarfaraz's bed.

He's awake now, and he's stretching his arms over his head. His shirt rides up, revealing a sliver of muscly skin. I force myself to look away from it and instead look at Sarfaraz's face. *You threw up on him, Maya*, I chant in my head. *Keep picturing his grossed-out face.*

His eyes widen when he takes my form in. He slowly lowers his arms. "You, uh…" He clears his throat. "You got your clothes back?"

I briefly study my outfit. I clear my throat and pretend like I don't notice he's trying not to stare at the slight dip in my cleavage. The clothes in the stores here aren't halal-girl friendly, but it's either that or walk around in my dirty clothes. "Yeah, I was surprised they cleaned them so fast, too. I was worried I'd have to go out and buy more. My bank account can't keep taking hits like this."

He snorts, but he quickly covers it up with a cough. He lowers his gaze so he's not looking at me anymore. "Nice. That's, uh, nice."

"Yeah." I pull on my fingers. "So…what are your plans now?"

"Oh." He sits up in bed, clearly eager to change subjects. "Probably going to stay here and get some work done."

"Really? But you're in Switzerland."

"And?"

"And…" I draw out. "It's a beautiful country. This stop may not exactly have been part of your plan, but it'd be a complete waste to not take advantage of what's essentially a free trip to Switzerland. After all, we're not paying for our ticket to get *back* on our flight to Pakistan." I gesture to the door. "You should go experience it while you're here. I did a whole day exploring Zurich yesterday, and while it didn't exactly end well, I still had fun."

Sarfaraz waves me off. "I'm good." He tosses the blankets off and swings his feet to the floor.

I pause. He's going to stay in here and work? We're in *Switzerland*! He can't pass up an opportunity like this. Plus, after all he's done to help me out, the least I can do is get the man to loosen up. I don't know much about him, but he seems coiled tighter than a boa constrictor choking its prey to death. He could probably use a good time. He can't *want* to be alone. Who wants that?

I don't like seeing people alone. It's partially the teacher thing—I don't like seeing a kid sitting off in the corner by themselves while a larger group of kids play. But it also makes me feel bad because I know how suffocating loneliness can be.

Sarfaraz has said more than once he likes his space, but from the way he insisted on helping me, watched over me to make sure I was okay, and took care of me, I know there's more to it than that. Maybe he's lonely, too, but doesn't know how to do something about it, so when he saw a stranger in need of help, he stepped in.

He moves past me to get to the bathroom, and the words come out before I can fully process them. "You should come with me."

Sarfaraz stops, hovering by the door. Slowly, he looks over his shoulder. "What?"

My mouth dries. "I'm going to Interlaken," I explain. "It's the plan I told you about last night. I'm going to go to Sigriswil and Iseltwald from there." I play with the edges of the towel. "Come with me. We can sightsee together. You'll get out of this stuffy hotel room, and when you get back home, you can be like, Ahh yes, I'm glad that total stranger I met on a plane made me go out and have some fun when I was stranded in Switzerland." I hold my hands out to the side. "It'll be fun. And I was planning to come back to Zurich very early tomorrow, so we won't miss our flight."

He sucks in his cheeks. "I don't know..."

"You're really going to tell me you'd rather be stuck in this crummy hotel room?" I cross my arms over my chest. "The answer is simple. Come with me." At his hesitating stare, I add, "I promise I won't be annoying."

Sarfaraz scoffs. "I don't know how you can possibly promise that."

"Okay, I promise I'll *try* not to be annoying."

He stares at me for another long moment, then slowly smiles. "Fine. Give me ten minutes to shower."

After Sarfaraz is ready, we pack the rest of our stuff and take the train to Interlaken. The journey was mostly quiet; I, of course, tried to make conversation with Sarfaraz, but he still responded with short answers. Eventually I gave up and just took some pictures of the beautiful scenery outside the compartment window.

Once there, we check into the hotel I booked, thankfully without any credit card hiccups. Unfortunately, there's only one bed, but Sarfaraz graciously agrees to sleep on the pullout couch.

After dropping our bags off, we get on the train to Sigriswil. I'm excited to get there; Zurich was so gorgeous, I can't imagine what the rest of the country is like. As predicted, there's very little rain in Interlaken, so the sky is much brighter. The stark contrast of the lush, leafy green against the grayish clouds makes everything look like it's right out of the pages of a storybook. It also makes the colorful buildings pop. In the Korean drama, I thought it was a filter over the shots, but the pastel-colored houses, ranging from baby pink to lavender to daffodil yellow, look incredible in real life.

When we find two free seats on the train, I stop Sarfaraz before he can sit down. "What?" he asks.

"I want the window seat."

"Why?"

"It's good luck," I insist.

"According to who?"

"Me!"

Sarfaraz rolls his eyes but moves out of the way. With a triumphant grin, I scooch past him and sit down. It may sound stupid, but as a person whose life has been one disaster after another, I try to seize every shred of good luck I can get. I pray to Allah for help, of course, but it doesn't hurt to indulge in a little superstition. I wish on eyelashes, I pick four-leaf clovers, and I always watch meteor showers. The only thing I don't do is carry around a rabbit's foot, because ew.

Sarfaraz sits down next to me, and I get another strong whiff of pine, and coffee, though the coffee isn't as potent this time, even though he had like two cups before we left the hotel.

We're quiet as the train starts its journey, but, much like when we were on the plane, I can't take the silence for long. "Are you excited about where we're going?"

"I don't even know where we're going," he points out.

Right. "*Crash Landing on You* is one of my favorite shows ever. It's a Korean drama, and they filmed some scenes here. The scenery in the show was so beautiful, and the moments that the leads had while here were so important to their relationship that I *knew* I had to come visit sometime. I wanted to come here for my honeymoon, but my fiancé didn't agree."

"And that's why you're braving the rain to sightsee?"

"Yeah."

Sarfaraz hums for a second, and I think he's going to stay silent, but then he speaks. "Why is this show so important to you, anyway?"

His question kind of startles me. "I just love it."

"But why? There has to be a reason if it made you want to come here for your honeymoon."

I tap my fingers against my lap. "So, I lived in South Korea for two years," I explain. "I went there to teach English. I watched it for the first time there. I started watching the dramas on Netflix to immerse myself in the language and the culture, and I found a lot of comfort through it. At first, I thought maybe I made a mistake in going so far from home, and that my mother was right, and that I wasn't ready to be on my own. But I related a lot to the main female lead; being in a new and foreign environment and being scared." I trace the flower design in the center of my palm. "But the show was great at making me feel comfortable. I watched it so many times that it became the one thing that was familiar to me. Plus, it was an extremely popular show, so a lot of people watched it, and I found commonality with people through it."

He's quiet for a second. "That makes sense… I guess," he eventually says, though I can hear him trying hard to keep the judgment out of his voice.

I didn't want to admit this part to Sarfaraz, but one of the other reasons I love the show so much is because of the romance between the two leads. The thought of gushing to him about how much I adore the lingering looks between Yoon Se-ri and Ri Jeong-hyeok—as well as their tender goodbye kiss right before Se-ri returns to South Korea, and their tearful final reunion in Switzerland—is kind of embarrassing. I know there's nothing wrong with a woman enjoying romance, but I've already thrown up on this man; I want to keep as much dignity as possible. Plus, I can tell by his tone that he wouldn't care.

Still, the chemistry between the actors—Hyun Bin and Son Ye-jin—is electrifying, and enough to make any cynic believe in love. If it can make someone like me, who doesn't think that real romance can happen for her, so enamored by their relationship, that's a true testament to how amazing their chemistry is.

After another long beat of silence, I ask, "Why are you going to Pakistan, anyway?"

"That's none of your business."

"Come on!" I pout. "I told you why I'm going."

"I didn't ask you to."

I grit my teeth. Why did I think asking him along would be a good idea, again? "Let me guess," I start. "Are you going there for a 'discover yourself' retreat? Taking photos for a magazine? Looking for tranquility?"

"Even if that *were* the case," he says, looking over to me,

"I got stuck sitting next to you, so clearly I haven't found my tranquility yet."

The barb stings way more than it should. "I didn't *have* to ask you along, you know."

"You practically harassed me to come."

"And now I'm regretting it," I grumble under my breath.

Thankfully, my phone ringing interrupts us. I pick it up when I recognize Ammi's name. "Assalaam-o-alaikum," I greet.

"Walaykum salam," she says back. "How are you doing? Have you found a place to stay?"

"Yes," I confirm. "And I'm doing okay. I had food poisoning yesterday, though. The only real meal I ate was an oyster pasta, so I think that's what caused it."

"Oh, no," Ammi moans. "Are you feeling better now?"

"Much," I reply. "I think it had to flush out of my system, but I feel fine now."

"That's good to hear. We wouldn't want the bride sick at her own wedding events." Something muffles the sound on her end of the conversation, then her voice is much clearer as she says, "Oh, here's Imtiaz."

I don't have the chance to say anything before I hear the cheery voice of my fiancé. "Assalaam-o-alaikum, Maya."

Sarfaraz stiffens next to me and briefly glances at me from the corner of his eye, but I ignore it. "Walaykum salam," I reply, scootching closer to the window and switching my phone to my left ear.

Imtiaz clears his throat. "How has your travel been?"

"Well, I'd rather be on a plane right now, but I'm doing okay."

"I hate the thought of you being alone," he says. "I know how much you don't like being by yourself."

A breath gets caught in my throat. "Yeah," I squeak. "But I'm not alone. I'm traveling with somebody."

Sarfaraz turns his head to me when I mention him, just as Imtiaz asks, "Oh? Who?"

"A guy I sat next to on the plane," I respond. I can't exactly say, *Yeah, the guy I sat next to on the plane, who was rude to me on the flight, and then saved me when I threw up in public, and then loaned me his shirt as we shared a hotel room, and who's sitting next to me now because I pitied him staying in said hotel room alone.* My face drops. "Don't tell my mom, though. I didn't tell her because I don't want her to freak out, you know? It's not that big a deal. It's mostly for safety."

"Yeah, yeah, of course," he assures me. "I wouldn't want you to be alone, either, and if you can trust this guy, then that's good enough for me. It's only until you get on the plane, right?"

"Right. Then we'll be going our separate ways."

"Cool. So, what are you and Seat Stranger up to?" he asks, and not in a suspicious way, thankfully.

"We've decided to make the most of our time in Switzerland. You know that Korean show I love? We're going to the places they filmed here."

There's a pause on the other end of the phone. "Ahh, yeah, yeah, *that* show," he falters, his tone uncertain.

My smile freezes. "You don't know which show I'm talking about, do you?"

"No, I do!" Imtiaz says, a slight panic to his voice. When I'm silent, he adds, "Yeah, fine, I'm sorry. I'm sure it's exciting, though!"

"It is." I glimpse the other patrons on the train, and a few of them are giving me dirty looks. "Listen, I should go—people are starting to get annoyed. But don't worry, I'm going to get to our wedding if it kills me."

"I believe you." He chuckles. "Hey. I love you."

My chest squeezes. "Back at you," I mumble before I quickly hang up. I rub my sweaty palms on my pants.

"Oomph," Sarfaraz teases. "Trouble in paradise?"

I frown. "Excuse me?"

He gestures to my phone. "You didn't say 'I love you' back."

The tips of my ears redden. "That doesn't mean anything."

"Doesn't exactly sound right, either," Sarfaraz counters. He runs his finger along his upper lip, and the action momentarily distracts me until he says, "You know, sixty percent of all divorces involve individuals ages twenty-five to thirty-nine. I'm guessing you and your fiancé are in that demographic?"

I glare at him so hard he cowers. "I didn't ask for a consultation," I seethe. "When I want your services, I'll ask." I stare out the window, hoping the gorgeous scenery will calm me down.

We continue to sit in silence for a while until Sarfaraz speaks. "Look, I'm sorry," he starts. I cautiously peek at him from the corner of my eye, and he *does* have an apologetic look on his face. "I get... I'm cynical. I'm just frustrated my travel plans got halted. I shouldn't take it out on you."

I huff, but eventually position my body so I'm not hugging the side of the carriage anymore. "No, you shouldn't, but this whole thing is partly my fault."

Sarfaraz raises a brow. "I didn't know you could control the weather."

I snort. "No, it's not that. I'm cursed."

He laughs, but when I don't, he stops abruptly. "Wait, what?"

"I'm cursed," I repeat.

"I'm sorry, how are you saying that with a straight face?"

"Because it's true," I insist. At his scoff, I sit up in my seat. "Like being late to the airport, my luggage getting left behind, and now being stranded in Switzerland. I have bad luck all around, but it's especially bad when it comes to my love life."

"Wait, wait, wait," he says. He makes a *rewind* gesture. "Back up. You don't actually think that, do you?"

I stare at him, completely serious. "Of course I do."

He tilts his head to the side. "But you *do* know curses don't exist, right?"

"Of course they do," I counter. "I know some people think it's stupid to be superstitious, but I can't help it. Not after everything I've ever experienced in life."

"I'm sure it's not *that* bad—"

"First month of university," I cut him off, holding up one finger. "I sit next to this super cute guy in one of my English classes, and I spend the whole month working up the courage to talk to him, and on the day I decide to say something, he's not in class. Turns out he got kicked out because he'd committed an academic offense."

Sarfaraz swallows back a laugh. "Okay, that's bad, but—"

"Second year," I go on, putting up another finger. "My roommate, who I didn't talk to much, persuaded me to go to a party with her. I spotted a very cute guy, and just as I went to talk to him, his boyfriend showed up and kissed him right in front of me."

I continue even as he tries to fight the grin on his face. "I managed to get a date with that same guy later that year, but his table manners were so bad that *I* had to end the date early."

I hold up another finger. "In my last year of university, there was this guy who I had lots of classes with because we were in the same program, and I always had a distant crush on him. We got paired for a group presentation and I thought it was my chance to talk to him, and one night while we were working, he told me he had something to tell me. I thought he was going to profess his undying love for me, but he said, 'The earth is flat.'"

Sarfaraz's face briefly contorts at the mention of the conspiracy theory, but otherwise it's red from how hard he's trying not to laugh. "Okay, okay, I get it," he croaks. "You have really bad luck."

I lean back in my seat. "That's nothing. You don't even wanna hear the horror stories I have from potential rishtas. Once, I accidentally insulted the guy to a woman who I didn't realize was his mother by telling her he was super boring."

Sarfaraz gives up and howls, his laughter filling the train car. He immediately gets a flood of dirty looks from the other passengers, but he can only wave his hand in a silent apology while a whistling sound comes out of his nose. He wipes uselessly at his face, because fresh tears replace the old ones. A couple of times he manages to calm down, but then he takes one look at me and loses it again.

I have to admit, as annoying as he is, his laughter is kind of sweet, like the first bite of an ice-cream cone on a sweltering day at a theme park. It's late, you're exhausted, your feet ache, and you're soaked with sweat, but the first bite of sugary sweetness that hits your tongue is enough to rejuvenate you.

I brush my bangs behind my ear. "Fine, make fun of my misfortune. I'll be waiting in the wings for you to get your retribution from Allah."

"Okay, okay," Sarfaraz relents. His chest hitches, but he finally stops to take in a few long, deep breaths. Once he's back in control, he says, "Fine, that stuff's…bad, but it doesn't mean you're *cursed*."

I cross my arms over my chest. "I'm stuck in a foreign country, on a train with a total stranger who I threw up on after getting caught in a rainstorm so bad they had to land our flight for multiple days. That's not exactly *good* kismet."

"Fair. But if you believe in that stuff, then fortune comes in fluctuations. Maybe for a while you've had lots of bad luck, but that means you have a long period of good luck coming." He points to my ring. "For example, you said you've had bad luck when it comes to love. But if you're getting married, doesn't that mean your luck's turning up?"

Theoretically, he's right; this is a great rishta, Imtiaz is a wonderful man, and my mom's starting to treat me like the adult I am—sort of. Doesn't that mean I should be happier? That I should feel like everything's all sunshine and rainbows?

The short answer: yes, it should. But it doesn't.

A shiver runs down my spine. I peer up at the vents above our heads. Air-conditioning hits my face full force, and I reach up and close it. "It's kind of chilly in here. Why is the air-conditioning on full blast?"

Thankfully, Sarfaraz doesn't bring up my deliberate change in subject. Instead, he closes his own vent. "Do you feel better?"

"A little," I respond. I press my palm against my lids. "I feel a headache coming on."

"Did you sleep okay last night?"

"No," I answer. "I don't sleep well in general, though."

"You could try sleeping now." He checks his watch. "We still have some time before we reach Sigriswil."

"I don't know." I hesitate. "I don't want to leave you alone."

"Don't worry about me," he says, waving me off. He holds his phone up. "I'll watch something on Netflix, and I'll wake you up when we get there."

"If you're sure." I sink down farther in the seat and rest my temple against the cold window, which sends a small shudder through my body. Even though the vent's closed, I still feel some of the forced air blowing on my face, as well as the air coming from the other open vents in the car. I close my eyes, hoping to catch at least a few minutes of sleep.

12

**Maya's Law #12:
Always bring a backup to your backup.**

I manage to sleep. It's peaceful. I'm warm, and I feel like I'm wrapped up in a really fuzzy blanket.

Wait. Warm? A fuzzy blanket? I fell asleep with the air-conditioning blasting and my arms wrapped around myself to keep the shivers away.

I open my eyes to see a light sweater spread over my front, covering as much of my chest and arms as possible. I look to my right to see Sarfaraz, sans sweater, leaning the back of his head against the seat. He's in a T-shirt, and his arms are crossed over his chest, but I see him shiver once or twice. Sarfaraz shifts every now and then, and I realize it's because he's trying to get out of the way of the direct stream of cold air coming out of the vent.

Reluctantly, I take the sweater off (I'm starting to become accustomed to his smell of lemons and laundry, which probably isn't a good sign). I'm about to drape it over his chest, but the train suddenly jerks like a car that's run over roadkill.

I scramble to regain my balance, but I end up sprawled on Sarfaraz's lap. My stomach flops on top of his legs, my hands flying out. Unfortunately, in my desperate attempt at seeking stability so I don't fall completely to the ground, I accidentally graze the bulge in the front of his pants.

Sarfaraz's eyes fly open, and he sits up so fast I lose my balance. The floor rushes up to my face, but at the last second, his arms wrap around my stomach. Sarfaraz touching my body brings heat to my face. I push up as fast as I can while he pulls me into a sitting position.

Once I'm back in my seat, Sarfaraz immediately draws back. The spot he touched scorches, like I accidentally touched a hair curler to my skin. He clears his throat, his ears bright red. "Are you okay?" he asks, looking straight ahead.

Allah ka shukar hai, he's not looking at me. I will my own face to go back to its normal color. "I'm fine." Keeping my focus ahead of me, I hold his sweater out to him. "Sorry about that. Just trying to return your sweater."

I feel him take it from me. Thankfully, the train slows to a much smoother stop a few minutes later, and the automated speaking voice says something in German before announcing in English, "Approaching Thun station."

That's our stop. Still not making eye contact, we shuffle off the train and find the bus stand for Sigriswil. Twenty minutes later, we reach our destination. At this point, the awkward air between us has started to clear, and I completely forget about it once I step off the bus and get my first glimpse of Sigriswil.

It's even more breathtaking than in *Crash Landing on You*. Kelly's right: there's a certain magic that only exists when you see something in person. The sky is bluer. The buildings are sturdier. The dewdrops on the grass shimmer even brighter.

A bunch of small buildings with russet slanted roofs scatter along the bottom of the large, looming mountains. I can't tell if the buildings are houses, offices, or stores, but I can make out one church, the telltale cross peaking at the top of the tall pillar.

The backdrop of the buildings looks like it came right out of a postcard. The mountains appear distant yet somehow close-up, hidden behind the swirling gray clouds. Snow speckles on the top of the peaks like sprinkles on ice-cream cones, somehow managing to glisten despite there being no sunlight. I can't help but tear up.

People clamber about, some carrying umbrellas over their heads despite the fact that it's not raining yet. They're not even paying attention to the weird tourist who's trying hard not to cry because the place they live is so beautiful. Well, not only because of that, but after such a turbulent forty-eight hours, it's nice to stop and stare at something so natural, undisturbed, and calming.

"Alright." Sarfaraz's voice breaks me out of the spell. "We should move out of the way of the people trying to get onto the bus."

I look to see a small line has formed during my ogling. A few of the people send glares our way. I quickly blink away my tears and sidestep to make room for them.

"So," Sarfaraz starts as we walk down the street, "did you have a place in mind you wanted to go?"

"I do," I admit. "But is there anywhere you wanted to go?"

"Nope," he says. For the first time in like forty-five minutes, he looks at me. "I had no plans of leaving the hotel room. I'm following your lead."

"That easy? So, you'll go where I want to go?"

"I'll follow you wherever," Sarfaraz confirms.

I pause at his phrasing. I don't think he's seemed to notice exactly what he's said, either; he moves his head this way and that, drinking in the scenery around us. I shrug it off. It's just a way of phrasing things. I reach into my backpack and produce the brochure I took from the Zurich hotel. "I want to go to the panorama bridge," I announce. I open the pamphlet and hold it out so he can see it.

He peers at the page, then shakes his head. "I take it back. I'm not gonna follow you wherever."

I pout, lowering the brochure. "Come on! You said yourself you have nothing else you want to do. Trust me on this."

Sarfaraz hesitates, and I take the opportunity to say solemnly, "I'm getting married. You might not know, but desi households are *very* specific on how they want their daughters-in-law to act." I sigh wistfully, pouting some more. "This might be the last shred of freedom I get before I have to be the perfect bahu."

I expect him to roll his eyes at me, to say I'm being dramatic, or even for him to ignore me completely and continue down the street, but his expression softens. I hold my pleading look, and he says, "Oh, trust me, I know how constraining desi households can be."

This time, I knit my brows together. "What do you mean?"

"I'm half-Pakistani, remember?" Sarfaraz says, then he shakes his head. "Never mind." He gestures to the brochure. "How does the pamphlet say we get to the panorama bridge?"

The pamphlet directs us to Grabenmühle. On the way up, we're mostly silent. I'd rather conserve my energy; seriously, this path feels like it's never going to end. In the show, Ri Jeong-hyeok and Yoon Se-ri never mentioned how freaking *long* the journey is.

Finally, we reach the bridge. A few people loiter around the end, while some people pose for photos in the middle. It's a long, narrow path, and the bridge looks like it stretches on forever. Tall metal boards with small holes pattern the sides of the bridge, and just about reach my chest in height. Greenery surrounds the area, from giant leafy trees along the bottom to the landscape on the other side of the bridge. A few houses peek through the trees. I wonder if the people who live there marvel at the beautiful place they live, or if they're used to it. I don't think I'd ever get used to living in a place that looks like it came straight from the concept art of a Studio Ghibli film.

At this point, I'm bursting with excitement. This is where the show was filmed! The actors stood on *this* bridge. This is where Yoon Se-ri and Ri Jeong-hyeok interacted for the first time as complete strangers, with no idea how much they'd eventually come to mean to each other.

My smile nearly splits my face in half as I step onto the bridge. I test the bottom for stability, and once I'm positive it won't bend under my feet, I continue. The height itself doesn't frighten me; in fact, the distance between the bridge and the ground sends a thrill through my stomach. Being so high up, enjoying the breeze you'd only get at this altitude, with a backdrop of vast streams and looming mountains, outweighs any fear in the pit of my stomach.

I'm about a quarter of the way down when I realize I don't hear the clomping of Sarfaraz's shoes behind me. I stop and check to see he's still at the end. His eyes are squeezed shut, and his hands rest on the sides of the bridge, but he can't seem to move his feet forward.

I walk back to Sarfaraz, stopping in front of him. I stay on the bridge, though. A sheen of sweat lines his forehead. "Is everything okay?"

"Yeah," he says gruffly, keeping his eyes closed. "Everything's fine."

I give him a once-over. "But you're just standing there."

His eyes crack open. "I'm fine," he insists. "I'm...uneasy when it comes to heights."

My face relaxes. Of *course* he's afraid of heights. He doesn't like flying, and he wasn't thrilled when I suggested coming to the panorama bridge. Actually, now that I think about it, his behavior before the flight makes a lot more sense now. His short, curt responses, his restlessness before takeoff, the way he squeezed his eyes shut so he wouldn't have to see the plane flying into the sky. It was so obvious I feel pretty dumb for not putting the two pieces together earlier. "Is this why you didn't want to come here?" I wonder. I dip my chin so he's forced to look at me. "Why did you say yes, then?"

"You wanted to come so badly." He swallows thickly. "You were dealt the short end of the stick, and then you were sick yesterday, and I felt bad about how I've been acting since we met, so I..." His grip tightens around the sides of the bridge.

Something sweet touches my chest, spreading through the rest of my body and leaving me pleasantly buzzed. "That's really kind of you."

"Yeah, well..." Sarfaraz grumbles, trailing off.

I scan the length of the bridge, then look back to him. "You can stay here. I'll go and take pictures by myself."

"No, wait. Give me a minute to work up to it."

I step forward. Gently, I pry his fingers off the bridge. As he opens his mouth to protest, I move them onto my shoulder and offer an encouraging look. "I've got you," I assure him. "Just lean on me."

He sucks in a shuddery breath, but he takes one step forward. Encouraged, I continue onto the bridge, and he follows me. His fingers clench around my shoulder with every step, but he continues to walk. He keeps his eyes trained on me, not straying to the side for a second.

As we make our way down, Sarfaraz trips over a stray pamphlet on the bridge. He jumps and wraps his hand around mine, holding tight. I want to protest, but instead I silently keep going until we reach the middle. Plus, the weight of his palm in mine is kind of...nice.

I stop when we get there, and my grin grows when I see a red plaque. Something is written in white in Hangul, but the text next to it spells *Crash Landing on You* in English. Next to the words are sketches of the faces of the lead couple in the show, Son Ye-jin and Hyun Bin.

I gleefully reach into my pocket and pull out my phone so I can take a picture of the sign. I only have one free hand, though, because Sarfaraz is still holding on to my other for dear life. While I want to spend longer on the bridge, I should wrap it up before the poor man dissolves from nerves.

The quality of the photos are good, but I'm still not satisfied with them. Stupid iPhone. I turn to Sarfaraz. "Hey, your phone is a Google Pixel, right? I saw it on the train."

He somehow manages to answer without exploding. "Yeah, it is. Why?"

"Can I borrow it to take photos? The camera quality is so much better on the Pixel."

Surprisingly, he doesn't argue with me, probably because he wants off the bridge. He produces his phone, types the password in with his thumb, then gives it to me. It's been left open to a website, though—the Wikipedia page for *Crash Landing on You*. I look up at him with an inquisitive stare. "I thought you didn't care about the show."

Alarm flickers in his face, and he temporarily forgets his fear as he snatches the phone back. "I never said I didn't care," he clarifies, his cheeks pink. "And, well...you kept going on and on about it, even braving the rain to visit the places where they filmed." He turns his attention to his phone so he doesn't have to look at me. "Plus, I was *vaguely* interested to see how the place we're at influences the show. I watched the first episode on the train ride up here, while you were asleep."

I can't quite believe my ears. "You did? What did you think?"

He scoffs. "The woman in the show is obviously a menace. She showed up and disrupted that poor soldier's life."

I choke out a noise of disbelief. "Or maybe she's what he needed to break out of his boring routine lifestyle and wake up and realize what's been missing his whole life." I gesture to Son Ye-jin's face. "His soulmate."

Sarfaraz hums, low in his throat. "So, you believe in soulmates?"

"Yes," I say plainly. "I mean, the actors who played Se-ri and Jeong-hyeok fell in love in real life and got married after filming the show together. They had a kid, too." I flatten my palm against the side of my leg. "You can't tell me you don't believe in soulmates after that." I tilt my head to the side. "Can you?"

He doesn't answer my question. He hums for a second and stares so intently at me I'm sure my face is gonna melt off, but then he asks, "So you think this fiancé of yours is your soulmate?"

My face flushes, and I can't look him in the eye. I pick flecks of dirt off my pants. "I never said *I* had a soulmate."

"But you just said—"

"I said I believe in them," I interrupt. "Allah created us in pairs, after all. But I don't think everyone marries their soulmate." My thoughts drift to my own parents' broken marriage. "But I think the people who do are the luckiest people in the world, though, and it'd be nice if I did, too."

When I peek up at him, he's looking at me with an expression that's part puzzled and part…intrigued. After a beat, he opens his mouth. "Can we please get off the bridge now?" he chatters.

I chuckle. "Yeah, let me take a photo first."

"Oh!" a new voice says, and I look to my left to see a young couple passing by us. The girl on the left steps toward us. "I can take a picture of you guys, if you want!"

Sarfaraz and I both start to refuse, but she plucks Sarfaraz's phone from him and pushes him next to me. Instinctively, Sarfaraz's arm loops around my waist, desperately searching for an anchor to keep him from freaking out. His palm against my hip burns a hole through my pants. A blush crawls up my neck, and I discreetly use my hair to cover it up.

After the girl snaps a few pictures, I ask her to take some pictures of only me. Sarfaraz reluctantly lets me go and steps off to the side, but he holds on to the side of the bridge. Once the girl has taken a couple photos, she gives me back the phone. "Thank you!" I say, then hurriedly lead Sarfaraz off the bridge.

Once we're off, he finally relaxes. "Ugh, sweet land!" he groans as he staggers around, probably waiting for the shaking in his legs to stop.

I roll my eyes, continuing ahead of him. "Oh, and *I'm* too dramatic?" I grumble under my breath.

"I heard that!" he calls after me. I guess he's feeling well enough to snark back at me, which honestly feels a lot more familiar than…whatever the hell happened on the bridge.

I'm about to suggest we go get lunch when a splash hits my cheek. I look up to see the clouds have darkened. Another drop of water pelts my eye. More rain starts to fall, hitting the ground and making the grass smell crisp.

"Damn," Sarfaraz murmurs. I stop to let him catch up with me, and he shrugs out of his coat as he brings the top half up to cover his head. "We're going to be soaked by the time we make it back down."

My bag suddenly weighs heavily against my back, and I gasp. "Oh, wait!" I swing my backpack to my chest, unzip it, and produce the two umbrellas I bought from the store. "Here we go!" I grin triumphantly and offer Sarfaraz one.

He frowns. "When did you pick up umbrellas?"

"I got them in Zurich. I bought one because I needed it, and then I bought the second in case something happened to the first, which, in my experience, is something very likely to happen." I hold it out. "Take it or get wet. It doesn't matter to me."

"No, I want it!" Sarfaraz insists. He takes it from me and opens it, smiling when the pellets hit the umbrella panel instead of his head. He smirks and looks back to me. "Maybe you're not so unlucky, after all."

I smirk and unwrap my own umbrella. I stuff the cover back into my backpack, then press the button that's supposed to open the umbrella. "Yeah, maybe not—"

I cut myself off as the runner goes up way too far. There's none of the usual resistance. Instead, the stretcher snaps, and the jagged tip of the metal goes straight through the outer canopy, shredding the material. I gape at the broken umbrella, ignoring the rain splattering against my bare arms. "What the hell?" I groan. I shake the umbrella in my hands. The broken pieces just flop around, the metal bits inside scraping against each other. I know it's useless, but better for me to take my anger out on this stupid umbrella than something else. "This was like fifteen bucks!"

Sarfaraz's eye twitches, as does the corner of his mouth. I glare at him. "If you laugh, I will beat you with this umbrella."

"Well, I wouldn't say it's much of an umbrella anymore,"

he says evenly, though a small chuckle underlines his tone. He presses his mouth into a firm line, but I can see it wobble.

I'm about to hurl more insults at him when the corners of his lips gently turn up. "Here." Sarfaraz closes my mess of an umbrella as best as he can, and then opens my backpack so he can shove it inside. Once he zips the bag closed, he circles back to my side, but instead of continuing forward, he wraps his arm around my back, his fingers grazing my arm. He huddles closer to me, holding his umbrella over both our heads the best he can.

I stare up at him, but the kind smile stays on his face as we continue down the path from the bridge. His hand is gentle against my arm, and somehow the left side of my body fits well against the right side of his.

I face forward, crossing my arms over my chest and enjoying the pitter-patter of rain against the umbrella.

13

Maya's Law #13:
Things are never what they seem.

The bridge is the biggest highlight of Sigriswil, so once we finish there, we're back on the train to head to Iseltwald. On the way, we both receive emails from the airport saying that the worst of the storm has officially passed and our flights are officially booked for tomorrow morning.

On the ride up, I fish out my iPad from my bag. I'd initially planned on watching something on the way up, but I was too tired. Now I'm too wired to sleep on the way back, so I load up the second episode of *Crash Landing on You*. As I stick one earbud in, I look to my right and notice Sarfaraz peeking at the screen. He quickly tears his attention away when I catch him staring. Instead of being upset he was staring at my screen, I smirk and offer him an earbud.

He stares at me for a second, but wordlessly takes it. His face is mostly stoic as we watch the episode, but every now and then from the corner of my eye, I see his face crack at a joke.

When we get to Iseltwald, we leisurely walk around for a while. I force Sarfaraz to take photos of me posing normal, silly, and completely ridiculous. He pretends to be indifferent the whole time, but I catch glimpses of amusement in his eyes every now and then. It's always gone within the next blink, though.

I step into a souvenir shop. Switzerland may not have been a planned stop, but I want something that'll remind me of the experience. Plus, I can get Imtiaz a gift that says, *Hey, sorry I'm late for our wedding, but I got this cool thing from Switzerland for you! We can find a place for it in our new apartment!*

Sarfaraz doesn't want to get any souvenirs, so he leaves me alone in the shop while he goes off to buy us some coffee. He clicks his tongue when I tell him my order (a coffee with lots of whipped cream and a caramel drizzle) and mutters something about how I'm tainting my drink with all that extra stuff before setting off.

I wander along the aisles, taking my time. I pick up a couple of magnets, a keychain, and a deck of cards with the gorgeous mountains printed on the back. I'm about to head to the counter to pay when I walk past a display of snow globes. I grin at the sight of them, but one captures my immediate attention.

It's a house, painted to look like it's made of wood, with a gray slanted roof. At the top of the roof is the Swiss flag. Green covers the floor of the globe. The bottom section has a man and a woman surrounded by trees and faraway mountains. Next to the man is a white flower I assume to be edelweiss. I gently pick it up and give it a light shake. Instantly, tiny flecks of white swirl around in the globe, making the world inside look just as majestic as it does in real life.

By the time I'm done paying for everything, Sarfaraz is back from the coffee shop. I step outside and accept my coffee from him.

"So," he starts while we continue down the street, "what did you end up getting?"

"A couple of things," I respond. I whirl around so I'm standing in front of him.

He stumbles to a stop. "Jeez, what?"

Unable to keep the grin off my face, I reach into the bag and pull out the snow globe. "Look!"

"It's…a snow globe," he says slowly.

"Yeah, I *know* it's a snow globe," I retort. I hold it out. "It's for you."

He stares at me, and I can't quite decipher the clouded look in his eyes. "You got me a snow globe?"

I falter, doubt creeping up on me. "Yeah? I thought you might like it."

Sarfaraz stares at me for a moment longer but then recovers quickly. "I don't collect sentimental junk."

This time, disappointment flares through my body. "But I already got it for you! It was final sale!" I pout. "I was trying to do something nice to repay you."

"You don't need to repay me," he says, then continues down the street.

I huff, staring after him, before looking back down at the snow globe. I guess that's that. I'll give it to Ammi, and she can figure out who to give it to. I shove it back into the bag with a little more force than necessary. Honestly, you try to do something nice for someone else, and you get wrecked for it.

We explore the town until sundown, which is when we decide to stop for dinner. Afterward, Sarfaraz wants to go back to Interlaken, but I manage to convince him to get some ice cream and take a nice walk. There's one place we didn't make it to during the day I want to see.

We end up at the lake area where Ri Jeong-hyeok played the song he wrote for his brother on the piano. Excitement buzzes in my toes, and I thrust my phone and ice-cream cone at Sarfaraz. "You've got to take a picture of me here."

I'm sure he's tired of being my personal photographer at this point, but he grits his teeth and gestures for me to go over to the port. I race over, and after I've posed for a few photos and I'm positive I like them, we sit down on the bench and enjoy our treats.

I lick my cone in silence as I flip through the pictures from the day, but my attention is quickly called by the small crowd forming in front of us. I get up from my seat and wander over, trying to get a better look.

I manage to get close enough to see a couple standing on the port area. A dark-haired woman is down on one knee, while the woman who I presume to be her girlfriend stands above her, her fingers pressed against her mouth. The woman proposing must be saying something incredibly sweet that I can't hear, because her girlfriend tears up. The woman on one knee holds the ring box up, and her girlfriend nods. The crowd bursts into applause as the dark-haired woman slides the ring onto her now-fiancée's finger and they share a celebratory kiss.

I clap along with everyone else. "Oh, that's so *romantic*," I breathe.

"Only if you're naive."

I startle, my head whipping to see Sarfaraz standing next to me. I hadn't even noticed him get up from the bench. He must've finished his ice cream, because both his hands are buried in his pockets.

I scoff. "Excuse me?"

The crowd around us begins to disperse, but we continue

to stand there as someone goes up to the couple and offers to take pictures for them. "You're kidding yourself if you think they're going to spend their whole lives together," he says.

"What is your *problem*?" I huff. "What do you have against love?"

"I don't have anything against love," he retorts. "It's marriage that leaves something to be desired."

"Oh, of course you fit the cliché," I grumble. I cross my arms over my chest. "Family lawyer who doesn't believe in marriage. Very typical."

His expression hardens. "Listen, in my line of work, you learn quickly the first rule of life is you can only ever count on yourself."

My jaw drops. "That's a terrible way to think," I blurt, even though his "rules of life" seem uncomfortably similar to my own laws. "We need to rely on other people in our lives. Humans are social creatures. We need companionship, otherwise we're going to be pretty sad for our whole existence." I raise a brow at him. "What, do you think love is stupid, too?"

Sarfaraz stares at me. "You think so, too. Didn't you say that not everybody has a soulmate?"

"Yeah, but that doesn't mean I don't believe in love," I correct with an annoyed sneer. "I've been going after it my whole life despite feeling like God is telling me it's never gonna happen for me. You know why?" I suck in a deep breath. "Because life by yourself is *miserable*."

To my surprise and annoyance, Sarfaraz doesn't say anything. He just stares ahead. I give him a once-over, and his bare ring finger gets my attention. I grin triumphantly and cross my arms over my chest. "Let's be real. The only reason you're so hard on marriage is because you've never tried it."

Sarfaraz whips his head to face me, and I swear I get whiplash from the force. Barely contained fury darkens his eyes as he narrows them at me. "Actually, I have, and it ended with her in another man's arms," he scowls. "If soulmates exist, I wasn't hers. If divorce stats are true, then fifty percent of the time, people don't marry their soulmates—and you won't, either." His brows stitch together. "Maybe when you're getting *your* divorce, you can tell me how great marriage is."

My jaw drops. Humiliation dries my mouth. Sarfaraz's back stiffens, and even in the nearing darkness, I can see his jaw-line harden as he grits his teeth. Based on the regret on his face, he hadn't meant to blurt that very personal and sensitive information.

I open my mouth to say something, anything, but all that comes out is a strangled noise of surprise. All I can do is stand there stupidly, my mouth opening and closing like a wooden puppet on strings.

After a full thirty seconds of this, Sarfaraz checks his watch. "We're going to miss our train." Without another word, he starts walking.

Reluctantly, I follow him. The silence is awkward and tense and so thick it wraps its fingers around my throat. I want to say something, but every time I glance at Sarfaraz I'm reminded of the look he had on his face during our spat, and I lose my confidence. No, it's probably better if I keep my mouth shut. Besides, after tomorrow, I'm never gonna see this guy again. We'll get back on that plane to Islamabad and go our separate ways. This surreal adventure will be a blip in the story I tell people after I get married. "Ha ha, it's a funny story, I spent a few days in Switzerland with a total stranger because our flight had an emergency landing. No, I don't know what he's up to now." Though, I'm not sure how well this scenario would go over with the people in my community.

Sarfaraz sleeps the whole way back. Or he *pretends* to sleep. Either way, he spends the whole time with his arms crossed over his chest and scootched as far away from me as possible. I huddle close to the window. I rest my head against the windowpane and try to convince myself what he said about marriage not working out isn't true.

I also try to ignore the stuff he said about his own marriage. Like his wife cheating? That sucks. Still…it makes sense why he's so anti-marriage. But just because the institution failed him, doesn't mean it's going to fail everybody. Plus, he's a family lawyer. He sees bad stuff day in and day out. Of *course* he doesn't believe in marriage as an institution.

Still… I can't help but think back to how sad he looked when he blurted out that his wife slept with someone else.

We return to the hotel. The silence between us thickens in the close quarters of our room. As I step out of the bathroom, my shoulder bumps into his, and I automatically look over to him. Something resembling pain creases his face, but he quickly schools his features when he sees me staring. The bathroom door shuts behind me, hitting my back on the way.

I go over to the bed, where I dumped the souvenirs I carried around all day. I stuff them into my bag, but I pause when I touch the snow globe, upside down in my bag. Slowly, I pull it out, and the tiny white flakes float around in the dome when I hold it upright. I stare at the man and woman on the bottom. I assume they're supposed to be a couple. But are they happy? Is she cheating on him with someone else? Are those handcrafted smiles on their faces fake? Is the glow in the man's painted-on dark brown eyes a show to hide his pain?

I peek at the bathroom door, but it's still closed. Maybe I *should* say something. I don't think it's necessarily going to be an apology, but something at least. What do I even say? "Hey, it really sucks your wife cheated on you, here's a snow globe?"

It's too late to go into that right now. We have a flight to catch in the morning. I can say something on the train ride back to Zurich. That'll give me some time to think. I don't know if I'll still be sitting next to him on the plane, but it would be a really awkward twelve hours if one of us doesn't try to clear the air before then, and because I can't see him being the first person to say anything, it'll have to be me. And I'll admit it…as much as he's pissed me off, the few sweet moments we've shared while here in Switzerland make me not want to end our encounter on a sour note.

I'm about to put the snow globe into my bag when I pause. I sneak a peek at Sarfaraz's suitcase by the pullout couch, then back down at the snow globe.

I mean, I *did* buy it for him. And for some reason, I want him to have a reminder of this trip. Yeah. He'll probably never forget this trip, I know that, but I can't bring myself to put the snow globe with my own things.

Keeping my eye on the bathroom door, I tiptoe over to his bed. I unzip his bag, then stuff the wrapped snow globe into his suitcase, nestled between a few articles of his clothing. That should be safe, right? It won't break, and by the time he gets to his destination and opens his bag again, it'll be too late for him to return it to me.

The sound of the doorknob turning interrupts my thoughts, and I jump into bed before he notices me by his couch. I roll over in the bed so my back is to him and feign sleep, drawing out exaggerated snores. I hear him move around, and then the sound of rustling as he lies down on the pullout couch.

I settle in to sleep, hoping when I wake up in the morning I'll know what to say.

14

Maya's Law #14:
You're always the one left behind.

My alarm buzzes softly. I pat the side table for my phone and turn it off. I stretch my arms over my head, then sit up. Automatically, I search for Sarfaraz. While I lay in bed, I thought about things I might want to say to him, but it was mostly me saying, *I'm sorry I didn't know about your wife. I'll stop being so happy-go-lucky about marriage and soulmates until we go our separate ways.*

But when my eyes land on the pullout couch, a jolt runs through me. The bed has been pushed back into a couch, and the sheets are folded neatly on top of it. Sarfaraz's suitcase isn't where he left it last night beside the dresser, either. I pull my sheets off and pad over to the bathroom, but it's empty. And his shoes aren't by the door. Sarfaraz is nowhere to be found.

It's hot in the room, but my blood runs cold. I stay rooted in place, swaying in the front hallway. That's…it? He left for the airport without me? I know I keep saying we're strangers, we owe each other nothing, but… I expected a goodbye. At least, that would've been the *polite* thing to do. But no. Instead, I've been left in the dark, alone, like always. I guess like my bad luck, that's something that'll never change, either.

My breaths come in short, uneven bursts. My head becomes light, and the world around me tilts. I press my palm on my chest and try the breathing exercise Dr. Khan taught me. I breathe in slowly through my nose, deeply and gently. I exhale that breath through my mouth the same way. I hold my breath, counting *one, two, three, four, five* in my head. Then I do it again.

I do this until the dizziness ebbs. I press the heels of my palms into my lids, then run my fingers down my face. I go over to my bag and pull out a fresh set of clothes. I change, then stuff the dirty clothes into a plastic bag and shove it into my backpack. I put on my shoes and head down to the lobby.

Because I was the one who made the reservation, I quickly check out, then take a cab to the train station. The whole time, I resist the urge to curl into a ball. I don't know why it's affecting me so much—being abandoned isn't exactly new to me. Plus, Sarfaraz objectively sucks. Okay, his attitude toward me has changed since we first met on the plane, but still, he sucks. He didn't even have the courtesy to leave a note. These past couple of days have been weird, but they've also somehow been the best days I've had in a long time. For a small amount of time, I could forget everything going on in my life. I could forget I'm alone in a foreign country, I'm about to become someone's wife, and I don't even know if I'm *ready* to become someone's wife. Instead, I could enjoy the beautiful scenery of a gorgeous country.

But I guess Sarfaraz didn't see it the same way. Why should he? This wasn't a mini vacation for him the same way it was for me. He was essentially guilted into letting a random woman stay with him because he felt obligated to worry about her after she puked on him, and then was unwittingly dragged into her plans to make as much of the time she had in the country as she could. Sightseeing is *my* idea of a good time; that doesn't mean it's his. Maybe his life is usually so busy I ended up ruining the single shred of tranquility he managed to find for himself, so he left before he had to deal with me anymore. He just…left, without considering that I'd wake up in that hotel room by myself, with no idea of what happened. Did he stop to consider I'd probably wonder why he left without so much as a goodbye? Did he think I'd brush our encounter off as a small blip in my travel plans? Is he going to do the same? Does it matter if he does? If *I* do?

I knock my knuckles against my temple. Inshallah, I don't end up sitting next to him on the plane. If I do, I'll beg the flight attendant to let me sit in another seat.

I get onto the train and find a seat near the back. The compartment is empty, which I'm super thankful for; I can wallow without worrying about dragging the mood around me down. I drop my bag onto the seat next to me and slump beside the window. I wrap my arms around myself and rest my head against the cold frame. I don't know how many times I've done this in the last couple of days, but this time I feel way colder, way more uncomfortable, way more…alone. I squeeze my eyes shut.

After a while, the train slugs awake and churns forward. Footsteps echo in the cabin, and my skin prickles when I feel a presence looming over me. I wait for a second, pretending to be asleep, because I don't want to move my bag and let a stranger sit next to me. But the strange feeling is still there, so I open my eyes to grudgingly move my bag.

I freeze when I recognize the towering figure to be Sarfaraz, carrying two coffees. A small plastic bag swings from his left wrist. His hair is slightly tousled, and he looks out of breath, but it's him, alright; I'd recognize those dark eyes anywhere.

I shoot to my feet. I didn't realize how close he is to me, because once I'm standing, there's only a small amount of space between our chests. I stare at him blankly while fighting off the blush creeping up my neck. "What are you doing here?"

"I'm *also* going to the Zurich airport?" he says like a question instead of an answer.

I huff. "Yeah, I know." I gesture to the space between us. "But what are you doing *here*?"

"I think the better question is—why did you leave without me?" he retorts, though the words lack bite. His tone is more confused than anything.

I wait for the anger I felt earlier to flood my face, but I'm also confused. "I thought *you* left without *me*," I explain. "I woke up and you weren't in the hotel room. I thought you ditched me and went to the train station." I pick at the mehendi lining my skin. It's been almost a week since Ammi's friend applied it, so it's starting to morph from a deep red to a burnt orange. "So, I left."

"I went to get breakfast." He holds up his wrist with the bag encircling it. "When we had breakfast at the hotel, you said a bagel with cream cheese was your go-to."

I can only stare at him, confusion marring my face. "Why did you take your whole suitcase with you, then?"

"Oh." He pats the handle of his bag. "I'm so used to traveling alone that whenever I leave a hotel room, I take my bag with me. I guess I can see how that made you think I left." His gaze drops from mine, and he shuffles his feet awkwardly. "I was hoping it'd be a peace offering after what happened last night," he reveals. Tentatively, he peeks up at me from beneath lowered lashes. "But when I came back to the room and saw it empty, I thought you were already gone." He looks around the cabin. "Figured there was only one place you were going."

I sniffle, trying but failing to keep the growing smile off my face. "Peace offering?"

Sarfaraz sighs. "I shouldn't have said all that stuff last night. You're literally on the way to your wedding. It was wrong of me to try to ruin your mood just because things didn't end well for me when I was married." He holds out one of the cups. "Look—I even got your disgusting coffee order."

A laugh bubbles out of my chest. "My coffee order isn't *that* bad." I drink in a deep breath. "So…even after all of that, you still came for me."

He smiles, too. It's a small one, but it's there. "Yeah."

We stare at each other for another moment before I break the spell and take the coffee from him. "Thank you," I say, sitting back down.

Sarfaraz looks to my bag, then back to me, cleverly concealed hope in his eyes. I pick up my bag and set it on the floor.

He sits down. "Honestly, I'm so happy I found you," he starts as he settles next to me.

My heart unexpectedly skips a beat. "Why?"

Sarfaraz flashes an annoyed smirk at me. "I'm now going to give you the silent treatment for what you did," he teases. "Do you know how embarrassing it was to walk back into the hotel room to find someone cleaning it because the occupant checked out already?"

I snort. "Serves you right."

"Hey!" Sarfaraz protests, but after I fix him with an expectant stare, he huffs. "Okay, fine."

That rouses a round of laughter from the both of us. Sarfaraz digs into his bagel, and I can't help the warmth that spreads through my belly the longer I look at him.

He gives me a once-over. "What?" he asks around his mouthful.

My cheeks redden. "Nothing." I stuff my bagel into my own mouth, hoping the flavor of the cheese will distract me from the tingles settling in my skin.

We eat in silence for a while before I pluck up the courage to ask him a question. "I know you won't tell me *why* you're going to Pakistan, but will you at least tell me where you're going? Are you going to stay in Islamabad?"

Sarfaraz chews for a moment, then swallows. He still doesn't say anything, though, and as I open my mouth to tell him to forget it, he says, "No. I'm taking a bus to Karachi once we get to Islamabad."

"What?" My jaw drops. A grin spreads on my face. "No way. I'm *also* taking a bus to Karachi when I get to Islamabad!"

"What?" he echoes. "That's…a wild coincidence."

"It is." I open my mouth to say something, but then pause. "Wait." I press a finger into the center of my chest. "*I'm* taking a bus to Karachi because it was the cheapest option. Why are *you* taking a bus to Karachi? I would have thought a lawyer would be able to afford a direct flight." I sit up in my seat. "And on that note, why did you fly Jinnah International? *I* had to because it's a cheap airline, but again, you're rich. Why wouldn't you take, like, Pakistan International Airlines?"

Sarfaraz tilts his head to the side, as if contemplating whether he wants to answer my question. "My trip to Pakistan was very last minute," he explains. "I wasn't planning on going, but I was convinced at the last second. There were no other flights available other than with Jinnah International. And because of that, I couldn't get a connecting flight to Karachi, so I arranged a bus."

I want to ask him more. More about why he's going, and about who convinced him to come. But he's opened up enough, and I'm afraid if I press too hard, he'll shut down completely. "Well, then. I guess we'll be travel companions for a while longer."

"Aww, man," Sarfaraz fake groans, hanging his head over the back of the seat.

My mouth drops open, but a laugh bursts from my chest as I smack him in the arm. "Hey!"

Sarfaraz sits up properly. "I'm just teasing." Then he holds up a hand. "But promise you won't puke on me again."

I chuckle. "I promise."

We drift back into silence as we finish our bagels, but this time, I don't feel the familiar sinking in my stomach when there's a long stretch of quiet. In fact, it's kind of…nice. I glance at Sarfaraz from the corner of my eye. I'm excited to keep going with him. Who knows? Maybe it'll be fun. Anything could happen in the time between us boarding the plane and getting off the bus in Karachi, but if I'm with him, maybe it won't be so bad.

15

Maya's Law #15:
Another thing that "almost never happens"?
It'll happen to you.

The seating assignments for the new flight are the same as the last one, so I'm technically supposed to be sitting farther back in the plane while Sarfaraz is up ahead. However, the thought of sitting by myself after being with Sarfaraz for so long unexpectedly twists in my gut, so I offer the father I initially changed seats with to switch again. He happily accepts, and while he goes to his family, I settle into the seat next to Sarfaraz.

He lifts his brows when he sees me. "I thought you were sitting closer to the back."

"Oh." I shrug, but my heartbeat picks up as I respond, "The guy who switched seats with me before asked to switch again so he can be with his family. I couldn't say no."

The beginnings of a grin touches Sarfaraz's face before he

schools his expression. "Well, as long as you don't bother me this time," he says, but the playful hint in his tone undercuts his words.

"Oh, I promise," I assure him. Out of curiosity, I lean forward so I can look past his chest, and my mouth curls into a smirk when I recognize Comatose Guy sitting next to Sarfaraz. A sleep mask covers his eyes, and his mouth hangs slightly open as he snores. The plane hasn't even taken off yet and he's already asleep. I shake my head and settle properly in my seat.

Sarfaraz tries to do more work, and at first, I *do* keep to myself, but I end up asking him to finish *Crash Landing on You* with me. To my surprise, he agrees, and we watch a couple more episodes before he decides he wants to sleep. While I'd rather not sit here alone with my own thoughts, he rests and I read on my iPad.

Thankfully, without any further hiccups, we make it to Islamabad. Islamabad is the capital of the country, though Lahore is technically more well-known. It's a shame I'm not staying in Pakistan for too long; when I used to come as a kid, I would spend at least a month here. I stopped going when I got older and it became harder to skip school, but I still miss the long afternoons spent at markets or the weekends road-tripping to the mountains in the north.

I head over to an information desk in the airport. The person working behind the desk confirms my luggage has made it from Toronto, so I go to baggage claim and pick up my suitcase. Sarfaraz has already grabbed his bag by the time I get there, and he helps me pull mine off the conveyor belt. Once we have all our stuff, we head for the exit. Before we step outside, though, I take a second to call Ammi. I updated her every now and then while we were in Switzerland, but I managed to avoid phone calls by saying I didn't want to spend more money on my international plan than I had to. It's supposed to be a quick call, but of course, nothing is ever quick with my mom.

"Ammi, for the last time, you don't have to send Mustafa Mamu to come get me," I insist.

"But it'll save you time!"

"How?" I demand. "It's way too far for him to drive to come get me. And what's he supposed to take? His motorcycle? Plus, I've already paid for the bus ticket to Karachi."

"I don't like the thought of you traveling alone," she sniffs. "It's dangerous!"

I almost tell her that I'm not alone, but that would involve telling her I've spent the last couple of days with a stranger, and then I'd have to explain *why* I didn't tell her, and it'll become way too complicated. Instead, I say, "It's very simple, Mom. The bus goes straight from the airport to the station in Karachi. I'll be on the bus the whole time. I won't even get off to pee. And I have my phone so you can reach me whenever you want."

Ammi grumbles on the other line. "Fine..." she relents, then her tone picks up. "But you have to text me updates."

"Don't worry, I will." I look back at Sarfaraz, who is waiting by the door. "Listen, Ammi, I gotta get on the bus. Inshallah, I'll see you soon."

"Okay. Khuda hafiz."

I say it back, then hang up and pocket my phone. I head over to Sarfaraz. "Sorry about that," I tell him. "Even though I'm an adult, my mother still thinks I can't take care of myself."

"No worries," he assures me.

We step out of the airport, and the brutal late-June temperature slaps us in the face. I choke out a breath. "Oomph, I feel like I stepped into a volcano."

Sarfaraz wipes his forehead. "It's a big contrast to Switzerland. I mean, it was still hot there, but nothing like this."

He's right; Switzerland was bad but endurable. The thickness of Pakistan's climate makes me want to submerge myself into the Antarctic Ocean and never get out. I can learn to live with penguins, but orca whales aren't friendly, no matter what SeaWorld tries to say.

We make it to the bus and find seats near the middle, and a small spark of pleasure lights up my chest when Sarfaraz automatically moves off to the side and waits for me to take the window seat. I giddily slide over and sit.

Once we're settled and the bus takes off, I crane my neck. It's stiff after spending so much time leaning against a window or uncomfortably on a travel pillow. I already can't wait to see my Parveen Khala, who gives the *best* massages. Ammi says it's one of her favorite parts of going back home to Pakistan, and I honestly can't blame her; that woman's fingers are magic. But for now, all I can do is press my own fingers against the sorest spots in my neck.

Sarfaraz notices me struggling. "Everything okay?"

"Yeah," I answer. I roll my neck out one more time. "I don't know how much longer my neck can handle leaning to the left while resting on a window."

Sarfaraz hesitates, then pats his shoulder. "You can lean on me, if you want."

My stomach clenches. "What?"

He rolls his eyes, indifference wrinkling his forehead, but I can tell by the way he doesn't look directly at me that he's a little…shy? "I'm just trying to save myself a round of your complaining; I still have to sit on a bus next to you for seventeen hours. So, you know." He shrugs. "Take it or leave it."

"Thanks," I murmur, before softly resting my temple against him. Sarfaraz stiffens under my touch at first, but then he relaxes. Encouraged, I close my eyes, welcoming the softness of his body.

★ ★ ★

I don't know how much time passes, but at some point, the bus jostles abruptly. I wake with a gasp. I grip my seat, and after a few more alarming stutters, the bus slugs to a stop.

My heartbeat slowly returns to a normal pace as I look at Sarfaraz. "What happened?"

Sarfaraz grabs the seat in front of him and hauls himself to his feet. "I'll go find out from the driver. Wait here."

"Where else am I going to go?" I tease, and he just gives me an annoyed look as he makes his way to the front of the bus. He's only gone for a few minutes before he returns, grumbling under his breath. "What did you find out?" I ask.

He looks like he's trying so hard not to curse in front of judgy Pakistanis. I mean, it's hard to say if any of them would know what's he's saying, but if Sarfaraz has taught me anything, it's to not assume people around you don't know what you're saying just because you're speaking in a different language. "Two flat tires," Sarfaraz announces, scowling. I open my mouth, but as I do, Sarfaraz holds a halting finger up at me. "If you say something about being cursed, I'm tossing you off the bus."

I clamp my jaw shut. Then I ask, "So what do we do now?"

"Nothing. Because there's nothing we *can* do but wait for another bus to show up and bail us out." He bites his lip, and I try not to focus on it. "But…"

"But?"

"But that could take hours," he reveals. "Apparently, we're in the middle of nowhere in between big cities."

A heavy feeling plunges down my throat and settles into my stomach, like I swallowed a rock. I sit there for a second, then nod once. "Alright." I get up and grab my backpack from the floor. "Move out of the way."

"Why?"

"Because I'm *walking* to Karachi," I announce. "If I have to get there on foot, I will."

"Don't be ridiculous." Sarfaraz sits back down, probably because he hopes I'll take the hint and do the same. I remain standing, though. "We have to wait for the bus. I'm sure it won't take that long."

"You don't know that! With my luck, it'll take *hours* for another bus to get out here." I gesture to the space around us. "There's no food and no bathroom," I point out. "I'd rather take my chances walking and hopefully end up at some village."

"And then what?" Sarfaraz questions. "Some of them don't even have electricity, let alone cars."

"I don't know," I grumble. "I'll borrow a horse or something."

Sarfaraz stares blankly at me for a long moment. "A…horse," he deadpans. He tilts his head to the side. "Have you ever *been* to Pakistan before?"

"Hey, I've seen the horses pulling carts on the road! I'm sure if I slip someone a few rupees, they'll help." I square my shoulders and squeeze into the aisle.

I'm about to walk to the front of the bus when Sarfaraz grabs my wrist. His palm against my skin sends a shock up my arm, and it distracts me long enough for him to tug me back. "If you go out there, you'll be on your own," he starts, and the severity of his words is bolstered by the stern pull between his brows. "That'll put you in even more danger than if you just shut up and sit your ass in this bus."

Ordinarily, I would have wrenched my wrist out of his grasp and gone down anyway. Who's he to tell me what I can and can't do? To insinuate I can't take care of myself?

What stops me, though, is the sincerity in his pupils. He continues to stare at me, his eyes urging, pleading.

With a long, defeated groan, I scootch past him and slump back into the seat.

16

Maya's Law #16:
Not everything is written in the stars.

The hours trickle by, and anxiety eats at the lining of my stomach.
I guess Sarfaraz is anxious, too, because he keeps tapping his fingers against his lap. I stare at the action for too long, and when he catches my eye, I look out the window instead. My throat dries as I watch the sun dip below the horizon. When the sky changes from a dusty pink to shadowy purple, I whip my head to face Sarfaraz. "Where is the bus? You said it wasn't going to take long." I gesture to the window. "The sun's gone down!"

Sarfaraz fixes me with an annoyed stare. "I don't know, Maya. I'm sitting on the bus next to you, not driving the bus on the way here."

I groan and bang my head against the seat. Pain prickles at the back of my scalp, but the frustration boiling in my body masks it. "What are we going to do?" I grumble. "It didn't take us this long to drive all the way out here; what's taking so long?"

"I don't know," he says again, but this time his tone is more sympathetic.

"This is all my curse's fault."

"Would you stop saying that? Curses aren't real."

I don't bother insisting that they are, because he's never going to believe me, so I might as well save my breath.

Then, one by one, people at the front start leaving the bus. Sarfaraz watches for a few seconds before speaking up. "Excuse me!" he calls out in Urdu.

A man helping his pregnant wife down the aisle looks over at us, so Sarfaraz asks, "Where is everyone going?"

"There's been another delay with the second bus coming to get us," the man explains. "But the bus driver has a new plan. Apparently, we're close enough to a rest stop, so the driver wants us to walk there. Once we get there, they'll call Ubers to take us to a nearby village where we can comfortably wait for another bus."

"What about our luggage?" I ask.

"The bus driver said it'd get delivered to the bus station in Karachi."

Sarfaraz thanks the man, who continues down the aisle. He dips his head toward the aisle. "Do you want to go, then?"

I peek out the window. In the distance ahead, people are already making their way along the dirt-stained road. I turn back to Sarfaraz. "If it's what the bus driver is saying, then we should."

We grab our stuff and make our way down the aisle. When we get to the front, I notice a gap between the bottom step and the ground. I brace myself for the jump I'll have to make. Sarfaraz goes first, and to my surprise, he turns around and offers me a hand. I hesitate but carefully accept. Tingles flush my skin as I brace myself and step all the way down and onto the dirt road. His hand lingers in my own for a moment before he pulls it away.

He puts his back to me, and I glance down at my hand. I flex my fingers for a moment before shaking the nerves off.

We start following the other groups of people walking in front of us. Sarfaraz and I make light conversation as we walk, but it quickly fades into silence because it's too much effort to keep up talking in the heat. The air is much cooler outside than it was on the bus, but it's still disgustingly hot. I twist my hair into a knot at the back of my head, and it provides some relief. We eventually make it to the pit stop the man on the bus told us about; it's a place where buses can stop to get gas, or truck drivers can rest if they're too tired to keep going.

The cars that are supposed to take us to a nearby village aren't here yet, so we have no choice but to keep waiting. There isn't really a place to sit, so I'm preparing myself mentally to keep standing when Sarfaraz reaches into his bag, pulls out the red sweater he wore on the plane, and sets it on the ground. He smooths the material down so it's flat, then sits down. When he's situated, he looks up at me. "We might be waiting a while." He pats the small spot next to him. "You can join me, if you want."

On the one hand, I don't know if it's a good choice to sit so close to Sarfaraz, not after what I felt when he helped me off the bus. On the other, I'm too tired to keep standing. I lower myself to the ground next to him. My side brushes his, and I edge away.

I wrap my arms around my legs and rest my chin on my knees. Right as I do so, however, my stomach growls and its alarmingly loud. The hunger gnawing at my insides reminds me that I didn't eat much on the plane ride to Islamabad. I thought I'd be able to grab something while waiting for the bus, or I'd suck it up and wait until I got to Karachi to eat something. But now that we're in the middle of nowhere, it's like my stomach's remembered that it's empty. Pain pinches my abdomen, and I run my palms over it, trying to soothe my body into relaxing. I've already experienced one bad stomach reaction on this trip; I don't want another.

Sarfaraz stares at the action. I go still, a blush coloring my ears. "I didn't eat on the plane."

His eyes suddenly light up, and he reaches into his own bag. With a triumphant grin, he produces two packs of airplane peanuts. "You're not allergic, are you?"

I splutter out a laugh. "No, I'm not."

Wordlessly, he holds out one of the packets, and I take it from him. We eat in silence. I'm so hungry I want to shove the whole bag down my throat, but I eat piece by piece, making each bite last. While we snack, the sky continues to darken, until it blackens completely around us.

Once we're done eating, I lie down, staring upward at all the tiny stars sprinkled across the sky. Usually there's too much smog in my city, so we rarely get to see them.

"I've always loved astronomy." Sarfaraz's voice breaks into my thoughts. I peek up at him but stay lying down. He looks down at me, the beginning of a smile on his face. "When I was younger, my dad, my brother, and I would go camping a lot. We would fish, roast marshmallows over the fire, find constellations in the sky for hours. My stepmom refused to go because she hates nature, but she always loved cooking up whatever we brought home." He sighs dreamily, like he was reliving lying underneath an open sky surrounded by family, the comforting scent of wood burning in the background.

I stay quiet, because this is the most he's ever said about himself, apart from the divorce thing, and I'm afraid if I say anything, he might close right back up again. When I don't speak, Sarfaraz tilts his face up so his gaze is to the sky. I begin to think I made the wrong decision in staying silent, but then he points to a scattering of stars. "That's Ursa Major," he explains. He looks back down at me. "It's always been one of the easiest constellations for me to spot."

"It's really something else. The only bright things in big cities you can spot at night are the airplanes." I let out a long breath. "My kids would love this."

Sarfaraz tenses. "You have kids?"

A laugh bursts from my chest. "No," I say, and he immediately relaxes. "I'm a grade one teacher. My class this year absolutely *loved* the astronomy unit. We made telescopes, even though I warned them in advance that it would be hard for them to really see anything in the city. They loved listening to me read books about space." My mind drifts back to the students I had this year. Sometimes they're a lot to deal with, but I love them to pieces. "I miss them."

Sarfaraz's mouth quirks up. "That's cute."

I snap my head up to look at him. His face reddens, and he clears his throat as he looks away from me. "I mean, it's nice you love your job so much."

I accept the explanation. "How much do you love your job? You must see some rough stuff."

"Of course," he says, and judging by the way his shoulders are noticeably less tense, he's glad I've taken the hint. "I handle divorces fairly often. The end of a marriage is usually tough, but sometimes divorce can be freeing."

At my confused look, Sarfaraz continues. "Sometimes it's better to be separated than to be stuck in a marriage you don't want, where all the love is gone," he explains. "People don't realize how much it affects their own mental health, as well as the mental health of their children, if they have any, if they stay in a marriage when they no longer love each other." He shrugs. "Sometimes divorce is better."

I mull over what he's said. After a few silent seconds of

tapping my fingers against my stomach, I open my mouth. I make sure to keep my focus on the stars as I ask, "Do you really think all marriages are doomed? I know we started this conversation in Switzerland, but we never finished it."

Sarfaraz hums for a moment. "Maybe not...*doomed*, but I don't know how realistic it is. Some relationships are fine until they add marriage to the mix. Such a permanent union... It changes things. Sometimes, it can even change *people*."

"Well, I think you're wrong."

He smirks. "Of course you do."

"I mean it." I push myself into a sitting position, balancing on my palms. "Marriage can be so beautiful. The idea of someone wanting only you for the rest of their life and knowing that person will be there for you is very sweet." I pause for a second, then add, softer this time, "And sure, sometimes it doesn't work out, and people leave, but the thought that someone is ready to forsake everyone else for you forever, and to proclaim as much in front of Allah, is amazing."

Sarfaraz stares at me for a long beat, searching my face. I almost cower under his attention, but I stand my ground. Eventually, he says, "But you can't know that it's forever. You can't see the future, so you never know if it's going to work out, or if something will tear you apart."

"That's what makes it even better." At his puzzled stare, I elaborate. "You can't promise what's going to happen in the future, but you can promise you'll be there for each other in the moment."

We share a look for a little longer, and then I tear my focus away from him. "Maybe we should see if we can find any more constellations." I lie back down.

To my surprise, Sarfaraz lies down next to me. When I raise a brow at the action, he just shrugs. "It's easier this way."

I grin. "Right."

17

**Maya's Law #17:
Not everyone is kind.**

Time passes. I debate whether I should call Ammi and give her another update, but it hasn't quite been seventeen hours yet, which is the time the website said it would take the bus to get to Karachi, and I don't want her nagging. All she'll do is tell me she was right, that I couldn't do this on my own. Plus, my phone battery is dangerously low, at like 18 percent. I turn it off and hope that it'll conserve some of the juice.

Sarfaraz points out all the constellations and planets he can see, and when there's nothing left, we settle into a comfortable silence. A few cars start showing up to take people to a nearby village, but Sarfaraz and I agree to let the families with children leave first; we can handle some more time in this weather, but small kids can't.

I rest my cheek against my palm. I've started to drift off when Sarfaraz shakes me awake. I groan and lift my head. "What?"

He points to a car pulling up in front of us. "Let's take that car."

I blink a few times while pushing myself into a sitting position. "Are the families all gone?"

"Yeah." He stands up, so I do, too. "We should take this chance to get out of here, too. I don't know how much longer I can go without water."

I adjust the strap of my backpack while Sarfaraz packs up his sweater, and then we make our way over to the car. The driver rolls the window down, and I offer my best teacher grin. "Salaam," I greet.

"Salaam," the driver says back. "My name is Muhammad Moiz."

"I'm Maya. Thank you so much for your help," I say. "I don't know what we'd do if we had to wait here much longer. At least in the village we can get some food and water."

He pauses for a beat, then replies, "Of course. It'll be my pleasure to take you." He peeks past me, then frowns. "Who's the guy?"

Sarfaraz speaks before I have the chance to. "Her husband," he responds curtly in Urdu.

I don't know who's more shocked: the driver at Sarfaraz's flawless Urdu, or me because he referred to himself as my *husband*. Wordlessly, he opens the door, and when he catches my bewildered stare, he sends me a look that says, *Don't argue.*

His lie is probably a good idea, but I can't let go of the nagging feeling in the pit of my stomach that feels less like a nagging and more like a...softness. One that absolutely shouldn't be there.

I peek through the door to see two other men in the car.

There's a man in the passenger's seat, and another man with a bushy beard sitting on the far left. I didn't realize there'd be other passengers in the car, but I dip my head awkwardly at them and climb in. I wince at how my skin sticks to the hot leather seats. I shift to the middle seat and my thigh brushes against the guy sitting next to me. I instinctively recoil.

Sarfaraz slides in after me, shutting the door. The driver clears his throat but starts the engine and begins driving.

We sit in silence for about twenty minutes until I ask, "So, what are your names?"

"As I said before, I am Muhammad Moiz," the driver responds. He jerks his thumb to the passenger seat. "This is Riyad." He moves his thumb in the direction of the man sitting next to me. "And that's Asad."

I swallow thickly. "Nice to meet you all," I mumble, my voice cracking.

"Where are you headed?" Asad asks.

"Karachi," Sarfaraz responds. "We're attending a wedding there."

They nod thoughtfully, and we drift back into silence. Something strange churns in my stomach, and it's not nausea or extreme hunger. It's something deeper, something more... worrying.

"So, is the company still Uber here, or is it called something else?" I ask.

"It's still called Uber," Muhammad Moiz quickly answers. His grip tightens on the steering wheel.

"Oh," I murmur, settling back. I peek at Sarfaraz. One look tells me exactly what he's thinking: there's something off here.

Muhammad Moiz's eyes flicker up to the rearview mirror and spot Sarfaraz and I exchanging a glance. We quickly break our stare. I try to look anywhere else in the car, and I happen to look at Riyad. The moonlight streaming in through the window catches on something metal in his lap. I squint harder, despite the darkness surrounding us. Once the form of the metal contraption registers, my heart leaps into my throat and a tiny gasp escapes me.

Sarfaraz's breath is in my ear within seconds. "What?" he whispers. "What is it?"

I keep my expression as neutral as possible, but in English, I choke out, "Gun. In Riyad's lap."

I guess I wasn't as quiet as I thought I was, because the next thing I know, Muhammad Moiz stomps on the brake. Sarfaraz shoots his arm out against my chest, pushing me safely back in the seat.

That feeling of security slips right out of my system as Riyad swings around in his seat and points the gun in our faces.

"What the hell?" Sarfaraz growls. He shifts his body in front of me as much as he possibly can, and I scramble behind him until my back is crushed against the window. I instinctively reach up to clasp his shoulders, and I press my chest as close to him as I can get. He puts on a brave face, but I can feel his heart thumping erratically through his back. "Let's calm down for a second."

Muhammad Moiz calmly turns in his seat. "Give us all the money and valuables you have."

"Okay, wait, hang on," Sarfaraz starts, but Riyad clicks the safety off the gun, pressing it toward us.

Sarfaraz's mood instantly shifts from negotiating to peacemaking. "Fine, fine!" he relents. Slowly, he reaches into his pants for his wallet. He takes out all the rupees he has, leans forward, and places the money in Asad's outstretched palm.

"Do you have a phone?" Muhammad Moiz questions.

Sarfaraz gives that over, too, then repositions himself in front of me.

Riyad dips his head at me. "What about you?"

"She doesn't have anything," Sarfaraz interjects. He presses his back to my chest, crushing me against the window. "I carry all the money with me, and I don't allow her to have a cell phone."

"Then what's in the bag she's carrying?" Asad demands.

Sarfaraz glares at him. "What do you *think* is in a woman's purse? It's her papers and medicines and other…feminine items."

Riyad sneers and digs the gun into Sarfaraz's cheek. "Don't test me, boy."

Sarfaraz grunts, and a shiver racks his body from the force of not showing that he's in pain. The feeling sends a worried shock through my body, and I speak up, "I do have something!"

"Maya, shut up," Sarfaraz hisses in English.

"No. I'm trying to help get us out of here."

"What are you talking about?" Riyad barks. He presses the gun closer to Sarfaraz's face. "Does the girl have anything, or not?"

"I do!" I insist. "I… I don't have anything in my bag…" I continue, hoping they'll buy Sarfaraz's *feminine items* line. I hold up my hand. "But if I give you my ring, you have to let us go."

Asad greedily reaches for me, but Sarfaraz bats him away. "Don't touch her," he warns with a hiss.

"Give us the ring, then," Muhammad Moiz orders.

"You have to let us out of the car first," I insist.

Riyad looks over at Muhammad Moiz, who nods. "Alright, get out," he grumbles.

I blindly reach behind me for the handle, and we tumble out of the car. The whole time, Sarfaraz stays between me and the men. Muhammad Moiz lazily stretches his arm out toward me while Riyad keeps the gun trained on us. "Hurry, now."

My lips curl back in disgust as I twist the ring off my finger.

"You're literally named after our most important prophet," I snarl at him. "Astaghfirullah. What will Allah say?"

"I guess I'll find out once I meet Him," Muhammad Moiz drawls. He curls his fingers inward. "You're testing my patience now."

I take one last long look at my engagement ring. I remember Imtiaz telling me he spent hours in a jewelry store trying to find one he thought would suit my tastes. It's a zero-point-nine-five carat total weight diamond, in fourteen-karat white gold. It encompasses a brilliant round diamond, with a sparkling halo and diamond-set shoulders. All in all, a beautiful and extremely expensive ring. Yet… I never really liked it. Of course it's gorgeous, but it never felt like *me*. Still, Imtiaz picked it with lots of love, or at least affection, and here I am about to give it to a thug in exchange for my freedom.

With a final huff, I give Sarfaraz the ring. Cautiously, he drops it into Muhammad Moiz's outstretched hand.

Muhammad Moiz examines the ring for a moment before curling his fingers over it. He gives us a mock salute. "Enjoy your stay in Pakistan!" he jokes, and then he hits the gas, the sound of his guffaws echoing through the night.

For a long moment, all Sarfaraz and I can do is stand there, utterly stunned. Finally, I say, "I'm starting to think they weren't from the bus company."

Sarfaraz whirls on me. "Are you trying to make a *joke*?" He waves his arm in the direction of the car. "We got *robbed* at *gunpoint*!"

"Hey, don't yell at me like it's my fault," I fume. "It's not my fault."

"It's not mine, either!"

"You were the one who chose that car, not me."

He grits his teeth because he knows I'm right. I guess that's not going to stop him from taking his frustration out on me, though, because he says, "You were the one who escalated the situation."

"What?!" I exclaim, my jaw dropping. "How?"

"You *had* to insist you had something to give them. You could have gotten us both killed. You should have kept your mouth shut."

I can't believe my ears. "I'm the one who got us out of there!" I snap. "Who knows if those guys would have let us go if I hadn't offered up my freaking *engagement ring*."

A loud crack interrupts us, and we both catch a glimpse of lightning above our heads. Within seconds, rain falls from the clouds, pelting our faces and drenching our clothes. Sarfaraz huffs. "Great! We're going to get soaked through, and we don't even have anything to change in to, because all our luggage is on a bus that's miles behind us." He clenches his hands into fists. "I don't know how you managed to survive on your own for two years, because it seems like your mother's right—you *can't* take care of yourself. You're an adult woman who apparently can't be trusted to do anything on her own without messing it up somehow."

Anger boils hot under my skin. "Hey! I was doing fine before I got stuck with you."

"Oh, you call what you were doing *fine*?" He laughs humorlessly. "Running late to the airport, talking to a stranger on the plane next to you because you can't handle being on your own, and then getting sick and not being able to take care of yourself. You call that *fine*?"

I hate how much merit his words have. I try to spin it around on him. "At least I'm not some emotionless robot who doesn't know how to interact with people without pissing them off."

"I don't think I was *that* bad." Sarfaraz's expression turns steely. "But maybe I should have been worse. At least then I wouldn't be stuck in the middle of nowhere with *you*."

That last sentence unexpectedly punches me in the gut, stealing my breath from my lungs. My jaw wobbles. I open my mouth to defend myself, but to my horror, I burst into loud sobs.

Sarfaraz freezes. "Why...why are you crying?"

"BECAUSE!" I explode, unleashing all the pent-up anger and frustration I've been trying to keep at bay since my plans derailed in Switzerland. "THIS IS SUPPOSED TO BE THE MOST BEAUTIFUL TIME OF MY LIFE AND I'M SUP-POSED TO BE WITH MY FAMILY IN A WARM HOUSE BUT HERE I AM IN THE MIDDLE OF *NOWHERE* BEING RAINED ON WITH AN ASSHOLE STRANGER YELLING AT ME!"

Sarfaraz stares at me blankly, and even in the darkness of night, I can see pink dotting his cheeks. "Oh," he says quietly.

I try to speak again, to shame him for his stupid *Oh*, but all that comes out is unintelligible blubbering. I can't catch my breath, and I continue to sob, burying my face in my palms, my hot tears mixing with the cold drops of rain. I fall to my knees, not even caring about the mud staining my pants as I sob.

All of a sudden, the rain stops pelting me. I look up at the sky. Rain continues to fall, but I'm not getting wet any-more. I crane my neck back, only to see Sarfaraz holding the sweater we sat on earlier over my head. He grimaces against the water plopping onto his body, but he continues to stand there patiently.

I sniffle loudly. "What are you doing?" I ask, my throat thick with tears. "I'm already wet."

He's silent for a moment. "I...don't know," he responds honestly. A helpless expression pinches his face. His eyes meet mine, and they're much gentler than they were before. "But I'm trying to do something."

We stay like that for a long while, me on the ground with tears slipping down my face, Sarfaraz hovering above me, allowing himself to get wet. I cry and cry and cry, and he remains quiet. All he's doing is standing in silence, letting me sob my brains out, but I realize I haven't felt so connected to someone in a long time. After years of faded friendships, failed attempts at relationships, and mismatched rishtas, here is someone looking at my truest, ugliest, and most vulnerable self, and still deciding to stick around. It feels good. I haven't let myself want anything like this before, and it's terrifying but I can't help but want more of it. It's exhilarating, emotional, and…dangerous.

18

Maya's Law #18:
If you're overtired, you'll always spill your guts.

After a while, I manage to pull myself together, and we decide the best course of action is to continue onward. We could try to walk back to the rest stop, but there's no guarantee anyone will still be there. With my luck, they'll be long gone by the time we get back. Then we'd have to continue forward anyway, but we'd have to cover that ground all over again. On top of that, we don't have any food *or* water, and the sun will be up soon; once it is, the scorching heat will return, and there's no telling how long we'll last on empty stomachs. Behind us, we know there's nothing, but if we keep walking, there's a better chance we'll stumble across the village we were supposed to arrive at to wait for a new bus.

We walk in the dark for what feels like hours. There are

lots of wild animals in the outskirts, and every now and then I cower behind Sarfaraz when we cross paths with something. Usually, it's a stray dog or a feral cat, but twice we encounter wild boars. Luckily they have poor sight in the dark, so we stay very still until they pass by us.

Thankfully, it stops raining, but after the sun starts to peek over the horizon, I wish the rain were back. I can barely raise an arm to block the rays from my retinas. A tortured groan rumbles my throat. "I wish I had some water."

"That's the third time you've said that in twenty minutes," Sarfaraz heaves, though his words lack their usual annoyance. Things must be getting bad if Sarfaraz is too tired to chastise my whining. "I'm sure we'll find a village soon."

I step on an uneven patch of road, and my foot slips. I don't have enough time to catch my balance, and I end up flopping to the ground with a hard thud. I manage to seal my mouth right before I hit the dirt, so thankfully I don't end up with a mouthful of dust. A moan grumbles my chest as I curl into a ball.

Sarfaraz hovers over me, tilting his head to the side. "Don't you think this is sad?"

My head spins, and black spots creep up on my vision. I don't even have the energy to defend myself. "Leave me alone to die."

"Come on. You're being overdramatic."

"I get low blood sugar." I bring my knees to my chest. "I've gone too long without anything real to eat."

Sarfaraz huffs a short breath through his nose, then holds his hand out to me. I huff and reach out an arm, and he hauls me to my feet. To my surprise, though, he loops my arm through his and secures my hand in the crook of his elbow. I stare down at our joined limbs, then look up at Sarfaraz. "What are you doing?"

"I don't want to be here when noon hits," he says simply. His expression is neutral, but I know him better at this point, and the pink tinting his ears isn't from just the hot weather. "It'll be way too hot, and I don't know if I'll have the energy to pull you along with me by then."

I gulp, but I let him lead us forward.

Even though it should be the last thing on my mind after everything that's happened, all I can think about is how this is the closest I've been to a guy before. Okay, so I've had my first kiss (Yahya Zafar when I was thirteen, and he said my breath smelled like cheese right after), but other than that, I've never gotten emotionally close enough to a guy to warrant this kind of close touch. Not only that, but because intimacy with the opposite sex is technically forbidden until marriage—even holding a guy's hand is enough fodder for gossip in our community. I didn't want to bring Ammi any more shame than she'd already received.

Still, if his feet weren't moving confidently and steadily forward, I'd still be on the ground, so I hold on. I rest my temple against him, and surprisingly, he lets me.

"So—" Sarfaraz's voice rumbles the side of my body, and a spark spreads through me "—how did you meet your fiancé?"

I must be totally out of it, because the words tumble out without me caring to stop and think about what I'm saying. "I was twenty-five and having such a hard time finding a permanent teaching position, and I needed to pay my mountain of student loans," I mumble. "And then I met up with an old friend from teacher's college. He'd just gotten back from teaching abroad, and he told me about how great of an opportunity it was. New city, new people, great money. After months of feeling like something was off, I thought a change might inject some real life into my life." I sigh heavily. "I wanted to go, but my mom said I had to be married first."

"Really?" Sarfaraz twists his lips. "That doesn't sound very fair."

"Yeah, well." I fist the material of his shirt between my fingers. "Having your father leave when you're ten isn't fair, either."

Sarfaraz is quiet for a beat before he says, "I'm sorry."

I sniffle but continue. "A young Pakistani woman typically doesn't leave the house before marriage. But I lobbied so hard, and my Hibba Baji was so supportive of me. Plus, Hibba Baji pointed out that I couldn't go into a marriage with debts. Ammi eventually relented, but her new condition was that I had to be engaged. We met Imtiaz through a mutual friend's matchmaker." I briefly pause when Sarfaraz's body tenses, but he readjusts my grip on his arm and keeps walking. "That was when we realized we remembered each other from a class we shared together in university. We were both quite surprised when we realized who the other person was."

"And then?" Sarfaraz asks, and his voice is noticeably tighter.

"Nothing, really." I stifle a yawn, then snuggle closer to Sarfaraz's arm. "We met up a few times, and we liked each other, so our parents secured the match. After the Baat Pakki, I went off to Korea. I stayed for two years, then came back and got a job working with first graders, and for the past year we've been planning the wedding. We decided to do it in Pakistan because all my relatives are here. Most of Imtiaz's family is in Canada, but he agreed to have the wedding here."

Sarfaraz pauses, and his Adam's apple bobs. Tension lines his forehead, and I swear for a brief moment, a torn expression twists his face. When he realizes I'm staring at him, though, the flash of emotion is gone, and he schools his features into a smirk that doesn't quite fill out his face like I'm sure he's hoping. "No offense, but your life sounds pretty wild," he says, and his tone is still strained.

I choose to ignore it…for now. "That's what my laws are for," I reply instead.

"Your laws?"

"Do you know the concept of Murphy's Law?"

"The idea that anything that *can* go wrong *will* go wrong?"

"That's the one." I inhale deeply, my lids drooping heavily. "Well, when I was a kid, I came across the saying in a book. It fit my life so perfectly I couldn't believe it. So, growing up, I made up my own laws in relation to Murphy's Law. It was the only way I could think to make sense of everything happening to me."

"That's…kind of sad," he says, sympathy in his voice. "You must have had a hard time growing up if you used an adult concept to cope through life."

I sniffle. "I guess I've never thought of it that way before. I saw it as a way to explain things because I grew up thinking God makes things happen for a reason." I stare down at the dirt road. "Guess that was me finding my reasons."

"I have to say, for someone who's had a lot of misfortune in life, and your love life, I'm surprised you even still believe in love." He keeps his eyes on the road ahead of us. "I would have thought someone like that would not believe in marriage at all."

I blink a few times, then stare straight ahead, too. "I guess, despite everything I've been through, I had to keep believing in it. Love may have failed me and my family in some aspects of our lives, but it was also something that kept us together. Pain is the price we pay for love, but with how happy love makes us feel, I think it's worth the risk."

Sarfaraz quiets down again. My shoulders relax, thinking he's satisfied with my answers, but he bursts, "You know, from everything you've been saying, it sounds like you don't want to get married." After another pause, he tentatively stops and peeks down at me. "Do you?"

We slowly draw to a stop, but neither of us says anything. I open my mouth, hesitantly, but before I can respond, a gush of laughter interrupts me. We both look straight ahead.

The sound came from what appears to be a village not too far ahead. The sun has made its appearance, creeping high enough that brightness stretches across the sky and casts a shadow against the short structures of the modest houses. Long, green fields cover the grounds, with tall stalks of crops, probably even taller than Sarfaraz, clustered together. Groups of cattle graze on the grass, and a man herds a couple of goats along the road.

"Oh, finally," Sarfaraz breathes, and my chest loosens when I realize he's forgotten about the question he asked me. I pull my arm out of his grasp, and we walk the rest of the way to the village side by side.

We stop the first person we can find, a woman around my mother's age carrying a basket filled with greens. "Excuse me," I start in Urdu.

She stops at the sound of my voice. Her hair, dyed red from mehendi, shines brilliantly under the early-morning sun. She gives us a smile. "Assalaam-o-alaikum."

"Walaykum salam," we say back. "My name is Maya." I gesture to Sarfaraz. "And this is Sarfaraz. He's my…" I peek at him, but before he can fill in his own answer, I say, "My husband."

When Sarfaraz doesn't stiffen or refute me, I continue. "We're trying to get to Karachi. We had some bus troubles a long while back, and we've been walking for a very long time. Are there any buses here that can take us to Karachi?"

"Well, we do have a bus that comes here and can take you

to a station in the next town over," she explains. "There, you can get on a bus that will take you to Karachi."

I brighten up. "Really? That's perfect!"

"But it won't be coming until the day after tomorrow," she adds.

The day after tomorrow? Despair weighs heavily on my back, threatening to drag me down to the pits of the earth. That'll mean by the time the bus shows up to this village and gets us to Karachi, there will only be three days until the actual wedding.

"Okay, is there a hotel where we can stay until then?"

"Unfortunately, no," the woman responds. "But you and your husband can stay with my family if you wish."

"Oh, no," Sarfaraz interjects. "We wouldn't want to impose."

"Impose? Nonsense." The woman waves off his concern. "You're in Pakistan, sir. I don't know what it's like where you're from, but in this country, we show out-of-town guests the best hospitality."

I look over to Sarfaraz. "It'd be rude not to accept," I say to him in English. "Plus, we don't have a choice."

"I don't know…"

"Look, it's either their house or the street. Now, I'm starving, and tired, and dirty, so if you want, you can stay here, but I'm going with the mother-looking lady."

Sarfaraz scrunches his brows, and at the sight, I pout. "Come on. Trust me."

His face relaxes at my words, and my heart skips a beat at how easy that was. Sarfaraz tips his head back with a defeated groan. With a grin, I loop my arm through the auntie's, then let her pull us along in the direction of her house.

19

**Maya's Law #19:
Showing your emotions on your face
never ends well.**

Like most of the houses in the village, the home of the woman—whose name we learn is Salama Kassab—is small. It's a little, one-story building; gray bricks, a slanted roof, and handcrafted windows with fingerprints smudging the glass. Salama leads Sarfaraz and me to a bedroom all the way at the end of the hall. It's really only big enough for a bed and a brown dresser tucked on the opposite side. My throat dries when I realize there is in fact only *one* bed. It's a good size, but still, there's only one.

"This is my daughter's old room," Salama explains when she notices me staring at the solitary bed. "She got married recently." She gestures haphazardly to the bed. "I know it will probably be a tight fit for you two, but I remember my own post-honeymoon time." She wiggles her brows at us. "Being closer to each other is much better."

The tips of my ears burn. Sarfaraz and I briefly look at each other, but I quickly look away when I feel my neck flush. "Well, congratulations to your daughter," I say politely instead.

"Thank you." Salama pauses, then gives us a once-over. "Do you two have anything to wear?" she asks, noticing our lack of suitcases.

"No," we both say.

She looks us both up and down again, then points to me. "You should fit into some of my daughter's clothes." She moves the finger toward Sarfaraz. "I think some of my husband's old clothes might fit you, but they'll be loose."

"That's fine," Sarfaraz says. He gives her a grateful smile. "We appreciate you helping us. You didn't have to, and may Allah reward your kindness."

Salama pinches his cheek, twisting his face from side to side. "So cute!" she gushes. "Such a polite boy." She looks over to me. "You're quite lucky, Maya."

"Oh, yeah," I tease with an affirming nod. "He's a real catch."

He begins to narrow his eyes before he remembers he's supposed to be in love with me. He dips his head at Salama. "Thank you again, Auntie."

"I'll be right back with some clothes for you two," she says. "I'll show you to the bathroom, and you can wash. In the meantime, I'll prepare some breakfast. You must be hungry."

At the mention of food, my stomach clenches. "Very."

Salama steps out of the room, leaving Sarfaraz and I alone. He immediately turns to me, pointing a finger at the door. "That is the raciest I have *ever* heard an auntie speak. And I certainly didn't expect it from one who lives in a pind."

I sit down on the bed. "Sorry I said we were married," I start. "I didn't know what else to say."

"It's okay. I told Muhammad Moiz that we were married, too." He sits down on the bed next to me. "Plus, I don't think she would have bought it if you told her I was your brother."

I snort. "Yeah, probably not."

Thankfully, before the silence can drag on, Salama comes back with shalwar kameez for us. Sarfaraz, graciously, allows me to bathe first. Salama heats up some water for me, then pours it into a bucket in the room they designated as their bathroom. It's not like a bathroom in the city, where there's a separate stall for the shower. Instead, the whole room is open. There's a drain in the floor, where water from the bath goes.

I feel way better after washing the dirt and grime and sweat off my body. I dip a ladle-like tool into the bucket and pour the water over my face. I scrub at my skin, washing away the events of the last couple of days. I pause when my fingers graze the spot on my arm where it was linked with Sarfaraz's. My skin flushes, even while a shiver racks my body. I brush it off and douse the spot with another ladleful of hot water.

Once I'm done, I wrap the towel around my body. I'm about to step out into the hallway when I remember I have to go back into a room with Sarfaraz while technically completely naked. I was so eager to be clean that I didn't think to bring my clothes into the bathroom, and because we're *supposed* to be married, Salama assumed we'd be fine staying in the same room. My hand freezes on the doorknob, and I jerk it back, instead using it to secure the towel better.

Okay. Okay. This is no big deal. I just have to put on my big-girl pants and go out there. Besides, he's going to leave for the bathroom as soon as I get in there so he can shower, and I can dress then. This is fine.

Checking one more time to make sure the towel completely

covers my body, I open the door and dash down the hall to the bedroom. I slip into the room, and as I do, Sarfaraz looks up from his spot on the bed. The clothes Salama gave him are draped over his lap, like he's planning on taking them into the bathroom with him, and for a second, I forget about my embarrassment and curse the fact that he thought of doing that when I didn't.

The embarrassment returns full force when Sarfaraz's eyes widen at my semi-naked form. I know the towel covers all the important bits, but to me, my bare shoulders and collarbone are just as private as the rest of me, so my face flushes. I'm trying to cover my collarbone with my hair when I notice his eyes are raking over my bare legs. The words tumble out before I can stop them, "What happened to not wanting to stare at my legs?"

Sarfaraz blinks, like my words have brought him out of a trance. He gulps, his Adam's apple bobbing, his face light pink. He clears his throat and stands up, lowering his gaze as he does so. He sidesteps me without a word, slipping out of the bedroom door. For a second, all I can do is stand there and stare at the door in half-disbelief and half-amazement. Have I done it? Have I stunned Sarfaraz into silence?

I quickly change into the clothes Salama provided, relishing in the softness of the outfit on my body. It's a lawn fabric, the typical material summer clothes are made of because of its light and airy feeling. The kameez is short and white, patterned at the hem with strips of gold. Diamond shapes line the chest vertically, going from my throat to my abdomen. It has long sleeves, which I'm not surprised about; Salama isn't a hijabi, but modesty is still practiced. The shalwar is plain white and cuffs at the bottom, though the cuff at my ankles is also encircled with gold.

I adjust the dupatta around my throat. The door suddenly

opens and Sarfaraz steps back into the room. I don't know how I expected him to look dressed in shalwar kameez, but a breath is stolen from my lungs when my eyes land on him.

The outfit Salama gave him is a hickory brown, like the shade of the trees in the forest behind the school I work at. I always take the kids there when I teach them about nature in their science class. A thrill rushes through my stomach when I realize that the color of his clothes nearly matches his irises. His sleeves cuff at the bottom, though he hasn't buttoned them yet. He also hasn't buttoned the lining at his throat—the slit itself dips nearly to his mid-sternum, offering a plain view of his chiseled chest. The clothes are loose on him, but they still manage to suit him very well.

Sarfaraz catches me ogling, and all of a sudden, the shyness he displayed earlier when I was semi-naked is gone. He smirks. "Like what you see?"

I swallow thickly. "I've seen better," I retort, though my voice is squeaky.

"On who?"

I clam up and say the first name that comes to mind. "Colin Firth."

Sarfaraz regards me for a long moment. "Colin… Firth," he says slowly.

It was stupid to say the first name I thought of, but I can't back down now. "Yeah, Colin Firth." I don't give him the chance to say anything else. I point to the door. "I need to get something to eat before I faint. We should go down."

I don't even wait for his answer; I circle around him, open the door, and step out. The only way I know he's following me is because I can hear his footsteps. I take a few subtle but deep breaths to calm down, and when we reach the end of the hall, my face feels cooler.

We follow the sound of light conversation and end up in

the kitchen. It's a tight space, but there's enough room for a stove, a makeshift sink, and a small wooden table with four chairs. Salama stands by the stove, frying eggs and toasting bread on a pan. An older man with wrinkles adorning his face and more gray in his hair than black sits at the table, sipping tea. He must be Salama's husband.

A girl, around fifteen or so, looks over at us from where she's setting two plates and utensils at the table. "Assalaam-o-alaikum! My name is Aqsa."

"Walaykum salam," we say back, still hovering in the doorway.

The father eagerly waves us both in. "Come, come, sit!"

We do so. Sarfaraz pulls my chair out for me, and I give him a shy smile as I sit. As he takes the seat next to me, the father says, "My name is Kenan. My wife says you are Sarfaraz and Maya?"

"Yes," I say.

"Whereabouts in Pakistan are you from?" Kenan asks.

"My family is from Karachi," I explain as Salama carries two plates to the table. Four fried eggs cover one plate, while a small stack of toast is piled on the other. My mouth practically salivates as the fresh smell wafts into my nose.

"Mine, as well," Sarfaraz adds. "That's where we were headed before we had bus trouble. We just got married, so we're making a visit to our family."

"That is unfortunate," Aqsa says. She places glasses in front of Sarfaraz and me. "To have your travel plans derailed."

Sarfaraz and I share a secret look. "Oh, it's nothing we can't handle," he says. "Let's say this trip hasn't been the easiest."

"Where are you coming from?" Aqsa wonders.

"We're from Canada," I answer. "But we thought it'd be nice to come see everyone after our wedding."

"Where in Canada?" Aqsa's eyes are filled with the familiar

twinkle of wanderlust; I recognize it, because I grew up seeing that same twinkle every time I looked in a mirror.

Salama sets the plates of food in front of us. "Hush, now, Aqsa," she says, and the girl deflates as she leans against the counter. Aqsa doesn't sit, however, and Salama sits down in the last chair instead. She pushes the plates toward us. "Please, eat as much as you'd like, and if you want more, let me know."

We dig in. I don't even know if I'm tasting the food; I'm so hungry I'm stuffing my face with as much as I can. Conscious of my table manners, I force myself to calmly bring the fork to my mouth.

After we've had our fill, Salama brews chai. She ladles some into a cup. "How do you take your tea, Maya?"

"Milk, and two and a half spoons of sugar."

Sarfaraz blanches next to me. "I can't believe your teeth haven't rotted yet."

I narrow my eyes at him as Salama places the cup in front of me. I pick up my cup and take a sip, letting the familiarity of the cardamom and clove wash over me.

Salama pours some for Sarfaraz next, then sits down across from us again. "So!" Salama begins. "Was your marriage a love match or arranged?"

"Love," Sarfaraz answers at the same time as I say, "Arranged."

Kenan, Salama, and Aqsa all exchange confused looks. Sarfaraz coughs. "Well, uh, it was both," he adds quickly. "We had mutual friends. We liked each other, so our parents formally arranged a match."

"Ahhh," the family choruses.

Aqsa leans forward from her spot by the counter. "Not to be rude, but how does a white guy like you know so much Urdu? And how do you have such a Muslim first name?"

Sarfaraz chokes on his tea while I have to swallow back a

laugh at the way the liquid dribbles down his chin. I stay quiet, though, because I want to know this story myself.

"Aqsa!" Salama scolds, her eyes narrowing to slits. Aqsa cowers back, and Salama holds out a tissue to Sarfaraz. "I'm sorry for my daughter."

"No, it's okay," he says. He accepts the tissue and wipes at his face. Then he catches Aqsa's eye. "I get that a lot." He leans back in his chair. "I'm half-Pakistani from my mother's side. My dad is white, and my paternal grandfather converted to Islam when he was in college because he learned about the religion in a class and loved everything about it. So, because both my parents were raised Muslim, I was, too. As for how I know how to speak Urdu, like I said, my mom's Pakistani, though I didn't have much contact with her after my parents' divorce when I was one. But my father remarried my Pakistani stepmother when I was three, so she spoke to me in Urdu. They both thought it would be useful for me to know, given that it's the primary language of her family."

I find myself nodding along with the others in understanding before I realize this is something I'm already supposed to know. But now so many of our interactions makes sense. How he knows Urdu so well. How he knows so much about the inner workings of desi families—he's part of one. Why he's even in Pakistan in the first place—he must be here to visit his stepmother's family.

Sarfaraz polishes off his tea. "That was delicious, thank you." He pushes the cup toward Salama. "Now, if you don't mind, I'd like to rest. We didn't get any sleep last night."

"Of course," Salama says as she stands. She takes my mug, too. "Would you like to rest, as well, Maya?"

Now that they've mentioned sleep, the back of my eyes ache. Maybe my body is tired enough to let me sleep more than a couple hours straight. I stand up. "Thank you again for all of your hospitality."

Salama waves us off. "Go, get some sleep now. I put extra pillows and blankets in your room in case you need them."

"Do you have a janamaz there, as well?" I ask. "We missed the Fajr prayer this morning."

"Yes, there should be one in your room," Salama answers.

Sarfaraz and I trudge back up the stairs. He opens the door and lets me in first. There's only one janamaz, though, so we take turns praying. When I'm finished, I fold the prayer mat and stand up. I turn to face Sarfaraz, about to ask what we're doing for the sleeping situation, when he picks up one of the extra pillows and spare blanket Salama brought for us, draping the blanket on the floor and setting the pillow at one end.

"What are you doing?" I ask.

"You should take the bed."

I pick at my mehendi, but before I can say anything else, he rests his head on the pillow. I know from experience he'll be asleep in no time, so I go over to the bed. I lie down without a blanket, too, because the thick heat extends into the house. I close my eyes and hope sleep comes quickly.

20

Maya's Law #20:
Sometimes people will tell you stuff
you don't want to hear.

I wake up to dying rays of afternoon sunlight peeking through the window. I tossed for a while, but I got more sleep than I thought I would. I sit up in bed, blinking heavily. I'm surprised to see Sarfaraz gone, the blanket he used to make his bedding folded neatly and left by the foot of the bed. I paw the side table for my phone. There's only 5 percent battery left, but I might as well use it to update Ammi. It's been enough hours since I left the airport for them to assume that I'll be getting to the house soon.

I stretch my back as I dial her number. She picks up on the second ring. "Assalaam-o-alaikum," I greet with a yawn.

"Walaykum salam," Ammi choruses back, smiling on the

video call. "Are you at the bus station? I can arrange for some-one to come get you."

"No, Ammi, I'm not," I say, and reluctantly, I update her on our new situation.

I swear I can see the giant vein in her neck pulse. "I knew I shouldn't have let you come on your own. Nothing good has happened to you since you left. There's only a few days left until the wedding, Maya."

"I know," I grit. "But I didn't plan any of this to happen. It was my kismet. Allah intended for all this to happen."

Usually when I bring "God's plan" into an argument she lets it go, but she must be really stressed, because instead she says, "Maya, I need you to be serious for once. How does this look to your in-laws? To Imtiaz? It looks like you're purpose-fully trying to stall the wedding."

"But I'm not," I insist. "And why would they think that?"

"Well, your wedding is happening three years after an en-gagement," she points out. "Most people only wait a year, sometimes six months! And you didn't want to do the nikkah before you left, either. It looks like you're trying to put it off."

"I didn't want to do the nikkah before I left because I didn't want to have to do a big party twice," I explain. "And I'm not putting it off! I'm trying my hardest to get there. It's my curse that's bringing every possible roadblock in front of me."

"I know, meri bechari bachee," Ammi bemoans. "You were too pretty as a baby. I've always said someone put their nazar on you when you were born."

I can feel my pulse quickening, so I force a deep breath in through my teeth. Calmer, I say, "I promise everything's okay, though. I'll get on the bus bright and early the day after to-morrow and should be there sometime in the afternoon. I'm so close to home. Just wait for a while longer."

Hesitation on the other line. Then, "Fine. But if you're

not here by then, I'm sending your mamu to come track you down."

"Fine." I check my battery, and it's at 1 percent. "Listen, Ammi, I have to go, my battery's—" I don't even get to finish the sentence; the phone just powers down. I stare at the blank screen for a second, then set it aside and crawl out of bed.

Because it's later in the afternoon, I know I've missed the Dhuhr and the Asr prayer, so I perform both before I leave the room. I walk into the kitchen, but Sarfaraz isn't there, either. Salama is, though, and she lifts her head from the spot where she's cooking. "Did you sleep well?"

"Very well, thank you," I answer, stopping next to her. "Is there anything I can do to help?"

"No, no." She waves me away. "I'm making chicken korma, and it's a very easy meal to prepare. Please, sit."

I feel guilty not doing anything, but I sit down in a chair anyway. "Where is Sarfaraz?"

"He's helping Kenan in our wheat fields." She sighs dreamily. "Such a kind, good man. Allah doesn't make men like him anymore, at least not as often."

My mouth twitches. "I know."

"You say you've come to Pakistan to visit family, right after your wedding?"

"Yes."

A pleased smirk crosses her face. "I thought you two might be newlyweds."

"You did? How?" I peer down at my hands. "Oh, could you tell because of my bridal mehendi?"

"Oh, no." The look Salama gives me is truly gentle. "Because your husband stares at you with such love and care in his eyes. It's the same way my husband looked at me when we first got married." She pauses, then adds, "He still loves me, of course, but there's nothing quite as special as the love between husband and wife right after their marriage."

A shiver touches my spine and spreads through the rest of my body, all the way down to my toes. She must be mistaken.

I wrap my arms around my body. "Was your marriage a love match?" I ask, hoping desperately she'll accept the subject change.

"No," she answers. "Out here, they rarely are. But at least I knew my husband. He and my brother were friends because we grew up in the same area."

I lean forward, too eagerly. "So, you fell in love with him after marriage?" I wonder, hope flickering in my chest.

"Yes." Salama stirs something in the pot, then lightly places the spoon on the counter. "But it wasn't easy."

I deflate. "It wasn't?"

"Of course not," she says, facing me. "It's not easy to love a stranger. Just because I knew *of* Kenan doesn't mean I knew *him*. He's older than me, and I didn't have much say in if I wanted to marry or not. But we were a poor family, and I was the eldest child, so I knew it would be better if I married and left the house. I wanted to help my family more than I worried about being someone's wife. I was scared when I came to live with him, worried if I'd ever be happy in this life."

"But are you?" I ask, my palms sweating. "Happy?"

"Yes. My husband is a good man, very patient with me. It took us some time to get to know each other, and over time, I did find myself in love with him." She shrugs. "But not everyone is as lucky as I am. Some people are forced into marriages through obligation and find they harbor so much resentment that it poisons the relationship, and they can never love their spouses." She checks on the food. "Love isn't always there in the beginning, but marriages are still something that need to be *wanted*. If you *want* it, then you can find happiness. But if you have doubts, if you think there's the slightest chance you're not marrying for the right reasons, then you will wake up every day miserable."

I stay silent even when she pauses to taste-test the korma. "That's why I think you're very lucky, Maya," Salama continues, drawing my attention back to her. "You found someone you loved whom you *wanted* to marry, so your chances of being happy are infinitely better." She smirks at me over her shoulder. "Not to mention that he's also a very handsome man. You two will make very cute children, should you want them someday."

I manage to somehow find it in me to chuckle. "Thank you, Salama," I say. "That was very…informative." I glance down at my toes. "More than you know," I mumble under my breath in English.

"Oh!" Salama's voice draws my attention back to her. "I almost forgot! Tomorrow, we are going to my brother's home. My nephew recently married, so we're going to his house for the dawat."

A dawat is a small party that people close to the newlyweds throw to celebrate the union. Marriage is a big deal in Pakistani culture; we party until we're all tired. Sometimes we don't even stop when we're exhausted. "That's wonderful."

"You and Sarfaraz should come with us!" Salama gushes.

My jaw drops and I bolt to my feet. "Oh, no, no, no," I hasten. "That's not necessary at all, Auntie."

"What *no*?" she admonishes. "It'll be wonderful!" She comes over to me and grabs my arms, giving them a tight squeeze. "It'd be so nice to have you there. Why stay here by yourselves when we can all enjoy a party?"

I open my mouth to protest, but Salama interrupts by calling out for Aqsa, who pads into the room. "Stay here and watch the korma, I'm going to go pick out some nice clothes for Sarfaraz and Maya to wear tomorrow to Baqar Mamu's."

She's gone before I can call after her. Aqsa passes by me on her way to the stove. "Your mehendi's starting to fade," she points out.

Sure enough, the redness has all but disappeared, and it's now firmly in the yellowing stage; barely any of the original color is left. Mehendi isn't meant to stay on your skin forever, and it doesn't help that I've been picking at it every time I get nervous.

"I'm a really good mehendi artist," Aqsa says. She peeks into the pot. "I can go over the design for you, if you want."

"Thank you. That'd be nice." I turn around. "Where are your father's fields? I want to see Sarfaraz."

She gives me directions, and I walk toward the fields we passed on our way here. I stop when I see Sarfaraz, his back stained with sweat, hunched over one of the stalks. I can't quite see what he's doing, but when he straightens up and wipes his forehead, he pauses. He squints, and then bursts into a grin when he recognizes me. Salama's words from earlier drift back to me, and my heart stutters in my chest. The sight of his smile makes my stomach flip-flop, and I drink in a steady breath before I go over to him.

I catch the end of their conversation: "If you spread the crops out more, they should grow taller and more bountiful."

"Ah, I see," Sarfaraz muses. "I have a small area for my garden, so there's not a lot of space." He draws a long square on the ground with his pointer finger to indicate to Kenan how big it is.

"You need more room than that." Kenan gestures to the small space between two of the crops. "Otherwise, they won't grow as well, and you'll miss out on better quality."

"That's very helpful—thank you," Sarfaraz says.

"Thank you for listening to my advice." Kenan slaps Sarfaraz on the arm and grins at me. "That's a good young man you've got."

"So I've been told," I say with a smirk, stopping in front of them. I dip my chin at Sarfaraz. "Can I talk to you for a second?"

Kenan looks between us, then says, "I think we're okay to stop for the day. I'll go on ahead."

I wait until Kenan is a good few paces away before speaking to Sarfaraz. "I didn't know you liked all this stuff," I say in English, my eyes sweeping across the fields.

"Oh, yeah," he says, a proud smirk on his face as he peels his worker gloves off. "My step-grandmother loved gardening, and she had the best plants on the block. My brother and I used to love helping her with it in the summer." He keeps his attention fixed on the gloves for a moment. "My ex-wife didn't like how much time I used to spend out in the garden. She didn't think it was a worthy endeavor for me to spend my free time on, especially because I had so little of it in the first place."

"That's stupid," I say, the words slipping out before I can register how inappropriate they are. But at Sarfaraz's chuckle, I relax. "I think it's very sweet. I can just imagine you in the whole farmer's getup." I gesture to his chest. "The plaid shirt, the overalls, the straw hat."

Sarfaraz laughs, and I feel that same thrill in my stomach as when I heard him laugh for the first time on the train in Switzerland. "What, would you be bringing me fresh lemonade every hour?"

I cross my arms over my chest. "Who says I'd be doing that for you?"

"You're my wife, remember?" he teases. "You can help out on the farm by bringing me lemonade."

"You can take that attitude and go right back to the fifties with it."

"I'm only teasing," Sarfaraz says. "I'd want you in the fields with me—gathering eggs, taking care of the cows, mucking out the stables."

I pause. "On second thought, I'd rather make lemonade."

He grins. "That's what I thought."

He has such a sweet smile; he doesn't do it often, but whenever he does, it takes up his whole face. His eyes brighten, like a flash of light in a dark tunnel. His lips look impossibly soft, curled up at the corners like that. I wonder if they feel as soft as they look.

"So, what did you need to talk to me about?" Sarfaraz asks, his voice interrupting my thoughts.

I blush, then explain the situation Salama's put us in.

"Okay, I can see how that's bad," he allows. "But we can go along with it."

I splutter a laugh. "That's the last reaction I expected from you. I thought you'd be against it."

"Look, we can't protest too much," Sarfaraz points out. He starts walking, and I stumble after him in the direction of Salama's house. "If we do, they'll figure out something's up. They're kind people; I would hate for them to find out we've lied to them." He looks over to me. "Plus, would *you* leave a couple of strangers alone in your house while you weren't there?"

From that perspective, I can see how suspicious it looks. As kind as they've been, and as nice as Sarfaraz and I are, they still don't know anything about us, and it'd be better to be safe than sorry. "That's true," I grumble. "They're helping us out of the goodness of their hearts, and they want to include us in their family celebration. It probably wouldn't feel nice for them if they found out the strangers they took in were bad people."

"Hey, we're not *that* bad," Sarfaraz protests. "All we did was lie. At least we didn't try to rob them."

A laugh bursts from my chest. "That's true."

"So, we're settled, then?" Sarfaraz stops at the front door. "We…go with it?"

"I mean, we don't have any other options. We'll try to stick to the sidelines as much as we can. Besides, we won't be the focus of the event. Everyone will be looking at the actual bride and groom."

"Good." Sarfaraz grabs the doorknob and pushes the door open. "We're only here for a couple of days. How bad could it be?"

21

**Maya's Law #21:
If you try to hide something,
it'll always be discovered.**

The next morning, Sarfaraz goes back out to help Kenan in the fields, and I sit down with Aqsa so she can go over my mehendi. I probably won't have time to do it once I reach Karachi, so I figure it's a good choice to take her up on her offer.

Aqsa gently applies the cool green paste from the cone to my skin. Her tongue pokes out the side of her mouth, her forehead scrunched in concentration.

"Where did you buy the paste?"

"Oh, I made it myself," Aqsa responds without looking up. "The people in the village usually come to me when they need their mehendi done for an event."

"That's nice."

She pauses to squeeze more paste from the bottom of the

cone toward the top. "What is it like being in love?" she abruptly asks, keeping her gaze fixed on my hands.

I freeze. "What?"

Aqsa shyly peeks up at me from under her lashes. "There's a boy who lives a few houses down from us. He's the son of our butcher. He brings me flowers sometimes when he can get away from work." She scans the living room, even though we're alone. Still, she drops her voice low. "Sometimes he comes, and we talk in the backyard at night, but Baba and Mama don't know."

I can't help but smile at their innocence. "That is very sweet."

She blushes. "Thanks. But I don't know if he loves me. I don't know if I love him. We've never said it to each other. I don't even know if what I'm feeling *is* love." She leans forward. "But you must know—you said yours was a love match."

"Technically, it was also arranged," I correct lamely, but I know that's not the answer this girl is looking for. I suck in a breath. "Being in love is...like walking through a field of sunflowers," I begin, gesturing toward the door and the fields beyond. The lines in Aqsa's forehead deepen with understanding. "It's full of bright colors and beautiful scenery, and the stalks are so tall it feels like things will go on forever." I scrunch my nose. "But sometimes you forget the stalks are clustered together, and you can scratch yourself, and you can trip over roots that burst from the ground. Sometimes it feels like you're stumbling through the field, unaware of which direction you're going in, and you get so scared and frustrated all you want to do is fall to the ground and weep." My chest swells. "But then you remember you have someone holding your hand. Someone who *also* sees the bright colors and the tall stalks, and who also scratches themselves and trips. And suddenly you're not alone anymore." My lips quirk up. "They may get frustrated, too, and say mean things, but they'll apologize by bringing peace offerings. They'll protect you and hold you when you're scared. When you break down in tears in the rain, they'll cover your head and let you cry." I blink out of my daze and make eye contact with Aqsa, who's stopped her work and now stares at me with rapt attention. "And at the end of the day, you'll emerge out of the field and remember that as long as you hold on to each other, you can get through anything."

"That makes a lot of sense," Aqsa says. "Is that how you felt with Sarfaraz Bhai?"

I squirm. "Yeah," I answer, my cheeks flaming.

We're silent as she goes back to work. As she traces over my previous design, I try to quiet my mind, but all I can think about is Sarfaraz. How he thanked me for helping him when it was clear that he's the type to struggle with showing appreciation. How he took me back to his hotel, so I'd have a safe place to sleep after getting sick. How protective his body felt pressed up against mine when Muhammad Moiz held a gun in our faces, and how my arm felt when it was linked through his. How safe and secure my hand felt in his.

When I think about him, I picture him in a field, fingers linked with mine, clearing the path in front of me before letting me go ahead. I bite the inside of my cheek, surprised by my own thoughts. When did his touch go from being uncomfortable to soothing? When did his smile change from irritating me to stealing my breath? When did the air between us start to shift?

I shake my head, trying to dismiss the images. I shouldn't picture anyone in that field with me other than Imtiaz, because he's my fiancé.

I guess more time has passed than I thought, because just as I think this, Aqsa grins triumphantly and leans back. "Alright, finished!"

I lift my hands to examine the design. It's the same as the one I had before, but I admire the darkness of the wet paste on my skin, going down to my left wrist, over my pulse, where Sarfaraz's name is sketched in Urdu—

Wait.

I bring my wrist up so it's right in front of my eyes. But no, it wasn't a trick of the light; Sarfaraz's name stares back up at me. My pulse skyrockets, my heart leaping up my throat and threatening to spill out of my lips. "Why did you do this?" I wave my wrist in Aqsa's face.

"The design was so faded on your wrist that I couldn't tell what it was before," she explains, the space between her brows pulled. "So I wrote Sarfaraz Bhai's name instead." She stands up. "What's the big deal? He's your husband."

I stare helplessly at the design. Arabic doesn't look like Western letters—it's scripture, written from right to left. The scripture itself looks quite beautiful. I went to Urdu school when I was younger, so I don't remember a lot, but I can recognize the letters and how they fit together to make his name. سارفراز

But no matter how beautiful I think the writing *looks*, it is *not* good that Sarfaraz's name is written on me. It's a tradition in Pakistani culture for the bride to have the groom's name written somewhere in her mehendi design, which he then is supposed to look for. It's meant to be an icebreaker for the wedding night. But factor in that the name written on my skin is *not* my fiancé's, and I'm about to enter some deep trouble when I get to my wedding.

How am I supposed to cover this up? I can't scrape it off; it's starting to dry, meaning the design is already seeping into my skin. All I can do is look up at Aqsa, who's staring at me in confusion, and ask, "Does your mother have any chudiyan I can borrow?"

★ ★ ★

Salama's brother's house is the biggest in the village; its bricks are gray, like the others, but it's nearly double the size of the other houses. The hallway is grand, with concrete flooring and a spiral staircase that leads to a spacious second level. The rooms aren't clustered together, either, and I know if I poked my head through, I'd find huge bedrooms. It even has electricity and indoor plumbing. When I ask how he can afford all these things, I find out that Baqar Uncle owns the most land in the village. I guess I've had a warped impression of villages in Pakistan.

The party is in full swing when we arrive. Salama's nephew Sajjid looks radiant in his white-and-gold sherwani. His new wife, who I'm told is named Naila, glows in her extravagant sea blue lehenga, though of course there's only a sliver of skin visible between her top and her skirt. They sit next to each other at the front of the room, with guests going up to them every now and then to congratulate them and give them a gift.

Like we agreed, Sarfaraz and I stick to the sidelines. We make appropriate small talk whenever Salama and Kenan introduce us to anyone, but otherwise we try to blend into the background.

I nervously tinker with the chudiyan adorning my wrist. The bangles clink against each other, but they also slide down my wrist whenever I lift my hands, exposing Sarfaraz's name. I can't let anyone, *especially* him, see it. It'd be so *weird*. I've known him for a week, and now I've got his name inked into my skin, albeit temporarily.

"I can't believe how easily these people have taken us in," Sarfaraz mutters under his breath.

I shrug, discreetly lowering my wrist so the bangles fall to the bottom. "That's Pakistanis for you. The people here are very kind." I pause. "Except for those guys who robbed us. They were jerks."

He smirks, his stare shifting over the crowd. "I can't believe the fanfare, even for a dawat. This is exactly the kind of thing my ex-wife and I wanted to avoid when we got married."

"Was she Pakistani?"

"She was," Sarfaraz confirms. "We met at university. I was Muslim and half-Pakistani, and that was good enough for her parents." He gestures to the boisterous laughter amongst the crowd. "This type of thing—party after party after *party* wasn't us. We didn't even do the standard three-day celebration."

The standard Pakistani wedding celebration is three days: the mehendi, the bharat, and the walima. Technically, the only days that really matter are the bharat and the walima; the bharat is when the nikkah—the signing of the marriage contract, which is the actual marriage ceremony part—takes place, while the walima is required because of the rukhsati— the official giving-away of the bride to the groom's family. It's also where the bride and groom are presented to the public as a married couple. "Really?"

"She wasn't the flashy type, and I don't know if you've noticed, but I'm not, either."

My jaw hangs open dramatically. "You? Not the flashy type?" My mouth forms an O. "I'm shocked."

Sarfaraz narrows his eyes at me, but the playful glint in his pupils betrays his amusement. "My stepmother was upset, because she wanted me to have the typical desi celebration, but there wasn't much she could do. We got married at the masjid, and then had a small reception on the same day. I know her family would have preferred the Big Fat Pakistani Wedding, but we wanted to keep things as small as possible." He scoffs. "Though I suppose it didn't matter in the end."

I hesitate for a second, then, collecting all my courage, I

ask, "You said in Switzerland that your wife cheated on you. What happened?"

His chest stills briefly. I open my mouth to tell him to forget it, but eventually, in a soft voice, he replies, "I was more married to my career than I was to her."

That's all he volunteers, so I nod, glancing down to readjust my chudiyan again. "I can see how you legitimately think that marriages are destined not to work out."

"I didn't say that," Sarfaraz says, and his comment makes me lift my head. He's watching Sajjid and Naila laugh and feed each other sweets. "I think that statistically, marriages fail more than they succeed, but that's not to say I think people shouldn't get married." When he looks at me, my throat closes up. "Sometimes you meet someone and you realize…you were living your whole life staggering around in the darkness and didn't even know it. Not until you met them."

When he looks at me, it's with a tenderness he's never had before. Soft, like the brush of a dandelion fluff blowing on the breeze and kissing your cheek while you're lying in the grass. His dark brown eyes are no longer piercing, but hungry, deep, ready and waiting to consume but being forced to restrain themselves, a sharp contrast to the gentle expression he regards me with. His hair, just as dark as his irises, kisses his brows, tickling his eyelids, but he doesn't move to brush it away. When he looks at me, a *swoosh* crashes against my chest, gripping it tight and shaking me with a realization I've never let myself think too long about.

He's beautiful.

Like, not *hot*, but *beautiful*. *Hot* is for guys who are all hard edges and jagged lines, who wear their ruggedness like a badge of pride. Guys who wear leather jackets and pick you up bridal-style and tell you over and over that you're perfect because it's exactly what you want to hear. *Beautiful* is for guys who are soft and smooth, who wear their gentleness with an air of humility, like they don't want to be praised for doing the bare minimum. Guys who wear shalwar kameez and let you lean on them, taking on extra weight even when they're just as exhausted as you are, and who will tell you over and over when you're being ridiculous because it's exactly what you *need* to hear.

"Maya! Sarfaraz!" Salama's voice breaks the spell. Sarfaraz and I both jerk out of our stupors and look over to where Salama's voice came from. She waves from her spot by Sajjid and Naila. "Come here!"

We exchange an awkward look but go over to them. Salama nods to us. "You haven't been formally introduced yet," she says. She turns to the young couple. "Sajjid, Naila, this is Sarfaraz and Maya. They're travelers from Canada who are staying with us for a couple of days."

Sajjid looks to Salama. "Really, Phuppo? You're picking up people from the street now?"

Naila whacks him in the chest. "Helping people in need gets you lots of sawab from Allah. Plus, the Prophet would always house travelers, so it's sunnah," she reminds him. He rubs the spot where she hit him while she fixes us with a sweet look. "Assalaam-o-alaikum. It's nice to meet you both. Thank you for coming."

I smirk. "Walaykum salam. Thank you for having us. Mubarak ho on your nuptials."

"You, too!" Sajjid says. "Salama Phuppo tells us you two recently got married, as well."

"We did," Sarfaraz confirms, and he doesn't even cringe when he says it.

"Well, then, can you give us some advice?" Naila asks. She looks eagerly between us. "I know you haven't been married long, but you must have something to share. Anything would be helpful."

I hesitate, looking to Sarfaraz. He gawks when he realizes I'm waiting for him to speak first, but he clears his throat and gives the happy couple a polite smile. "Well, one thing you should keep in mind is that you're not going to agree on everything." A mischievous spark twinkles in his eyes. "Sometimes your spouse will speak up when you tell them to stay quiet, even if it's a dangerous situation."

I scoff, my brows lifting in challenge. I turn to Sajjid and Naila. "And sometimes your spouse will reject a gift from you when you're trying to be nice."

Red pools in Sarfaraz's face, but he says, "Sometimes your spouse will insist on buying things that don't hold value, just because they think it's pretty."

I glare at Sarfaraz. "And sometimes your spouse will disagree with you just to disagree and then get confused when you get mad."

"Sometimes your spouse will get impatient and dramatic, and you have to do your best to work around them."

"And sometimes your spouse will act like a know-it-all who somehow knows exactly how to wind you up and make you cry."

I expect him to say something else, but he grimaces. The silence lingers for a moment, and Sajjid clears his throat. The anger between us cools when we remember we're not alone. Sajjid and Naila eye each other warily, but Sajjid still asks, "Okay…do you have any *nice* advice?"

Reluctantly, we look to each other. This time, Sarfaraz's tone is softer when he says, "Comfort your spouse when they need it, even if they're too proud to ask."

My stern expression gentles. "And protect your spouse. You know you lucked out when you find someone who will literally use their body as a shield to protect yours."

Sarfaraz smirks. "Make each other laugh, especially when it seems like humor can't be found."

"Be brave for each other," I add, thinking back to the panorama bridge.

"And support each other when the other person wants to be brave," Sarfaraz says. "And above all—" when he looks at me, it's like he's staring right into my soul "—love each other, even when it's hard."

My heart stutters. It's too hot in the room. I can't breathe, the thick air around me choking my throat. I stumble back. "Excuse me," I mumble, and I take off without another word.

I gratefully gulp in the fresh air when I step out the front door. Thankfully, there's no one here, so I sit down on the steps and put my head between my knees. The air outside is way hotter than inside, but I still suck in deep breaths, willing my shakes to stop. I try my best to brush off the feelings swirling in my chest, but I can't. The tingles absolutely refuse to leave, instead attaching themselves to my skin and leaving imprints behind like the mehendi.

What the hell is happening to me? I've only ever felt like this a few times before, in the beginnings of a new crush, but those emotions never lasted long enough for me to know what to do with them. I always had to remind myself that because of my curse, it would never work out. But it's not like I'm *crushing* on Sarfaraz. I can't be. Not only would it be totally ridiculous because I haven't known the man for long, but I'm getting married. And not in the "oh, I'm engaged" type of way, but literally the "my wedding is in a few days" way.

But I can't brush off the sparks on my skin when he touches me. I can't ignore the fuzzy feeling growing in my chest when he looks at me. And I can't stop the emotions threatening to pull me under.

My wedding is in a few days, and all I can do is think about how this stranger I met on a plane has made me feel more things in a week than my own fiancé has in the three years we've been engaged.

Dr. Khan is going to be so overwhelmed when I get home.

"Maya?"

I whip my head up to see Sarfaraz towering over me. Worry wrinkles his forehead, and even in the darkness of night, the concern lining his face stands out. "Are you okay? You kind of ran out of there in a rush. I thought you might need space, but I didn't want you to be out here on your own for too long." He squints. "Are you...*crying*?"

I wipe my cheek, and sure enough, it comes back wet. "I'm fine," I assure him. "I need to be alone for a minute."

"Maya, you're panicking about something," he says matter-of-factly. "Is it because of what happened in there? Because I know it was uncomfortable, but—"

I ignore the pang in my chest. "I'm *fine*," I reiterate, my tone sterner.

His fingers wrap around my wrist, and I whirl my head to see him crouching down next to me. "What are you doing?" I demand.

"You said you get low blood sugar, right?" Sarfaraz says. He moves to push my chudiyan out of the way. "Let me check your pulse."

The chudiyan ride up my arm, and my eyes widen when I remember the arm Sarfaraz grasps is the one where his name is written on my wrist. I move to pull my arm away but judging by the crease in his forehead, I'm too late.

Slowly, Sarfaraz opens his mouth. "Uhhhh..."

"It was a mistake." I rip my wrist out of his grip. I hastily push the chudiyan back down my wrist. "Aqsa did it without me even realizing it. Let's not make a big deal out of this. It doesn't mean anything."

Sarfaraz stiffens next to me. I don't expect him to react—why would he care about something like this, after all?—but to my surprise, his face falls. "Yeah, of course not."

"Of course not," I repeat firmly, though I think it's more for my sake than his. "You're right, I'm feeling off because of what happened back there. Everything we said was just acting, and I felt bad that we were lying to these people who were genuinely asking for advice. That's it."

The more I talk, the harder his face becomes. He clenches his jaw. "Right." He pushes himself up. "I'm sorry you felt so poorly about it, but don't worry. We don't have to act for much longer after this."

My jaw falls open as I watch him walk away. Tension rolls off his retreating back, and the door slams shut behind him, leaving me alone.

Remember your curse, Maya, a stern voice stresses in my head. *Nothing good ever works out for you. You're going to end up alone.*

For a couple of days, I thought maybe…maybe I wasn't alone. But given my experience, I don't know why I thought things would start working in my favor now.

With a shaky breath, I head back inside.

22

**Maya's Law #22:
Sleep will always elude you
at the worst moments.**

When we get home, we go to bed right away. The bus will be here early in the morning to pick us up, and there's no way we can miss it.

But as I lie in bed, I find myself unable to fall asleep. I roll around for a while, kicking the blanket I stupidly lay down with off but then pulling it back over my body. I growl, low in my throat, and pull the blanket over my head despite the fact that I'm now ten times hotter.

"Please stop moving," Sarfaraz's tired voice calls from his spot on the floor. "I can hear every noise you're making."

I huff, dragging the blanket down my face. "I'm sorry, but you know I don't sleep well."

He doesn't say anything after that, and I nestle deeper into the mattress. Eventually, my back starts to hurt, and I turn on my side with a barely stifled grunt. I flop onto my back and stare at the ceiling. Why is this mattress rock-hard? How did Salama's daughter sleep on this thing?

Sarfaraz groans, then stands up. I lift my head, about to ask him what he's doing, when he picks up his pillow and lies down next to me. The bed is so small his shoulder touches mine. My face flushes, and I'm grateful we're plunged in darkness. My body stills. "What are you doing?"

He settles into the bed comfortably, and a pang of envy hits my chest at how easily relaxation comes for him. "If you're going to be moaning and groaning so much that I can't sleep, I might as well be comfortable."

A few minutes tick by, but neither Sarfaraz nor I sleep. I know he's not asleep because his breathing is short and shallow, and he won't stop moving. I can't sleep, either. As if I weren't having a hard enough time before, now I'm too warm. I'm warm from the extra body in the bed, and from the fact that it's Sarfaraz, and from the fact that I want to grab his hand, but I know I can't.

I have to distract myself. There's something I want to ask him, but I've been too afraid to be *this* vulnerable with him. He's someone I barely know, yet in a strange way, I feel like I've known him forever. It's dumb, and I know it, but I can't help how I feel. Plus, I know that tomorrow, once we reach the bus station in Karachi, we'll go our separate ways. I don't want awkwardness to be what's between us when we part. So, in a tiny voice, so soft he'd miss it if he weren't lying beside me, I ask into the darkness, "What's marriage like?"

He starts, his body shifting slightly on the bed. I expect him not to answer, but he responds, "You really want my opinion? My marriage ended terribly, and I work with dysfunctional families and handle divorces for a living."

"Well—" I fight the urge to squirm "—that's how I know you'll be honest with me."

He goes quiet again. I want to know what the expression on his face is, but I'm too tense to look at him, afraid of what I'll see. Then, after a beat, he says, "Marriage is…hard. Even with love in it, it's hard."

I hesitate, but decide to be brave and ask, "You never said—was yours a love match?"

"Yeah," he answers, his voice heavy, wistful, like his mind has wandered back in time. "I told you we met at university. I wanted to wait until I finished law school to marry her, but her parents didn't like the idea of a long engagement. So, we got married, but I was always so busy with school and cases that I didn't give her as much attention as I probably could have." A tiny shudder racks his body, moving the bed. "So, she went and found that attention from someone else. Our marriage ended by the time I graduated law school."

"That's awful," I breathe. "I'm sorry."

"Yeah." I wait for him to add more, but instead he asks, "Why aren't you in a love match?"

My heart stutters. "What?"

"You're smart, pretty, tolerable," he lists off. "Why didn't you meet anyone before you subjected yourself to an arranged marriage with a guy you barely know?"

My stomach clenches at the reminder, but I ignore it by latching on to something else he's said. "You think I'm tolerable?" I ask, hoping for a light tone in my voice but unsure if it's working.

He laughs into the dark. "*That*'s what you focus on? Not the fact that I called you pretty?"

If I focused on that, I would never focus on anything else again. Cheeks burning, I nervously ask, "Do you *want* me to focus on the fact that you called me pretty?"

"No," he replies hastily. "I'm just saying."

I save us both from this nightmare by moving on. "It's my curse," I say. "It's doomed me to a life without a love match."

"Maya, this whole *curse* thing is…foolish," he says, in the same matter-of-fact tone he uses when he doesn't think he's going to be contradicted. "There's no such thing as curses."

"I think there is," I grit, irritation blooming in my chest. "It's fine if you don't, but I *do*. You can't look me in the eye and tell me that after everything we've been through since that first plane ride that I don't have the worst luck in the world."

"I don't think it's the curse you're worried about," Sarfaraz says instead. "There's something more that's bothering you about being in a relationship that you don't want to admit."

I frown at the ceiling. At this point, I want to look at him, but the cowardly instinct in me keeps me firmly on my back. "You've known me for like, a week. How much do you really know about me?"

"Enough to know that you're running from something," he says, and his words cut deep into my gut. "Trust me, no one can recognize a runner better than another runner."

I sink my teeth into my lower lip. "So, what are you running from, then?"

I don't think he expected me to turn the tables on him, because he's silent for a long moment before he says, "A lot of things."

I snort. "That's very detailed."

"Come on, maybe you're not trying hard enough. When's the last time you *really* tried? Who was the last person before your fiancé that you tried to pursue?"

I stay silent. Even though I'm staring up at the ceiling, I can practically see the smug smirk on his face. I'm so confident, in fact, that without checking, I say, "Wipe that grin off your face."

Nothing. Then, "How did you know I was smiling?"

"I had a feeling."

We're quiet again, and the ensuing silence slithers down my back. With my heart drumming impossibly fast against my chest, I whisper, "Do you think love can happen after marriage?"

A beat passes. "Maybe," he admits. "But that's a pretty big gamble."

I gather all my courage and turn on my side. To my surprise, I come nose to nose with Sarfaraz. I thought he was facing the ceiling like I was, but instead, he'd been lying on his side, staring at me, watching my reactions. We're so close, barely a breadth of space between us. I stare at his lips, which appear so soft in comparison to the rough stubble on his face, because I don't know if I can look him in the eye when I ask next, "What about love at first sight?"

He hums softly. "Maybe," he says again.

I meet his gaze, and I wish I hadn't, because his eyes, so dark from far away, are even deeper up close. I can make out the lighter flecks of brown around his pupils, and I probably wouldn't have ever noticed had I not been so close to him. It's such a peculiar detail, but I guess it's fitting for a man who uses shadows to hide the light in him. He stares at me with an intensity that scorches a path from my belly to my face.

I quickly school my features. After a beat, Sarfaraz adds, "But if you tell anyone I said that, I'll deny it."

That makes me chuckle, and Sarfaraz grins in response, the action so bright it lights up the whole room, even in the darkness. His breath fans against my face, and for a moment, I finally understand what it's like to be drunk. His breath is soft, sweet, intoxicating, and once you take one sip, it's over. You'll experience a high like never before, see colors you didn't know existed, and risk the blackout you know will inevitably come, but wake up and know it was worth it.

I want to move closer, to keep drinking him in, but if I did, I'd have to kiss him, and I can't do that. No matter how easy it would be to close the gap between us, to feel his stubble on my skin, to run my fingers through his soft hair. No matter that I don't love my fiancé, and while I don't love this man, either, he awakens nerve endings in my body that I didn't even know were dormant. No matter how much I want to, yearn to, *need* to. None of that changes the fact that I'm engaged to someone else.

So, with an ache that reverberates throughout my whole body, I whisper, "We should get some sleep. We have an early day tomorrow."

For a moment, his face falls, then he straightens his expression. "Good idea." He rolls onto his back, and instantly, I miss his body heat.

Still, I force myself to lie on my own back, and I'm staring up at the stupid ceiling again. Softly, I say, "Good night."

As I drift off, I hear him echo back gently, "Good night, Maya."

When I wake up, the bed's moving. Why is the bed moving?

I open my eyes sleepily, and for a second, all that registers is the sun peeking through the boards of the window. The sun? When did the sun come up? I'm usually awake by sunrise (obviously not by choice) but I didn't even notice when it rose. And the sky isn't the early soft yellow and light blue of the dawn; no, the sun's been up for a while. How is that possible? I've never slept well enough to completely ignore the sunrise.

I blink a couple of times, and that's when I realize I don't feel the usual heaviness of my lids that sleep-deprivation gifts me. In fact, I feel incredibly well rested—way more than I have been in a long time, maybe even in my whole life.

I inhale deeply and get a huge whiff of lemons and fresh laundry. I freeze; there's only one thing that smell reminds me of. Slowly, I look upward, and that's when I realize I'm lying on Sarfaraz's chest. It moves evenly, his breathing quiet. His arm is snaked around my waist, his grip tight. I look down to see our legs somehow got tangled up at some point in the night. One of my hands rests on the spot between his neck and his shoulder, while the other curls around the side of his body. His chin brushes my forehead, and the scratchy sensation of his facial hair against me causes a burst of tingles to shimmer on my skin.

I should move my body away. I *need* to move my body away. Instead, I stare up at Sarfaraz's face, my heart thumping louder and louder the longer I look at him. In a few short moments, he'll wake up, and then in a few short hours, we'll go our separate ways, and we'll never see each other again. And I'll never know. I'll never know if what I feel is because of proximity or because he helped me or because there's *something* there.

Sarfaraz wakes slowly, and I jolt when he turns his sleepy smile to me. "G'morning," he yawns.

With shaking fingers, I touch his face. His facial hair prickles under my fingertips, sending a wave of pleasure down my spine. He stills under my touch. He doesn't move away from me. He doesn't move, and I take that as an invitation to cup the side of his face. I gently run my thumb along his cheekbone, and I feel him shudder under my touch.

Dr. Khan's words echo in my head. *When was the last time you did something for yourself?*

Softly, I say, "I'll never see you again after today."

Sarfaraz doesn't say anything.

"I'll never see you again," I repeat. "So, I'm going to do this."

I shift upward so I'm closer to his face. This close to him, his stubble grazes my chin, and the nerves there explode and travel down the rest of my body. His breathing, light and even earlier, now stutters under my palm. His heart thunders wildly against my chest, and my confidence rises when I realize he's as nervous as I am.

His beautiful dark eyes maintain contact with mine, apprehension lining his irises. I wait for him to stop me. For him to push me back. For him to say that this would be a bad idea.

But he doesn't.

When I touch my lips to his, Sarfaraz doesn't move at first. But then, slowly, his mouth presses against mine. Light at first, as if he's waiting for me to change my mind. Gentle, like he's afraid if he uses too much pressure I'll break.

But when I grasp his face, and my nails dig slightly into his stubble, something seems to snap in him. He sits up faster than I could have believed, and his hands move to my hips. He pulls me onto his lap, so I'm angled higher than he is. The sudden movement makes me gasp, and he uses the opportunity to slip his tongue into my mouth. A noise I didn't even know I was capable of making squeaks out, and I feel Sarfaraz laugh against me.

That first night we spent together in Zurich, I wondered what it was like to kiss the grown-up way. Well, it's exactly like this. It's his fingers tangled in my hair, moving to the base of my skull. It's my hands gripping his shoulders, desperately clinging to him. It's our bodies, hot and flushed against each other, pressing closer and closer like we can't get enough.

"Maya," he moans against my mouth, and suddenly I don't want anyone to say my name ever again, because they'll never say it the way this man says it. It's like everyone I've ever met has been saying my name wrong, and I never knew it until now.

"Sarfaraz," I groan in response, and he grins before swallowing my moan with his mouth. All thoughts about how I shouldn't be doing this, about how this is a bad idea, about how this is going to bite me later, go straight out the window when fireworks erupt in my belly. I thought that a one-time kiss would be fine. But now I want more. I want his soft and slow kisses, *and* his hard and rough kisses. His quick goodbye kiss, and his long welcome-home kiss. His kisses that make me forget my own name, and his kiss that keeps me grounded on earth, in his arms. I want everything. All of it.

Sarfaraz's lips move to my jaw, my throat, my collarbone, his stubble scratching against my skin making my toes curl. His mouth, open and hot against me, makes my core ache with longing. I grab his face and pull him back up to me, but as I'm about to kiss him again, I stop. Sarfaraz's face hovers in front of my own. Our noses brush, our panting breaths intertwine. Our mouths are inches away from each other. But I know if I kiss him now, I won't be able to stop myself again. I squeeze my eyes shut as regret settles into my skin, replacing the tingles Sarfaraz's kisses left. I let out a long sigh, and when I open them again, I see the same regret echoed in Sarfaraz's face. He sighs, too, squeezes my hips one more time, then rolls me to the side and lies back down.

We both stare up at the ceiling for a long moment, until Sarfaraz gets out of bed. He doesn't speak, and I watch his retreating form leave the room. I let out a groan and cover my face, already missing the sensations of his touch on my body. That was a mistake. That was a big mistake.

But at least I know now, and I can move on with my life.

23

Maya's Law #23:
What happens will always be
the last thing you expect.

We have a quiet breakfast, and as we finish, Kenan shows up to let us know the bus to Karachi has arrived.

We all linger in the doorway, doing step three of the desi goodbye. The "desi goodbye" usually consists of declaring your intention to leave, sitting on the couch for another fifteen minutes, getting up and lingering by the doorway for another ten minutes, and then saying your actual goodbyes at the end of the driveway.

Salama kisses my cheek. "It was so nice to have guests for a few days."

I give her a hug. "Thank you so, so much for your hospitality."

"Really, we don't know what we would have done had we

not met such nice people," Sarfaraz adds. He does a "manly handshake" thing with Kenan. "We're very grateful."

Salama cups the side of my face. "May Allah grant you and your husband a lifetime of happiness."

I peek at Sarfaraz, who has a neutral expression on his face. We can barely look at each other after what happened this morning. He nods at Salama. "Thank you."

After one last round of hugs, we depart, heading for the bus. When we get to the high steps of the bus, Sarfaraz offers me a hand, and I take it as I climb up. I don't want to let it go, but of course I have to, and I clench my fingers into a fist as I find a place to sit. I slide into the window seat, and I wave again at the Kassab family. Once their figures are too small to make out, I smile sadly. "I'm going to miss them."

"So will I," he confesses. He's acting totally normal, so I force myself to, as well. "You don't meet good people like them that often."

I look at him. Despite the drumming in my chest, and the memory of his mouth searing my skin, I reply, "Yet, here we are."

He dips his chin, looking away from me. I don't know why I'm being so reckless with my words. Maybe it's because I know once we step off this bus, I'll never see him again. He'll go off to see his relatives, I'll go get married, and the past week we spent together will be a distant memory.

Sleeping next to Sarfaraz has left me so well rested I don't even feel the urge to nap on the bus. Instead, we chat lightly, reminiscing about the last few days and pointedly ignoring the lingering tension between us from this morning. Okay, so Sarfaraz carries most of the conversation, but if I've learned anything, it's okay for once to be the one who stays quiet. I sit and listen, absorbing his laughter, staring at his smile, and committing the color of his hair to memory. When he talks, he doesn't quite look at me, his words coming out fast and shaky. I wonder if it's because he's trying hard not to think about this morning. The thought worries my stomach, and I rub at my abdomen.

All too soon, the bus pulls into the station and chugs to a stop. Sarfaraz leans over me to peer out the window. "I'd say this is the best luck we've had so far," he says. He sits back in his seat, waiting for the people in front of us to get off first. "We made it to our destination with no hiccups."

"Yeah," I mutter under my breath. "The best luck."

We get off the bus and head inside the terminal building. The bus company sent us an email saying our luggage was left here, so we collect our stuff from the customer service workers. While I'm grateful that I've finally gotten my actual luggage after being without it since I left Toronto, sadness lingers in my chest because for once, there's no unexpected delay.

We walk outside, and I quickly forget about the sweat dripping down my back as Sarfaraz and I awkwardly turn to each other. We both just stand there for a second, not quite making eye contact. "Well, I guess this really is goodbye this time," Sarfaraz begins.

A heavy weight settles in my gut. "Yeah, I guess so."

Sarfaraz's grin struggles to stay in place, but he holds his hand out to me. "Good luck on your wedding. I hope you manage to find happiness with that guy."

When my skin touches his, I feel a wave of longing so strong it threatens to pull me out to sea. I remember how only a few hours earlier, his body was pressed up against mine, and my core aches. I shake his hand once, and then let go. "I hope you have fun with your relatives here."

"Ooh, that may be hard," Sarfaraz teases, and I chuckle before we lull back into a silence.

We're prolonging the goodbye. Neither of us wants to say

it, but Sarfaraz sucks in a deep breath and starts walking backward, away from me. "Alright. Khuda hafiz, then."

I blink my tears away. "Khuda hafiz," I choke out, not even caring if he can hear the emotion in my throat.

At the same time, we turn our backs on each other. It takes everything in me to put one foot forward, followed by another, and another. I can't look back. If I do, I'm afraid I'll see him looking back at me, and I don't know what I'd do if I met his gaze.

But honestly? I think I'm more afraid that if I *do* stop, if I *do* peek over my shoulder for one more look, I'll realize he *didn't* look back, that he just continued on his way, without giving me a second glance.

So, I keep walking, and I don't look back.

After traveling with someone in the seat beside me for ten days, the back of the auto rickshaw I ride to Imtiaz's house feels especially spacious. Rickshaws aren't even big vehicles, either. The cab, which is attached to the motorcycle that the man uses to power the rickshaw, rests on three wheels, two in the back—one on each side—and one in the front. A small window separates my seat and the seat of the rickshaw-wallah in front of me. Thankfully, he doesn't try to make conversation with me, so I stare out the windshield and try to ignore the fact that my stomach feels like it's shrinking. The traffic is insane; either that or the rickshaw driver is intentionally taking the least convenient route possible. Of *course* I ended up with a driver who is trying to make my life harder.

You know what? He's not trying to talk to me, and he's going fast enough that there's a breeze coming in through the front of the rickshaw. He gets a five-star rating from me for that alone.

The rickshaw pulls up in front of a large house. I pay the

driver and then climb out. The house's outer walls are a muted yellow with screen-covered windows, presumably to keep the bugs out. It's only two stories, but the fact that the house stretches outward, covering lots of land, makes up for it. A tree, tall and green and leafy, sits in front of the house, its height nearly blocking one of the windows. The gates are a dark brown, and for a second, all I can do is imagine Sarfaraz's eyes, staring at me in the dark, face so close to my own…

"Maya Khala!" A voice breaks me out of my thoughts. I blink, and that's when it registers that the gates are opening. Iqra, my niece, clambers through the doors and launches herself at my waist.

I make an *oomph* sound and stagger back, but when I recover, I grin and hug her tightly. "I'm so happy to see you!" I gush.

"Maya!" I hear again. A few more people step out of the house, including Ammi, Hibba Baji, and Imtiaz.

Ammi throws her arms around me, holding on so tight I see dark spots for a moment. Iqra squeezes out from between us, and that gives Ammi the opportunity to hug me harder. "My baby!" she cries dramatically. Ammi pulls back from the hug, her eyes wide and wild. For a second, I can't help but marvel at how much we look alike: the same long face, the same small nose, and the same panicked expression whenever something goes wrong. "What took you so long to get here?" she demands.

"I'm sorry, my phone died," I apologize. "Everything went so wrong after I left home. But I did update you every chance I got, and I promised I'd be here by today when we spoke on the phone last, didn't I?"

She sniffs. "I suppose. But what happened?"

"It's a long story, and I'll tell you all of it, I promise," I assure her. "The important thing is I'm okay."

"I *knew* I should have waited to travel with you," Ammi groans. "I knew you couldn't handle it on your own."

I grit my teeth. "Everything's fine, Mom. I made it here."

She huffs. "Well, yes, I suppose so." She pats my cheeks. "You're going to put me in an early grave."

"Mom! Don't talk like that," Hibba Baji chastises. She wraps her arms around me. "I'm just glad you made it here in one piece."

I gratefully accept the wave of calm rolling off my sister. I break the hug and look to Imtiaz, who has stepped over to us in the meantime. A flash of guilt runs down my spine when I remember I made out with a different man this morning. I push that guilt away, reminding myself that it was a one-off, and that I'll never see Sarfaraz again. I smile at Imtiaz instead, even though it's weak.

He tentatively returns it, and with a quick look over at my mom to see if she'll object, he leans over and hugs me.

I've shared hugs with Imtiaz before, of course, but the moment he puts his arms around me, my mind flashes to Sarfaraz touching me a few hours ago. The memory stiffens me for a moment, delaying my reaction. At the confused wrinkles on Ammi's and Hibba Baji's foreheads, it quickly registers. I bring my arms up around his back, ignoring the fact that his arms feel foreign around me.

We break the hug, and he takes a respectable step back, earning a look of approval from Ammi. I resist the urge to groan; we're engaged, and we'll literally be married in two days. It's not scandalous if he hugs me.

Imtiaz's voice breaks my thoughts. "I was so worried about you, Maya. Are you okay?"

"I'm fine," I assure him. "I'm sorry it took me so long to get here."

"I'm happy you're safe." He gives me a once-over, and apparently satisfied by the fact that I have no obvious injuries, he nods firmly. "Well, you're here now. That's all that—" He pauses as his eyes land on my left hand. "Wait—where's your ring?"

I look down and remember my finger is bare. Honestly, so much has happened over the past few days that I somehow managed to forget I had to exchange my ring for my own protection. I clench my fingers. "That's *also* a long story," I admit, biting the inside of my cheek.

Imtiaz raises a brow but doesn't press further. "Well, I guess as long as you're okay," he relents. "I'm just glad you've arrived before the nikkah."

"*You* can be glad," Ammi grumbles. "But now we have an even tighter schedule than before. There's so much that needs to be done still!"

"Then let's get inside and not delay any longer, yeah?" I suggest. I step toward the house, but at the last second, Imtiaz grabs my wrist and pulls me back. I frown at the action. "What is it? Is something wrong?"

Ammi's glare deepens, but now it's directed at Imtiaz. "Tell her, Imtiaz."

My stomach sinks. "Tell me what?"

Imtiaz scrunches his face. "Do you remember how my parents and I told you I was an only child?"

I bob my head suspiciously. "Yes."

He focuses on my forehead so he's not looking me directly in the eye. "It was a lie."

My jaw drops. "What? You have a sibling?"

"Yes, he does," Ammi answers for him. She sneers at Imtiaz. "An older half brother."

"He's not really a part of our family anymore," Imtiaz cuts in before Ammi's saltiness can leak any further. "He got into a huge fight with our father shortly after he got married, and they haven't really spoken since then, so Dad pretends that I'm his only son. You know what it's like—once you're disowned, it's like you never existed."

Okay, while it wasn't cool that his family lied about only having one son, I knew exactly what he meant. When people have too much pride, they say things they might not mean or might regret, but then because of that pride, they won't apologize or acknowledge that they did anything wrong. "True," I allow.

His back relaxes. "Thank God you understand," he breathes. "I really wanted my brother to be at my wedding, so I asked him to come without my parents knowing. Remember that person I spoke to you on the phone about? The last-minute guest I wanted to add to our list?"

The memory vaguely prickles at the back of my mind, and the more I tug on it, the clearer the conversation in my kitchen becomes. I whistle low. "Yeah, I remember. But I didn't realize you'd be going behind your parents' backs in order to do it."

"Yeah, well." He shrugs. "It's not their decision. This is my wedding. He's my brother, I love him, and I want him here. I broke down and told everyone yesterday that I invited him."

"You see, this is the kind of drama you miss when your phone is constantly dead," Hibba Baji teases.

"Sometimes it's *good* to unplug," I tease, trying to make light of the situation. I face Imtiaz again and delicately squeeze his arm. "If you need my support, you got it. Like I said on the phone—I'm cool with whoever you invite. It's your wedding, too. And this guy is your brother. If you want him here, so do I."

Imtiaz grins in relief. "It's so good to hear you say that. He'll be here any day now, and I wanted to tell everyone before he comes." He peers over my shoulder, and his eyes light up. "Oh, here he comes now! You guys can meet." He shouts, "Bhaiyya!"

I turn around so I can properly greet my future brother-in-law. When I do, my stomach twists like I'm going to puke, and my heart stops in my chest.

He steps through the gate, his hair ruffling in the light breeze, his eyes boring into me with the same intensity they had when he kissed me this morning.

24

Maya's Law #24:
Always assume danger is lurking
around the corner.

"Hi, Maya," Sarfaraz says, standing at the threshold of the gate. After a few seconds of us staring intensely at each other, he turns to his brother.

I gape at him blankly. My fingers fly to my lips, my skin flaming. My mouth burns like I stuck a curling iron down my throat. Any words that escape me come out garbled, like I'd gargled them.

Imtiaz doesn't seem to notice because he grins and gestures between us. "You two know each other?"

Oh, yeah. We've only spent the last seven days together, with him making me feel things that I've never felt toward you. Oh, and I kissed him.

Sarfaraz answers for the both of us, stopping next to his brother. "We met on the plane."

He's not shocked, not in the same way I am. Which means... he knew. He *had* to have known. There's no way that he didn't.

"Oh!" Imtiaz grins at me. "Maya, was Sarfaraz the guy you said you were traveling with?"

My jaw drops, and Imtiaz realizes a second too late what he's said out loud—and in front of *whom*.

Ammi's mouth forms an O.

"You were traveling with a man?"

I gnash my teeth and send a mini-glare in Imtiaz's direction. "Yes, but my fiancé knew about it, and he said it was fine," I say in a steady voice. I'm hoping that mentioning I had Imtiaz's approval (not that I need it) will calm her down and cause her not to freak out. "We were just helping each other out."

Ammi brightens slightly, though one eyebrow stays lifted. "Oh, if Imtiaz was okay with it, then fine," she says. "But my, what a coincidence! You ended up traveling with your future bhaiyya. You'll have to tell us all about it."

Oh, God, the thought of Sarfaraz being referred to as bhaiyya, meaning *brother*, churns my stomach. I resist the urge to cover my mouth to keep down the breakfast I ate this morning. He finally looks me in the eye, but I can't decipher what he's thinking.

I'm *this* close to losing it when Hibba Baji wraps her arm around me. "Come on, let's go inside. It's too hot to be standing out here. You can tell us all about how the two of you met."

I want so badly to talk to Sarfaraz about this new development, but I'm not left alone for a single second. First, I'm bombarded by relatives who all express how worried they were for me when my travel plans got derailed, and then I have to sit and catch up with them and pretend like what they're saying isn't going in one ear and out the other. Then I'm taken to the room where I'll be staying until the wedding and forced into a new pair of shalwar kameez. *Then* we go back downstairs to the dining room, where a meal has been set up.

Mr. Porter sits at the head of the table, with Mrs. Porter next to him, and Imtiaz across from her. My mind immediately registers Sarfaraz's distinct absence. Where is he? Has he hidden himself away in the house? Or has he left entirely? He can't have left without talking to me.

I blink the thoughts away when everyone at the table stands up. Mr. Porter is a tall man—it's obvious where Sarfaraz got his height from. Thick gel keeps his salt-and-pepper hair pushed back, and relief relaxes the lines in his face when I walk into the room. "Oh, Maya," he greets. He hugs me, and I hug him back. Mr. Porter may *seem* scary, and some bad stuff must have gone down for Sarfaraz to be completely dismissed from his family, but he's the closest thing I have to a father now. He breaks the hug and pats my head. "We were all so worried about you. We're so glad you're here, and in one piece."

"I'm glad I made it, too, Dad," I say. I call him *Dad* at his insistence since the engagement.

I hug Mrs. Porter, too, who I call *Mummy*. When I pull away from the hug, I move a step back and take the whole Porter family in.

Now that I'm looking at the three of them properly, I can't believe I didn't figure it out earlier. The Porter men all have the same cheekbone structure, the same forehead, the same nose. The only difference between Sarfaraz and the others in his family is his extremely dark brown eyes; Mr. Porter's are green, which Imtiaz inherited. Mrs. Porter has brown eyes, too, but hers are brighter, more on the hazel side. Sarfaraz must have inherited his from his own Pakistani mother. His skin is lighter than Imtiaz's, which is something that can happen with mixed kids. The mixture of genes can make siblings look wildly different from each other—and forget siblings who have different mothers. With a jolt, I remember how Sarfaraz said that his stepmother is Pakistani. He also said he came here to visit family. I don't know why I didn't connect the dots earlier like he must have.

"Well, I think we need to talk." Ammi's voice interrupts my thoughts. We all take our seats at the table.

"Before you say anything," Mrs. Porter says to us, but it's mostly in Ammi's direction, "we're very sorry we didn't tell you we have another son." Sorrow haunts her face as she adds, with a mini glare toward her husband, "Sarfaraz hasn't been a part of our family for years now."

My heart twists. In all the time we've known each other, I never asked Sarfaraz about his family. Of course, there's no telling if he would have opened up to me about them. I thought him telling me about his ex-wife, clearly a sensitive subject, was good enough. But I feel terrible; how long has he been alone?

"What happened?" Ammi asks.

Mr. Porter looks like he would rather eat a bowl of nails than discuss this, but he says, "You know that I have my own law firm, yes?"

When we nod, he continues. "Well, I wanted Sarfaraz to go into corporate law with me." Mr. Porter's expression sours. "But he didn't want that. He wanted to be—"

"A family lawyer," I automatically finish, earning me a confused look from Hibba Baji. I ignore her and focus my attention on Mr. Porter.

"Yes, he wanted to be a family lawyer," he finishes gruffly. "But I didn't know until *after* he had finished law school, *after* I paid for all his schooling *and* his wedding, that he lied to me the whole time. He didn't study corporate law at all, despite the fact that he told me he did. So, I cut him off; I would not tolerate such behavior from my son."

I pause, the new information conflicting in my gut. It's not right that Sarfaraz lied to his dad, but it also seems like an overreaction to cut him off. But what do I know about the relationship between father and child? I don't exactly have a dad myself.

Mr. Porter flashes an angry look to Imtiaz. "So, you can imagine how it feels to know my other son invited Sarfaraz to his wedding."

Imtiaz balls his hands into a fist, presumably to contain his annoyance. "For the last time, Dad, I'm not apologizing for inviting Bhaiyya. I'm a grown man, and I can make my own choices about who I want at my wedding. Besides, if Maya and I are fine with it, that's all that matters." He looks directly at me. "Right, Maya?"

Red blooms on my face. "Right," I squeak, my throat dry.

Though his brow quirks momentarily, Imtiaz ignores my strange behavior and turns to Ammi. "Auntie Ji, I'm so sorry that my family lied to you about me being an only child," he begins. "But if you can look past this, I'd still like to marry Maya."

Ammi's poker face is immaculate; her lips are in a straight line, not curling up or down. Her eyes are relaxed, not a lick of tension in her pupils. Her forehead is line free. She taps her fingers on the table, then looks to me. "Maya? What do you think?"

I gulp when everyone turns their attention my way. I clear my throat. "It's fine with me," I answer, because what else *can* I say? If I say I don't want Sarfaraz here, he'll be forced to leave, and I won't be able to confront him. "If it's important to Imtiaz, then it's important to me."

"Then it's settled," Imtiaz declares, sending his father a firm stare.

Mr. Porter's nostrils flare, but Mrs. Porter touches his arm. "Jaanu, we can't force him to leave." She gives him a pleading look. "Besides, I want to spend time with him. I have not seen my other son in many years."

Mr. Porter still doesn't look happy, but he mumbles, "Fine," before pushing himself away from the table and leaving the room. Mrs. Porter shakes her head and follows him.

Imtiaz rubs his face. "What's a wedding without family drama, huh?"

"Exactly," Hibba Baji teases. "We were missing our dose of it."

Imtiaz gets to his feet. "I think I'm going to go track my brother down and have a talk with him."

That sounds like a good plan. I open my mouth to say that I'll come with him, but Ammi grabs my wrist and pulls me up with her. "Come, Maya, we need you to try on your mehendi dress to see if it needs any last-minute alterations."

"Oh, Ammi, I need to—" I start.

"We were *supposed* to have had this done last week," she cuts me off. "But your travel chaos put everything off course. The maiyun is tomorrow, so we won't have any other time to get this done. Now, come."

Stomach sinking, I allow her to pull me along.

25

Maya's Law #25:
Coincidences are never just coincidences.

Once everyone's gone to bed, I casually ask one of the servants if they know which room Sarfaraz is staying in. I guess she's been instructed not to talk about him by Mr. Porter, because she pretends like she doesn't understand me, even though I'm speaking Urdu, and quickly shuffles off.

I plan on talking to him in the morning, but as I try to sleep that night, I have an extremely difficult time. The longer I toss, the more anger bubbles in my stomach. I had a perfectly fine time sleeping last night; what's the problem now?

I throw the blankets off and get out of bed. I stick my feet in a pair of slippers and leave my bedroom, heading for the roof. One of my favorite things about Pakistani houses is how the roofs are set up; they don't get snow or a lot of rain here, so the houses are built with flat roofs. That allows people to use them as a second storage space, or to hang wet clothes up to dry on a clothesline. Or, like many families, they use it as a place to sit and enjoy the evening breeze.

I climb the stairs but stagger to a stop when I recognize the figure standing near the edge of the roof. Even in the dark, I can make out the outline of his back.

Sarfaraz must feel my eyes on him, because he looks over his shoulder. He doesn't look surprised or startled, though; his expression is completely neutral, though it's clearly forced based on the way the lines in his face twitch. We stare at each other for way too long, until he breaks the silence. "Let me guess—can't sleep?"

A tiny growl rumbles my throat as I stomp over to him. "Don't joke," I seethe. "Do you know how *ridiculous* this all is?"

"What?" He looks away from me to stare at the moon. "That the random woman I sat next to on a plane is the woman marrying my brother?"

Hurt unexpectedly hits my chest, and I swallow thickly. "That's all I am?" I ask, trying not to let the pain show in my voice. I hate that it's even there. "A random woman you sat next to on a plane?"

"Fine," he relents. He looks over at me, and in the pale light, I see a muscle in his jaw working. "Does *sister-in-law* work for you?"

I cringe. That word is forever going to be ruined for me. "This is such a mess," I grumble. I scrunch my face when I remember a crucial detail. "You didn't seem surprised to see me. Did you know?"

His face drops, but I press on. "Did you know this whole time who I was?"

Sarfaraz hesitates but looks at me. For the first time since we saw each other standing at the threshold of his family house, I can see how he's feeling. Pain momentarily flashes in his eyes, but it's gone just as quick. At my unrelenting stare, he breaks. "I didn't know when we first met on the plane," he reveals.

I gape at him. *"Unbelievable!"*

He quickly backtracks. "I thought it was weird that I was going to Pakistan to attend my brother's wedding and *you* were going to Pakistan to *have* your wedding, but I thought it was a coincidence. Lots of people get married, and people travel to weddings every day. You're not the first or last person to have a destination wedding."

"When did you figure it out?"

"Well, I suspected when you spoke to your fiancé on the phone when we were on the way to Sigriswil." He bites his bottom lip. I pretend like the action doesn't drive me crazy as he continues. "I thought it sounded like my brother, but I convinced myself that there was no way." His fingers still, his throat bobbing. "And then there was that long stretch of time where we walked after we got robbed, right before we got to Salama and Kenan's village…" When I nod, he says, "You mentioned that your fiancé's name was Imtiaz. I think I knew then, but I was really, *really* hoping that it was all a random coincidence."

It never is when it comes to me. "And you didn't think to say anything?"

"What difference would it have made?"

"A *huge* one!" I exclaim. "I would never have acted the way I did if I'd known."

"And how did you act?" Sarfaraz demands. He crosses his arms over his chest. "How did you act that you're so worried now?"

Tears wet my lashes. "That is not fair," I seethe. I press my finger to my chest. "I'm not the one who knew that I was his brother's fiancée and still kissed me anyway."

Sarfaraz grimaces. "As I recall it, *you* were the one who kissed *me*."

"You still kissed me back, knowing who I was!" I toss back. "I may be in the wrong here, but you are way wronger than I am. You knew what we'd have to deal with once we saw each other again. I had no idea. I was blindsided while you had time to prepare yourself."

He pinches the bridge of his nose. I want to smack his hand away. He's not the one who gets to be frustrated. I'm the one who opened up to him about my feelings and my insecurities and hopes and fears while he was keeping this huge thing from me. I thought I was getting emotional vulnerability from him, too. Now he knows all these deeply personal things about me that even my fiancé—his *brother*—doesn't know. I was fine with Sarfaraz knowing all that stuff before because I assumed I'd never see him again. But now I have to see him at family functions, birthday parties, holidays.

It feels like the time we spent together has been tainted. I was open and honest. He deliberately withheld information that definitely would have stopped me from kissing him and thinking it was a big romantic gesture I'd keep secret for the rest of my life and only think about on my deathbed.

I shake my head free of the thoughts. "Do we tell Imtiaz?"

He freezes. "Tell him what?"

I clench my jaw. "About the kiss."

"Were you planning on telling him before?"

"No," I admit. "But that was before, when I thought you were a stranger and not one of my future in-laws."

"Look, telling him wouldn't do anyone any good," he points out. "What happened this morning was—" he sucks in a breath "—something that won't happen again, and something that was irrelevant. It's useless to waste time thinking about it anymore."

Even though anger at him flushes my skin, his words still twist in my gut. "Okay, then."

"Okay. Besides, it's not like we'll be seeing much of each other after the wedding, anyway."

My breath hitches. "Why not?"

"I'm only getting a pass to be here because it's Imtiaz's wedding," Sarfaraz explains. "Our dad is *not* happy that I'm here, but he won't say anything more on it because it's a big enough event for this to be Imtiaz's call. But after that..." He huffs. "I don't know if Imtiaz has the bravery to keep fighting against Dad."

I should hold on to my anger, but after letting him keep his secrets, this, at least, is something I deserve to hear. "What happened between you guys, anyway?" I explain. "I mean, your dad gave us the rundown, but what *happened*?"

Sarfaraz sighs, then takes a seat on the dusty roof. I slink down, too. "I knew going into law school that I didn't want to do corporate law. The *last* thing I wanted to do was be *Mr. Porter's son* at his office, and I didn't want to succeed him in his company because it wouldn't have been something I earned on my own merit. I could have been the worst corporate lawyer at the firm, but he still would have made me managing partner." He shrugs. "It wasn't something I wanted. I know you think of me mostly as a divorce lawyer, but it's just part of why I went into family law. I want to help families— whether that's keeping them together, helping them figure out a path apart, or working something out that makes everyone happy. As a Pakistani, I know how important family is. It's something I've always loved about our culture and it's why I wanted to help others."

It makes sense; it explains why he said divorces can be helpful for families, and why he enjoys what he does so much, even though family law can get pretty dark. "So, you thought your best course of action was to lie to him about what you were studying and hope desperately he wouldn't find out the truth until *after* you graduated?" I ask, disbelief widening my eyes.

"I'm not saying it was a good idea, and I'm not saying I'm proud of it," he clarifies gruffly. "But I didn't know what else to do. I felt so...*suffocated* by the pressure he put on me." He picks at a loose button on his kameez. "I didn't let him put any of it on Imtiaz, because I knew how crushing it was and I didn't want him going through the same thing. But I couldn't think of anything else to do. I was desperate, and I needed an escape."

"That sounds intense. What ended up happening?"

"Dad obviously found out when I graduated. He called me no son of his and forbade anyone else from having contact with me." Sarfaraz tries to speak casually, but I see the hurt brimming in his eyes. "I've kept in secret contact with Imtiaz, meeting with him every now and then. I was the one who encouraged him to pursue biology, which is what he wanted. I knew it was going to disappoint Dad that he didn't want to do law, but I told him it was his life and he needed to do what made him happy."

I stare up at Sarfaraz and, briefly, sympathy washes over me. "I hate that you felt so trapped that you had to lie about what you really wanted to do. I can't imagine how that must have felt."

He raises a brow. "Don't you? I assumed you know exactly how that feels."

"What do you mean?"

"Maya, you basically told me you got engaged because you wanted to escape the pressure your mom was putting on you," he states plainly, and the words cut deeper than they should.

"You wanted to be treated like the adult you *actually* are, and you couldn't see any other way to do it than to get married."

"That's not true," I blurt, though the words sound fake.

"Try looking at yourself in the mirror and say those words again. You'll see how ridiculous you look."

Anger rushes to my throat. "I'm not having this conversation," I seethe. I rise to my feet. "I just wanted to talk to you to make sure we're on the same page, and that we're saying nothing. If you keep your mouth shut, so will I."

I don't wait for a response. I head for the stairs, go back to my room, and pray that I make it through the next two days.

26

Maya's Law #26:
You should always hide
how you're really feeling.

The next day, I wake up bright and early for the maiyun. It's a ceremony where Imtiaz and I will be covered with turmeric paste by our family and friends. The application is supposed to bless us, and turmeric is said to be good for the skin, too. I don't know how much I'm looking forward to being smeared with paste by my family, but I have to suck it up and put on a pretty smile. That's all I have to do as the bride, anyway.

I don't bother to do my makeup, and once I'm dressed, I head downstairs. The song "Ballay Ballay" from *Bin Roye* blasts through the house as I'm led down the hall to the backyard space. The maiyun is a more laid-back event, so we're doing it at home. Because the ceremony is less formal, I'm in simpler clothes. I'm in a blouse and a lehenga, but the material is much airier and lighter, not as weighed down by heavy embroidery or beads. The ensemble is red, which is unexpected, because traditionally the bride wears red on the day of the bharat, when the actual nikkah will be read. Plus, the traditional color for the maiyun is yellow. However, I'm already wearing yellow to the mehendi, and I found a wedding dress I liked better, and because it isn't red, I can wear the color today and no one can accuse me of being a palette repeater. My hair is in a simple braid down my back, to keep it out of the way when the haldi is applied to my face.

Ammi wraps her arm around me, holding me tight to her side. "I'm so happy you're getting married, Maya," she coos. "I thought I'd never see the day, what with you always shutting down rishtas."

"Yeah, neither did I," I mumble.

"No, really, Maya." Ammi stops when we reach the doors to the backyard. A few people bustle around us, arranging food and drinks and carrying bowls of turmeric paste. She leans forward and curls my hair over my ears. "After everything you went through with your baba..." she continues, and my back tenses. "After that kameena left us, I thought you'd never want to get married." She rests her hand on my cheek. "But I'm glad to see that you changed your mind. Getting married is part of completing your deen, I know, but it's wonderful to know that you got to fall in love with your man first."

My breath hitches. I reach up and pull Ammi's hand away. "Yes," I say through gritted teeth. "That's exactly what's happening. I'm very happy, too."

Ammi furrows her brows, and it looks like she's going to say something, but before she can, I pull the door open and step outside.

The air is already incredibly thick, but some of the uncles managed to set up fans outside. I don't know what kind of good it's doing, but it's better than nothing. The backyard isn't that big; not many backyards in Karachi are. But we invited only immediate family to the maiyun ceremony, so there's enough room for all of us. Tables line the back, with rose petals scattered in the middle as the centerpiece. Strings of hanging pink and purple lanterns hover above our heads, dangling on a line that connects from the tree closest to the fence to the top of the roof. Set up right in front of the fence is a swing, adorned with dahlias and more paper lanterns. A long wooden table sits in front of the swing, ready for the materials to perform the rasam. Imtiaz is already sitting on the swing, wearing a smart white kurta.

"There she is!" Imtiaz booms as I approach him. "You look absolutely beautiful."

I grin at him as I sit down. "You look really handsome."

"Thanks." He places his arm on the backrest behind me. His fingers barely touch my skin, but I force myself not to cringe. After a few quiet, calming breaths, my body relaxes, and I lean more into his touch.

We have to wait for the older adults to bring the haldi over to us, so we silently swing on the seat. After a while, though, I can no longer handle the silence. "How have things been going for you? We haven't had much opportunity to talk since I got here."

"Good," he responds. He taps his foot against the ground. "I'm glad Bhaiyya is here, but the tension is pretty obvious. I'm trying to figure out a way to smooth things over, but I don't know if that's going to happen."

I knot my fingers together and casually watch the yard. "Where *is* Sarfaraz, anyway?"

Imtiaz squints for a moment, scanning the crowd. He points in the direction he's staring. "He's over there."

I follow his gaze, and sure enough Sarfaraz is in the corner, far from any of the other guests. He's tucked himself into the corner of the couch he's on, trying not to wrinkle his white shalwar kameez. Some auntie takes the seat next to him and taps his leg enthusiastically. I have no idea what they're talking about but based on how hard he's clenching his jaw, it can't be anything good.

"What happened, by the way?" Imtiaz's voice brings me out of my thoughts.

I snap my attention back to him. "Huh?"

He points to my bare left finger. "Your engagement ring. You said you'd explain what happened, but you never got around to it."

"Oh." I try to casually run my fingers through my hair, but there's so much hairspray in it they get caught in the tangles. "It's a funny story. So, Sarfaraz and I were traveling together, and our bus got a flat tire in between Lahore and Karachi."

Imtiaz whistles low. "I don't think I've ever met someone with luck as bad as yours."

"*Tell* me about it," I grumble. I go back to the story. "We ended up walking to a rest stop, and the driver told us that cars would be showing up to take us to a nearby village to wait for a new bus to arrive. But it turns out that the car we got into wasn't part of the service the bus driver arranged for us, which we found out after we'd been driving for a while, and then the guys…kind of robbed us. I had to give them my ring so they'd let us go."

Imtiaz blinks once, and then exclaims, *"What?"*

That draws attention to us, and my face reddens as I gesture for him to calm down. "It's not that big a deal, okay? They were threatening us, so I did what needed to be done. That ring wasn't worth our lives."

"No, no, I don't care about the ring," he dismisses. "You

did what you had to. But, oh, my God, why didn't you tell anyone you were in that kind of danger?"

"I didn't exactly have the opportunity to make a phone call," I grumble. "I was kind of busy. Plus, I wasn't alone. Sarfaraz was with me."

Imtiaz places his palm on top of mine. I wait for tingles to rush to the spot where his skin meets mine, but nothing happens, no matter how hard I will it to. "I'm happy that Bhaiyya was with you, but it should have been me. I'm sorry I wasn't there for you."

Surprise fills my chest. "It's okay. You couldn't get a flight out with me, so you couldn't have traveled with me. It's not your fault."

He opens his mouth to say more, but before he can speak, Ammi's chipper voice exclaiming "Time for the rasam!" interrupts him. Our parents come to a stop in front of us. Mr. Porter stands off to the side, but Ammi excitedly rests the platter with a pot of haldi and some mithai on the table in front of us.

I glance at Imtiaz out of the corner of my eye, but he hasn't dropped the concerned look on his face. I clear my throat and gesture to the pot. "Who's going first?"

Ammi steps forward; as the mother of the bride, she's the one who's technically "losing" a daughter. She picks up the spoon, cuts a small piece of a gulab jamun, and then feeds it to me. We pose for a photo, and then she scoops up some of the haldi. She spreads it along my cheeks, and I relax under her touch. The relaxation morphs into a fit of giggles as Hibba Baji goes next, purposefully cutting a huge piece of barfi and stuffing it into my mouth. She grabs my chin and smears the haldi all over my face. I squirm in her grip, but she maintains a firm hold. By the time she lets me go, most of the tension snaking my gut is gone. I look at Imtiaz, who is also covered in haldi. Some of the tension rushes back, but I force it down.

I'm going to enjoy this. This is one of my last moments as a single woman, and I'm not going to let it be ruined.

People continue to come up and feed us mithai and put haldi on us. Ammi and Hibba Baji have already covered my face, so other people move on to my neck and my arms—though I'm careful when it comes to my left wrist.

It's also customary for the bride and groom to apply some haldi to their unmarried family members and friends, so when my cousin Fizza comes up and puts some on Imtiaz and me, I make sure to swipe some on her, as well. I also make sure to use my right hand, so my left wrist is in no danger of the chudiyan slipping. Telling that story about Sarfaraz's name on my skin once was mortifying enough—especially because it exposed my not-quite-certain feelings about Imtiaz. But still, this is my choice, and I'm going through with it.

I've just finished applying haldi to Fizza when Sarfaraz strolls over. His hands are in the pockets of his kameez, and I have a strong feeling his fists are clenched. Still, he offers Imtiaz and I both a happy look when he stops in front of us. "How are you guys enjoying the party?"

I stay silent, but Imtiaz says, "Oh, you know." He gestures to his turmeric-covered face. "It's great getting covered in paste."

"Well, I guess it's my turn, then." Sarfaraz steps forward, and because he came pretty much dead last, there aren't any sweets left to feed me, nor is there much paste left in the pot. He dips his fingers in, scooping the excess paste from the bottom of the pot.

Sarfaraz smirks as he grabs Imtiaz in a headlock and smooshes the haldi paste to his face, smearing it all over his skin. Imtiaz erupts into laughter, and he playfully pushes his brother away. "Come on, man!" he protests. He wipes the yellow paste off his mouth. "You didn't have to do me dirty like that."

"What can I say? We have a lot of years to catch up on, little brother," he jokes.

I watch the two brothers for a moment. When apart, it's easy to see how I wouldn't have made the connection that they're related. But seeing them together, it's impossible to deny that they're siblings. Sarfaraz may have a lighter complexion, but they both have the same sturdy square face shape, the same arched brows, the same full lips.

The similarities don't just end with their physical appearance, either. Their postures are the same; ramrod straight, held-back shoulders, torso turned all the way when facing someone. When they move, it's in tandem, their bodies clearly not registering all the time they've spent away from each other.

While I feel incredibly dumb that I didn't figure it out before, it's sweet to watch the two of them together. How long has it been since they were together like this? How long have they felt ghosts in their lives where people they loved should have been?

How do we all just get used to people not being there anymore?

I jolt when Sarfaraz looks over at me, and any trace of laughter leaves his face when his eyes meet mine. It's my instinct to look away from him, but I force myself to keep his stare and ignore the tension brimming between us.

He gestures to the pot. "May I?"

As I nod wordlessly, Imtiaz smacks Sarfaraz in the stomach and asks, "Why did you ask her permission and not mine?"

"Because she's your future wife," Sarfaraz points out. He kneels in front of the pot again. He doesn't take his eyes off me as he scoops the very last bit of haldi onto his fingers. "I can't exactly touch her like that."

My mind involuntarily flashes back to our kiss, and a rush of anger blooms under my skin. He certainly had no problem doing that when he kissed me back.

Those thoughts leave my head when he crouches in front of me. He doesn't even tremble as he lifts a hand to my face. Softly, ever so softly, he grazes my cheekbone with his fingertips. The paste from his fingers blends with the paste already on my face, but his touch burns my skin. I'm grateful there's so much haldi on me that it covers up my reddening face. He runs his fingers down my cheek, stopping at my chin. Reluctantly, he moves his fingers from my face, then smirks. "There. Now you're officially a part of the family."

My stomach sinks. "Thank you," I say in an uneasy tone.

He gestures to his own face. "Well? Aren't you two going to put some on me?"

Imtiaz, who has been watching the whole exchange with an unreadable expression, snaps back to attention. "Yeah, of course." He reaches into the pot for some paste but frowns, pulling his hand out haldi-free. "Huh. I guess we're out."

I touch my fingers to my cheek, right where Sarfaraz had spread it on me. The paste easily slides around on my face, and I brighten up. "I have an idea," I say. I rub some of the haldi onto my own fingers and pull it away with enough to apply to Sarfaraz's face. "We can reuse this. It'll save the hassle of making enough haldi for one more person."

Imtiaz stares at me for a second, but then shrugs. "Sounds like a good idea."

While Imtiaz wipes some excess haldi off his own face, I face Sarfaraz. With shaky fingers, I touch the spot beside his nose. I run my thumb sideways, spreading the paste across his under eye. My fingers tingle where they touch his skin and the feeling runs up my arm. The intensity in his focus makes me shiver. I stop when I reach the spot under his temple. I continue to stare up at Sarfaraz, the knot in my stomach becoming tighter and tighter.

"Alright, my turn," Imtiaz declares.

I jolt, quickly pulling away from him. I pretend not to notice the flicker of disappointment on his face as I curl a loose strand of hair over my ear and smile at his brother. And I ignore the strange look Imtiaz is flashing the both of us as I gesture to Sarfaraz. "He's all yours. Go for it."

27

Maya's Law #27:
If you bury your problems,
they'll dig themselves out of the dirt.

Back in the day, the mehendi ceremony was a small gathering of only the women of the bride's family, who were responsible for adorning her with henna. Nowadays, it's a joint effort between both the bride's and groom's sides of the family, and everyone attends. It's basically a day for both sides of the family to present performances to show off whose side is better. All our relatives live in Pakistan, so I haven't had many chances to participate, but once in a while we were able to make it back to Pakistan for a family member's wedding, and I would dance with my cousins to show that we were the best side of the family.

After a restless night, I'm summoned early in the morning and ushered into the first of three bridal outfits I'll wear over the next couple of days. It's usually tradition for the bride to wear yellow on her mehendi day, and I'm no exception. The blouse, known as a choli, is long-sleeved and stops at my midriff, meeting the high-waisted skirt and leaving only a sliver of skin visible. Pink flowers decorate the choli, from the chest all the way down to the wrist. The skirt is purple, with yellow and pink swaths along the bottom and more elaborate pink flowers stitched into the fabric. I sit still while my hair and makeup are done. Gold covers my lids, with layers of mascara and a cold swipe of jet-black eyeliner to make my eyes look bigger than they are. My hair, straight and flat before, now rests against my back in elaborate thick curls.

Ammi tears up as she fixes the pink jewel-studded choker around my throat. "You look so beautiful," she sniffs.

Hibba Baji pauses from where she's adjusting my tikka, the large piece of jewelry that rests in the middle of my forehead. "Ammi, the mehendi hasn't even started," she reminds her. "Don't start crying yet. You'll ruin your makeup."

Ammi blinks away her tears. "Right, yes, of course." She tilts my chin up. "You do look beautiful, beta." She takes a few rupees out of her clutch and waves them over my head. I politely dip my head down so she has easier access. This is something done to ward off nazar, and though I've long given up on avoiding the evil eye's cruel gaze, it makes my mother happy. Once she's finished, she puts the money back into her clutch. "Remind me to give this to Awais so he can give it to the poor."

Hibba Baji grabs the chudiyan from where she left it on the vanity in front of me. "Okay, Ammi, I think Maya and I are almost done here. You can go down and we'll meet you there."

"Okay." She kisses the top of my head, careful not to move the tikka, then leaves the room.

Hibba Baji picks up my wrist to slide the chudiyan on, but

at the last second, my stomach drops and I remember. "No!" I screech, but before I can pull away from her, she's lifted my sleeve up.

Her eyes widen when she catches sight of Sarfaraz's name written there. She whips her head up. "Maya, what is this?"

I wrench my arm out of her grasp. "Nothing," I mumble. "I told you guys what happened on our way to Karachi." I told them, including Imtiaz, the *bare* minimum. Just that Sarfaraz and I had bus trouble, we'd been held hostage at gunpoint, and that we stayed in a village until a new bus could show up and bring us here.

I take the chudiyan from her, fiddling with them. "Remember the family we stayed with? The daughter redid my mehendi, but she thought Sarfaraz was my husband, so she wrote his name. By the time I noticed, it was too late."

I meet her worried stare. "Baji, it's nothing," I assure her, trying to regulate my erratic heartbeat. "It was a mistake, that's all. It'll wash off in no time."

Hibba Baji stares at me for such a long time, sweat trickles down my neck. Her voice is a sad whisper when she breathes, "Maya...do you like Sarfaraz?"

I freeze. "Of course not," I say, a beat too late. I stare at the beauty mark under her left eye. "That'd be dumb. I've only known him for like a week."

Hibba Baji's jaw drops. "Oh, no, Maya. You *like* him." She lifts her fingers to her face, pressing them against her mouth. "Oh, I knew there was something different about you when I first saw you in the driveway. You seemed more chill, and you didn't slump around as much. That, plus you guys were acting really intense during the maiyun. I thought I was imagining it, but I guess not. Sarfaraz must have had a profound effect on you in such a short time."

"I don't like him!" I insist. "And I'm certainly not acting different because of him."

"Oh, please," she says, clearly exasperated. "You're practically walking around with a stormy cloud hovering above your head. You haven't been carrying yourself the same, and it's very noticeable."

"It's not!"

Hibba Baji crosses her arms over her chest. "You're really going to try to lie to your sister? You're acting as if I haven't caught you in every lie you've ever tried to tell me."

"Name one time!"

"Remember when you took money from my wallet to buy snacks from the convenience store when we were kids?" she lists. "You said that the jinn in our house took it, but then I found the receipt in your waste bin."

"In my defense, we *did* have a jinn in our house. Stuff was always going missing, and doors opened on their own."

Despite my interjection, she continues, "When you borrowed my CD player without permission and broke it, when you used my hairbrush, when you eavesdropped on my phone calls—"

"Okay, okay, I get your point, I'm a terrible liar. But I'm not lying about this."

Hibba Baji sighs. "Maya, do you know how I always knew you were lying to me?"

"No."

"You never look me in the eye when you lie. You're good at not making it look obvious sometimes, but you can never look me in the eyes when you lie to me."

Damn it. I hate that she's the older sister. I set my chudi-yan onto the vanity table before facing her. "Okay, fine," I grit through my teeth. "*Maybe* I have a little...crush," I finish, cringing at the fact that I admitted it out loud. "But I don't like him enough to leave my fiancé for him. Besides, he figured out that I was Imtiaz's fiancée and then didn't even tell me. I can't trust him after that."

"If you loved Imtiaz, you wouldn't be looking at any other man days before your wedding." She crosses her arms over her chest, and the chudiyan on her wrists clink together. "Do you even *like* him?"

I hesitate. "I like him *enough*," I reply, though there's no life in my words.

Hibba Baji's jaw drops. She pauses, then cups my face. "*Enough* is not a good reason to marry the man, Maya," she insists, her tone as gentle as her fingers on my face.

Somehow, the softness in her voice is worse than if she yelled at me. I push her away. "Well, what was I *supposed* to do?" I huff. "Ammi wouldn't have let me go to Korea if I hadn't agreed to get engaged first. And I felt so trapped at home, so alone, so…so *lost*, that I knew if I didn't do something, I was going to lose it."

The exasperated noise that comes out of Hibba Baji sounds like a choked wheeze. She draws a deep breath. She clasps her hands together, like she's pleading with me to understand what she's saying. "Maya, we're standing here, in Pakistan, about to go celebrate your mehendi ceremony. And you're not even sure if you want to marry the guy!"

"I never said that! Why do people keep saying that?"

"*People?*" she splutters. "Who else has said it?"

I grit my teeth. "Sarfaraz," I answer reluctantly. "But he said that because we were trying to figure out what to do about the fact that we kissed—"

"You *what*?" If Hibba Baji's jaw fell any lower, it'd hit the floor.

I clamp my mouth shut. "I wasn't supposed to talk about that," I whisper.

"Maya, your wedding is tomorrow, and you kissed another guy! And not *just another guy*, but your future brother-in-law!"

"Okay, in my defense, I didn't know that when I kissed him."

"That doesn't matter!" Hibba Baji carefully covers her face so she doesn't smudge her ridiculously expensive makeup. After she takes a few deep breaths, she lowers her hands, and when she turns her attention to me, pity deepens the lines in her face. "Maya, be honest with me. Do you love Imtiaz? Can you really see yourself being married to him, for the rest of your life?"

I open my mouth to answer, but all that comes out is a resigned huff. "It doesn't matter now, okay? There's nothing we can do. We're in Pakistan, all our relatives are here, we've spent thousands of dollars, and I'm not going to be the reason Ammi bears any more humiliation."

Hibba Baji stares at me for a second. "I know you want to protect Mom, but you can't sacrifice yourself to do it."

"This isn't just about me," I remind her. "I may not have romantic feelings for Imtiaz yet, but I have a lot of respect for him, too much to risk hurting his feelings or humiliating him. Besides, I made a promise to him and to God that I would. A vow of commitment like that *means* something to me." I huff, tears brimming my lids. "Unlike our father, who made those same vows and then…left." My eyes water, and I blink the tears away as fast as I can because I'm not wearing waterproof makeup. "I don't know if I love him, but at least I can trust him."

Hibba Baji has to work to get her tears under control, too. She steps forward and cradles my face. "I know it hurts that Dad left…so bad," she starts. She uses the pad of her thumb to wipe at a tear threatening at the corner of my eye. "But just because he left doesn't mean you have to overcompensate for it, and it doesn't mean you're doomed to bad things always happening to you." She gestures to herself. "I mean, look at me. I'm happily married, with a daughter who brings me so much joy."

"Yippie for you," I grumble. "But you never had my track record, Hibba Baji. Guys have been falling at your feet for years. One of us had to bear the brunt of the nazar, and it ended up being me."

Her face crumples. "Maya—"

"How did you do it?" I cut in. I shake my head in wonder. "How did you...walk around like everything was okay after Baba left? And how did you find someone who you could trust enough to marry?"

Hibba Baji draws a deep breath before answering, "I guess it's the older sister thing. I had to keep it all together for you and Ammi." She tilts her head to the side. "As for trusting someone... You just have to trust other people will still be there."

My mind flashes to the hurt that cut my chest wide open when I realized that Sarfaraz knew I was his brother's fiancée, but I didn't know he was my fiancé's brother. "But how do you do that? How do you know you're trusting the right person?"

"You just...know," she explains. "You have to make it a habit and a routine to trust, and then it happens naturally. There's nothing wrong with routine."

My throat closes up, but I choke out, "Do you remember the night Baba left?"

She blinks, shifting from foot to foot. "It's not something I like to think about."

"Well, no matter how hard I tried to forget, I never could." I bite my bottom lip to keep it from wobbling. "Because it wasn't anything big or loud or scary. It was just...any other night." My throat thickens, and I clear it. "We ate dinner. I did some homework. And then I got ready for bed. He read me another chapter of *Charlotte's Web*, kissed my forehead, said he loved me, and then turned the light off and left the room." I choke back my emotion, thick in my throat. "It was our routine. It was any other night. And then I woke up in the morning and he was gone. How can I trust a man to stay when our own father couldn't?"

Hibba Baji grabs my arms and gives them a firm squeeze. "Because that's one man," she declares.

"But what if it's not?" I blubber. "What if it's every man I come across? What if I'm doomed to meet people that can never stay in my life? How can you trust that the love you give people isn't going to hurt you in the end?"

Hibba Baji pauses for a brief moment. "Maya, every action we take in the present is a gamble. We can never know what will happen in the future." She tucks a strand of hair the stylist missed behind my ear. "But you need to stop thinking the worst will happen. Maybe the future holds something beautiful for you."

"Or maybe I'm doomed to be cursed forever," I grumble.

"You are *not cursed*," Hibba Baji insists. "You just act like you are because it's the only way your brain could make sense of what happened. I dealt with Baba leaving differently because I was a teenager, but you were still a *child*. You didn't know how else to cope with the fact that our father left us, so you made up a curse. In fact, you didn't even start *talking* about being cursed until after he was gone."

I look up at Hibba Baji, her words swirling in my head. I desperately rack my brain. The memories of my young childhood are fuzzy, but as I flip through each image in my head, I realize Hibba Baji's right. I didn't start considering myself cursed until I was ten years old, when Baba left. I read Murphy's Law in a book around then, as well, and that's when I came up with

my own laws. That was how my younger self made sense of the
world around me, and then as I got older they became habit
until it was the only lens I had for the world.

Red rims Hibba Baji's irises, but the smile that held me
together when we were young is still there. "Baba leaving
wasn't your fault. And you were never alone. You always had
Ammi and me."

"You're right." I sniffle. "You're absolutely right. My whole
life, I felt like I couldn't keep any lasting relationships but…
I guess I have."

"You don't have to take on the world alone, Maya," Hibba
Baji reminds me. "And if you don't want anybody else right
now…if you don't feel ready for it…all you have to do is say
the word. Imtiaz will understand."

The mention of his name cracks my chest open again. "It's
fine," I assure her, though I don't quite believe the words myself. "I'm going to marry Imtiaz, and everything's going to
be fine. Everyone will be happy."

"Everyone but *you*."

I suck in a breath. "That's something I'll have to live with."

With that, I pick up the chudiyan from the vanity and slip
them on. They slide on easily, clinking against each other,
and perfectly covering Sarfaraz's name tattooed on my wrist.
No one's going to notice, and I intend on keeping it that way.

I meet Hibba Baji's eye, and her face falls when she realizes
that I'm going to go through with it. She just turns me around,
pushing me in front of her so she can pick up the train of my
dress and help me out of the room.

28

**Maya's Law #28:
Positive affirmations don't always work.**

There really isn't much of a difference between the mehendi and the maiyun ceremonies, but because we invited more people to the mehendi, we needed more space than we had at our house. In my uncle's neighborhood, there's a large patch of undeveloped land, so we pitched a very large tent there to have the mehendi. It's the evening now, so the air has begun to cool off. I would have absolutely refused to wear this dress in the heat. Instead, I take the air-conditioned limo over to the location.

As the bride, it's okay if I'm the last one to arrive. I know Imtiaz left earlier, so he must be sitting on top of the loveseat on the stage. Behind me, Hibba Baji grabs the bottom of my skirt and lifts it up so it's not dragging on the dirty ground.

She gives me a worried look, but I ignore it as I approach the front of the tent.

The music thumping the ground stops, and I hear the emcee, my uncle Tariq, announce, "Ladies and gentlemen, please find your seats! The bride has arrived!"

Ammi places her hand on my shoulder and gives it a delicate squeeze. "This is going to be great!" She pinches my cheek lightly instead of kissing it, which would have ruined my makeup, then loops her arm through mine. Hibba Baji comes around to my other side. She flashes me a worried look, but when I keep my expression firm, she wraps her arm around mine. At the tender look in her eyes, I sniffle.

With my sister and my mother on either side of me, I step through the flaps of the tent.

The decorator we hired was worth her money—the interior of the tent is breathtaking. Gold and purple sashes meet in the middle at the top of the tent, alternating colors. Attached to each end of the sashes are purple and gold lights. The mixture of the two lights casts a dreamlike aura over the whole place. Sofas are arranged in front of the stage with coffee tables in front of them for people to sit and eat, but there are also some regular tables and chairs available. The tablecloths are a deep blue, embroidered with gold swirls along the edges.

Ammi and Hibba Baji escort me over to the stage, where Imtiaz sits regally on top of the white loveseat. He's dressed in purple shalwar kameez, with a gold vest on top. He smiles as I sit down, and I briefly return it before going back to stoicism. Thank God it's *normal* for the bride to look miserable during her wedding in desi culture. I have no idea why, though. It's her wedding day; shouldn't she look *happy*?

Still, for now I'm glad that I don't have to fake being happy. "How's everything going for you?" I ask Imtiaz.

"Good," he answers, though the air between us is awkward.

"You look great," I compliment, giving him a once-over. "White really suits you."

"I hope so. It *is* my future uniform, after all."

I chuckle. "True."

An awkward silence lulls between us. "You look beautiful, by the way," he says, though it's more of an afterthought, something he's obligated to say rather than something he might actually believe.

"Thank you," I reply out of politeness, also because we're now surrounded by our family.

We sit in silence for a while, posing for pictures every now and then. When Imtiaz's parents and Sarfaraz come up to the stage to take photos with us, tension coils in the air around us. Mr. Porter quietly glares at Sarfaraz, but Mrs. Porter ushers them both onto the stage so we can take the picture.

A pang of disappointment hits my chest when Sarfaraz chooses to stand behind Imtiaz, but I brush it off. I have no business feeling disappointed by something like that. I just pose for the camera.

Mr. and Mrs. Porter give us both hugs, and Mrs. Porter is teary-eyed as she pulls away. She cups my cheeks, pinching the skin. "I'm so excited for you to be part of our family!" she gushes.

I accept the praise with a stuttering heart. "I am, too," I tell her.

She grins at us both before stepping off the stage. Once she's gone, Imtiaz leans toward me. "I'm sorry about her. She can get sentimental."

"It's the desi mom thing," I assure him with a wave. "My mother does it all the time, too. The weeks leading up to the Pakistan trip, she would burst into tears at random moments when she remembered I was getting married."

"I think my mom's so emotional because she won't have a

child in the house anymore," Imtiaz suggests. "But she won't be alone for long. She'll have you to keep her company, and vice versa."

I freeze. "What? What do you mean *keep her company*?"

He frowns. "I told you about my surgical schedule, didn't I?"

When I shake my head, his frown deepens. "Well, when we get back home, I'll have a lot of work to catch up on for my residency. I'll be pretty busy studying both at home and at the hospital. You'll be alone a lot, which is why I was going to suggest my mom come stay with you on nights when I'm working. I know you get spooked being alone."

No, I don't get *spooked*. I can't sleep alone not because I'm afraid someone's loitering outside the window, but because I feel like I don't have anyone around to be with me. No one to go to bed with, and not even in a sexual way. In a "when I wake up, I know you'll be there" kind of way. And I can't do that with my mother-in-law.

My breath hitches at the thought of being alone in that empty apartment. Imtiaz startles at the action. "Maya, are you okay?" He puts his hand on my back. "If you don't want my mom to come stay with us, she doesn't have to."

Then I'll be labeled as the wife who ruins the relationship between a mother and her son and forces him to choose between them. I don't think Imtiaz would do that, but then again, I don't really *know* him. He could be completely different once we're married and settled into our lives, but I knew that was a risk, and I was willing to take it.

I inhale deeply a few times, then lift my chin. "It's fine," I assure him. My mouth stretches and I hope that I don't look like the Joker. "Thank you for telling me now—I might have been shocked to go back home and find out that we're cooking for three instead of two."

He tilts his head to the side, his expression torn. "If you're sure…"

"I am." And I am, really. At least he had the decency to tell me something big like this. Sure, he forgot to tell me, but the point is he planned to tell me. And he did it out of consideration for me. He knows that I don't like being alone, so he tried to figure out a solution for that. He didn't knowingly hide anything from me. He didn't listen to me bare my soul while knowing that we wouldn't be parting at the end of it all. He didn't hold my hand while knowing that he'd have to let it go. He didn't kiss me while knowing I was someone else's.

If Imtiaz ever left me, I know it wouldn't hurt. But if he stays, then we can figure it out. It's a win-win scenario either way.

Imtiaz has my best interests at heart. Imtiaz is willing to make things work with me. Imtiaz is my future.

Maybe if I say it enough times, it'll finally feel right.

29

**Maya's Law #29:
You have to stand up for yourself.**

When we get home, I want to go right to sleep. But instead I find myself on the floor in Ammi's room, leaning against the foot of the bed. It's 10 p.m., yet the room around me bustles with activity. With the wedding officially tomorrow, my whole family is in hyperdrive, making sure everyone has the right jewelry and shoes and clothes. All the girls have also gathered to sing a few songs, play on a dhol, and spend some time with me before I join someone else's family.

I stare blankly at my feet. I hadn't gotten mehendi done on my feet at home, but Fizza did it for me the first night I arrived. I study the rich, intricate design swirling on my skin. It was a tedious process to sit through, and I couldn't move for a while after it was done because I was worried I'd smudge the wet paste, but I'm super grateful she did it. Now I have something to look at while Ammi slathers my skin with coconut oil. I refuse to take the bangles off my wrist, though, in case she sees Sarfaraz's name written on me.

With the mehendi out of the way, all that's left is the bharat, the day the nikkah would be read. Technically we'll be doing our nikkah at Dhuhr at the masjid and then have our reception in the evening. And the final event is the walima, but that won't be until two days after tomorrow, to give everyone a break.

"Oi, Maya!" my mother's older sister, my Kinza Khala, calls out.

I snap into focus, blinking heavily. "Jee?"

Kinza Khala fixes me with an annoyed stare. "I've called your name three times. What's wrong with you?"

I stammer, my mouth opening and closing a few times. I'm saved when my younger cousin Faryal speaks up for me. "Oh, Khala, bechari ko chodeya," she says. She plops down on the floor next to me. A mischievous twinkle flashes in her eyes as she nudges me with her arm. "She's getting married tomorrow. I'm sure her focus is somewhere else."

My face flushes while everyone goes, "Ahhhhh," laughter in their voices. I duck my head, then nudge Faryal back, harder. "Why are you like this?"

Faryal giggles. "I'm sorry, Maya Baji."

"No, no, don't be sorry," my mom's cousin, my Amira Khala, interjects. She's a woman even older than Ammi. Her gray hairs are well disguised with brown dye, but there's no hiding the wrinkles forming on her forehead. "You're right. A young woman right before her wedding *should* be somewhat worried at least."

My face heats up. I nudge Ammi, who sits beside me, with my elbow. "Ammi, get them to stop," I plead.

Ammi pauses, her hand stilling on my arm. She flashes both Faryal and Amira Khala stern looks. "Leave my daughter alone," she demands.

I'm about to thank her when she grins. "She already has enough on her plate to worry about."

That causes another round of laughter, and I want to sink into the floor. They'd never say the word *sex* out loud, but it's annoying enough that they're heavily implying it. I rip my arm out of Ammi's grasp, ignoring her confused pout. I grab the bottle of coconut oil, then look for Hibba Baji. She's standing in front of the vanity on the other side of the room, sifting through pieces of jewelry. "Hibba Baji!" I say, and she looks up at the sound of her name. I hold the bottle out to her. "Will you?"

She looks at me and our mother, but she ultimately puts the earrings down and comes over, taking the bottle from me and sitting down. She squeezes some into her palm, rubs her palms together, and then begins to massage my other arm, the one with Sarfaraz's name. She moves the bangles out of the way and slathers my skin as quick as she can before letting the bangles cover the scripture up again. "The coconut oil's going to make your skin super smooth," Hibba Baji says, an encouraging smile on her face. I know she still thinks what I'm doing is wrong, but at least she's being supportive. She looks from me to Ammi. "I remember when Ammi did this for me right before my wedding."

"That was a special night." Ammi sighs dreamily, her eyes glazing over like she's returning to that time in her life. "But you cried so much."

Kinza Khala laughs. "Can you blame her? Your mother-in-law's house is *very different* from your mother's house."

Ammi snickers, as well. "It's a good thing Maya is moving into her own apartment with Imtiaz after the wedding," she says, rubbing my arm. I don't look at her, but I don't shrug her off, either. Ammi takes that as a good sign, giving me a gentle squeeze. "She's much smarter than I was."

My back stiffens, my breath hitching. I stay silent, hunching forward slightly as Hibba Baji moves from my arms to my legs. She pulls up my black shalwar to expose my skin. Hibba Baji, noticing my lack of response, quickly fills in, "I think what Maya is doing is great. You know, it's not required in Islam for a woman to move in with her husband's family. It is the woman's right to ask for a home."

Amira Khala clicks her tongue. "Yes, yes, that is all fair. But we mustn't forget that in our culture, people would call Maya chalaak."

Chalaak—the word means "too smart for your own good," and it's mainly used toward women who are trying to be themselves or voice their own opinions. "Canada isn't Pakistan, Amira Khala. The mentality is different for people who grew up over there, like Imtiaz and I did."

"Oh, yes, you kids growing up in the West, forgetting our culture," she sneers, and I force myself to bite back the insult rising in my throat. Amira Khala has always thought that Ammi moving to Canada after her marriage and raising her children there would make us lose our culture. She always finds some way to dig at the country where I was born and raised, and it irritates me to no end.

"I'm not forgetting our culture," I say through clenched teeth, trying to keep my voice as polite as possible. Hibba Baji flashes me a warning look, but I ignore it as I continue. "Just because I didn't grow up with the air from this land in my lungs doesn't mean that I don't feel it in every breath I take. I live my life differently and as true to myself as I can." I stress my tone as I add, "But that doesn't mean I forget my values *or* look down on the people from here."

Amira Khala sniffs at me. "I'm just saying, if you lived here, things would be different for you." She shifts in place. "For example, are you quitting your job after you marry?"

My mouth puckers like I've eaten something sour. "Why would I do that?"

Kinza Khala stares at me. "But you're going to quit after you have kids, right?"

I bite the inside of my cheek, hard. "No, Kinza Khala," I tell her. "Again, why would I do that?"

"Because you love your children!"

I stare blankly at her. She's talking about children who don't even *exist* yet. "I'm sure whenever I *do* end up having children, they're going to know how much I love them regardless of whether I'm working or not," I say slowly. "Besides, why would *I* have to give up my work? You'd never ask Imtiaz to drop out of his residency to raise his kids."

"Of course not, silly girl," Amira Khala cuts in. "He's the man."

If I grit my teeth any harder, they'd break. "But because *I'm* the woman, I have to do it?"

"Exactly," Amira Khala says, a pleased look on her face like she's glad she got through to me.

Keeping my expression neutral, I carefully lock eyes with Ammi. My face may be calm, but she's my mother; she can tell when I'm ready to explode. Ammi clears her throat. "Maya is not going to give up her work. She can find a balance." She gestures to my sister. "Hibba found her balance perfectly."

"Yes," Hibba Baji says eagerly. "I still work, and my daughter knows how much I love her. Huzaifa works, as well. We found a good balance for the two of us."

"But let's not forget Maya is marrying a doctor," Amira Khala argues. I can't believe she's still on this. "The workload is different. The expectations will be different. Maya's *life* is going to be different."

Maya's life is going to be different. My khala's words are true, but I've never wanted something to be false so badly.

My chest tightens, the walls of the room feel like they're closing in. I can't be in here anymore. I shoot to my feet, ignoring the looks of the people around me. "I need some air," I explain.

"Maya, wait—" Ammi starts getting to her feet, as well.

I don't wait for her to stand. I dash over to the door, grabbing a shawl off the hook next to it. "I won't be gone long," I promise. I twist the knob and pull it open. I pause, glancing over my shoulder. Thankfully, Ammi remains rooted in place, but her confused expression is going to be one that'll haunt my nightmares. "I'll be back soon. I need a second."

With that, I close the door firmly and wrap the shawl around me, speed-walking down the dark hall. The last thing I want is for someone in the room to catch up with me when I'm not in the mood to speak to anyone. I need to calm my anger before I can face any of them.

I'm about to round the corner when the door I pass by opens. I flinch at the glaring white light, lifting a hand in front of my face. It takes a second for it to register that the figure stepping out of the room is Sarfaraz.

He stares at me. "You're not going to hit me, are you?"

His teasing tone cools some of the anger in my chest. I lower my hand. "Don't tempt me," I fire back, earning a smirk from him. "I just walked away from a conversation that was about to become *really* ugly, and after the way you treated me when we first met, you'd deserve the punches."

Sarfaraz doesn't respond to my teasing threat. He leans against the open doorway, crossing his arms over his chest. "What'd the aunties say to make you so mad?"

I try not to stare too long at the muscles in his arms flexing. "Some...stuff. I don't want to talk about it, not until my anger's cooled down." I gesture to the hall in front of us. "I was about to go get a snack from the convenience store around the corner."

Sarfaraz's jaw slackens. "You were going to go alone?"

I shrug. "It's not that far from here."

"Do you have any idea how late it is?" He peers at his watch. "It's nearly ten thirty. It's not safe for you to be out by yourself."

I know he has no way of knowing the conversation I just had, but his words reignite the fire in my chest. "And why not? Women aren't incapable of defending themselves. I am perfectly capable of walking ten minutes to the convenience store and getting myself a frozen treat."

"I know you are," he agrees. "But you have to remember these aren't the streets of Toronto. I've heard too many stories of women being attacked while alone, *especially* at night. And remember what happened to us? I can't let you go alone."

"I *told* you—"

"Yes, you can protect yourself," he interrupts, his tone growing aggravated with each word. He pinches the bridge of his nose, squeezing his eyes shut. When he opens them again, most of the frustration is gone, replaced by genuine worry. "Please, Maya. Let me go with you. If not for your peace of mind, then for mine."

I stare at him for a good long moment. It's risky; we could easily get caught, and while we can play it off as the "brother-in-law" thing, that might not stop people from whispering. If those whispers get back to Imtiaz, it wouldn't be good. Plus, I'm still upset with Sarfaraz for keeping so much from me.

But at the pleading look in his face, I cave. "Fine. But *you're* paying."

30

**Maya's Law #30:
You have to fight for your identity.**

We're quiet as we walk along the dirt road. I cross my arms over my chest and keep my gaze forward. The walk is a lot longer than I thought it'd be; I should have taken a rickshaw. But because I was so insistent that it was an easy walk, I have to keep my mouth shut or I'll never hear the end of it from Sarfaraz.

"So," he starts, swinging his hands, "do you want to talk about it yet?"

"Not until I have kulfi goodness in my system."

He pipes down again, and we reach the convenience store in record time. We go in, grab a couple of kulfis, and Sarfaraz pays while I step out. Once he's done, he joins me, and we wordlessly begin our walk back to the house.

"Okay," he says. He licks the end of his almond kulfi. "Are you ready to talk now?"

I huff, nibble on my mango kulfi for a second longer, then slide it out of my mouth. "Why are girls always required to sacrifice things?"

"What? Sacrifice how?"

"Like, why are we always the ones expected to give things up?" I clarify. "Why do we have to give up our jobs to raise kids? Why are we expected to raise kids all on our own, while the only expectation from the father is that he provides money for the family? Money isn't the only important thing in life."

"That's true," Sarfaraz agrees. "Did one of your aunties tell you to stop working after you get married?"

I grit my teeth. "My Amira Khala was appalled when she found out that not only do I plan on working after marriage, but I plan on working even when we have kids," I reply, my mouth souring despite the sweet flavor of mango on my tongue. "I know the mentality is different because they grew up here, and that's not to say that because I was born in Canada I know better, but it irritates me so much."

"Some people have a hard time differentiating between culture and religion," he offers. "Like, they think some of the things that are cultural come from religion, and if we push back against the culture, then we're disrespecting our religion. And those mentalities are passed on to women because we live in a patriarchal society."

"That's a good point," I say. "But that doesn't excuse it. Women all over the world have been gaining power, and my family can't exactly ignore that. So many Pakistani dramas are about female empowerment and doing more than what other people expect. It's not just something that belongs in fiction."

"You're right, it's messed up," Sarfaraz agrees. "That must be the hardest part of living in a diaspora. I've seen how hard it is for the girls on my stepmom's side to reconcile the teachings of their family and the teachings of society where they live."

"It *is* hard," I insist. "It's so hard because if you're a woman, you can never do *anything* without being criticized. You're either too Western or you're not progressive enough. You're too docile or you run your mouth too much. You're too independent or you're too needy." I slump. "It sucks, and it's something I try so hard to get my mother to see. Most of the time she's good, but some things…some things she's just too hardwired to change."

"Like what?" he asks.

"Well, like the whole marriage thing. She wanted me to get married when I was much younger, but every time I mentioned wanting to date, she shut it down. But then when I reached marrying age, she was shocked that I was no good with guys." I pause. "Of course, my curse contributes to that, too, but still."

Sarfaraz rolls his eyes. "Your whole…*curse* thing aside, maybe she feels this way because your dad left. She worries about what's going to happen to you after she dies; she doesn't want you to be alone."

I stop walking, causing Sarfaraz to halt a few steps away from me. "What's so wrong with a woman being on her own? What's wrong with her wanting to be independent?" I ball up my hands so tight that my nails dig into my skin. "Why does she have to be the one to give up what *she* wants? How much can a woman give before she has nothing left for herself?"

He stares at me, hesitant. "I don't know what I can say to you," he eventually admits. "From what I saw growing up, I get that the pressure the culture puts on women is incredibly unfair, but how are we going to change the mentality of people who grew up in a different time than us?" He steps over to me, and gently, he rests his hand on my arm. A spark shoots to my chest at the contact and I hate that it does. I hate that his touch still has such an effect on me. "All we can do is try to change our own way of thinking, and then pass that on to the future generation, and hope that it all works out for the best. You have to figure out how to assert your own independence, how to fight for what *you* want." He shrugs. "It might not be in obvious ways, but you'll figure it out. You just have to know what you want." He gives me a once-over. "*Do* you know what you want?"

"I know what I *don't* want." I suck in a strangled breath. "As much as I believe a woman *can* find happiness on her own…" I kick a rock out of the way. "I don't want to be alone. I have my mother and my sister, yes, but…it feels like I've been alone my whole life. I don't want to feel that way anymore. Is there something so wrong with that?"

I don't look at Sarfaraz as he says, "There's nothing wrong with not wanting to be alone."

This time, I snap my head up. "What did you say?"

"What?"

"It's just…" A laugh of disbelief rumbles my chest. "Sarfaraz Porter, the guy who, not even a week ago, didn't believe me when I said that humans can't be alone."

"Yeah, well…" He polished off his kulfi earlier, and now he plays with the bare yellow stick. A cloud of indecision practically storms above his head, but when he looks at me again, he has a polite expression on his face. "You're annoyingly persuasive. Plus…these last few days have really showed me that while I like my independence, maybe…maybe I don't want to be alone, either."

An ache tears through my chest, so strong and so overwhelming that I nearly run into his arms and hold him tight like we're in an old Shah Rukh Khan film. In a movie, we'd embrace, clutching each other for dear life, and that's when our dreamsong sequence would begin. Me dressed in a bright orange sari, frolicking in the fields, not unlike the ones in Salama's village. Sarfaraz following behind me, wearing a snazzy black kurta and white pants. We'd meet in the middle and my dupatta would float in the wind as he dipped me.

But no. No matter how insane this past week has been, my life isn't a movie. There would be no last-minute romantic declarations. There would be no one running to an airport or a train station or, hell, even a *bus* station to stop someone else from leaving. And the happy ending isn't going to be one that I expected.

I look down at my fingers, picking at my nails. "Well, I hope you won't be alone for long," I eventually reply.

His expression is soft as he stares at me. "Yeah," he breathes, his voice impossibly soft, strange for a man whose voice is usually sharp and stern.

I clear my throat, eager to change the subject. I curl a strand of hair over my ear. "Well, while I don't want to be alone, I also don't want to be defined by my relation to someone else. But sometimes it feels like people don't know the difference."

"You don't have to care about what other people think, you know." He gestures to himself. "Look at me—if I did what my father wanted, I know I probably would have been more successful, but I would have hated my life. I feel like parents equate money to happiness, but you could have all the money in the world and *still* be miserable." He shrugs. "And even if becoming a family lawyer didn't make me as much money as it does, I would have been okay with it. Because at the end of the day, at least it was *my* decision. I did what was best for me, and I know I can live with myself because of it."

That's the whole crux of the situation, I guess. "I don't want to end up being seen as only someone's daughter, someone's mom, or someone's wife." I draw my shoulders back and hold my head high. "I'm Maya Mirza, and I'm whole on my own."

Slowly, the corners of Sarfaraz's lips turn up. "Thank God."

I give him a once-over. "What?"

"I've spent the last few days watching you run around doing whatever anyone tells you to do. I thought the Maya I met on that plane was a fabrication, and that the real you was just someone who lives by the words of everyone else." His smirk grows. "Thank God that first woman hasn't faded away."

Sarfaraz's hand moves from my arm; briefly, I wish it were back, and then a rush of anger hits my chest at that wish. "And I can only hope she doesn't fade away completely," Sarfaraz adds, "because I know if she loses any part of herself, she'll never be okay." We reach the gate of the house, and he pushes it open for me. "You don't need someone to find you, Maya. You'll find yourself. It may take a while, and it won't be easy, but when you find who you are, you'll know in that instant." The ghost of a pained smile touches his face. "And that's when you'll truly be okay."

31

Maya's Law #31:
Sweet things can never mask bitter truths.

When we get back home, Sarfaraz goes up to bed, and even though I just had kulfi, now I'm craving some chai. I don't feel like going back up to the room with the other women yet, either, so I head for the kitchen.

It's nearing 11 p.m. now, so I'm surprised that the light is on. I peek into the room, one foot poised to make an escape in case it's someone I don't want to talk to.

It's Mr. Porter making himself a cup of chai. And like, not in the kettle with a tea bag, but the desi way; fresh ginger root, whole cardamom pods, and cinnamon sticks litter the counter while a pot boils on the stove. He looks over at the sound of my footsteps and grins tiredly. "Ahh, hello, Maya."

I linger in the doorway. "Hi, Dad," I say, though the word

still feels foreign on my tongue. I haven't called someone *Dad* in years, so to get into the habit of doing it again is difficult. I know it'll probably take some time getting used to seeing these people as another set of parents, but it's so *strange*.

I tap my fingers against the wooden frame, then gesture to the stove. "I see you're making chai."

He glances at the pot. "Ahh, yes. I'm afraid I couldn't sleep." He gestures to it. "Would you like a cup?"

I nod, making my way over to the table in the middle of the kitchen. I sit down in one of the chairs. "This is weird," I say.

"What is?"

"Well, I've been told my whole life that I'm going to be making chai for my in-laws, like, every day," I say, a laugh teasing my tone. "But here my future father-in-law is making tea for me."

Mr. Porter smirks as he expertly crushes the cardamom pods with the side of a knife. For a brief moment, I imagine Mrs. Porter standing beside her husband in a kitchen, supervising his technique. I imagine Mr. Porter laughing as his wife puts her thin arms around his burly back, resting her hands on top of his and gently correcting his movements. Two people who come from different backgrounds teaching each other the things that make up how they live their lives. Culture is so personal; people don't usually think about it as such, but there's something so private about the details we learn from others, taking them for our own and molding them so they fit us. And then there's something so incredibly intimate about sharing that culture with someone else. To give someone you deeply care about a glimpse into your soul, knowing that that person will take those glimpses and be grateful for them, because they love everything that makes you *you*.

Blending two cultures is difficult; most of the time one ends up dominating the other. But these two loved each other enough to commit to making it work, and instead of things being too much or too little, they managed to meet in the middle, like all good relationships should.

"I've always found that aspect of desi culture strange," he says, coming back to the present. He looks over at me. "I mean, I want a daughter, not a servant." He swipes the pieces into the pot. "Even with my wife. When we married, it's like all she wanted to do was wait on me, and she *expected* me to want her to do that." He pulls out a stirring spoon from a drawer. "I was a grown man, on my second marriage. I knew how to take care of myself. All I wanted her to do was live for herself."

I smile. "I feel bad for the desi girls who don't have a father-in-law with your perspective."

He dips his chin at me. "That's kind of you to say, Maya."

We're silent as Mr. Porter continues prepping the chai, and soon enough, the spicy aroma fills the kitchen. I inhale the scent deeply, and it's like coming home after a long day at work. Ammi always had a cup ready and waiting for me as soon as I came home and changed into something more comfortable. It's one of the things I'm going to miss the most about living with her. We may have our differences, but the realization that I'm not going to live with my mother anymore settles heavily in my stomach. Ammi, Hibba Baji, and I agreed that it makes the most sense for Ammi to move in with Hibba Baji and her husband after I marry, because she has a kid. I'm sure Ammi will come stay with me when I have kids, whenever that is, but for now, Ammi will be going to Hibba Baji's house. And instead of a warm cup of chai to come home to every night, I'll be coming home to an empty apartment. To a cold lonely place.

A shiver runs over me, sprouting goose bumps on my arms. I rub at them over my kurta as Mr. Porter goes over to the fridge, pulling out milk. "I do hope you've forgiven our…

ah...*indiscretion*," he begins. He unscrews the cap of the carton, pouring some into the pot.

I pause my rubbing. "You mean where you left out that you had a whole other son?"

Mr. Porter sucks in his cheeks at my tone. I don't mean to get snarky, and I know it's rude, but I can't help the rush of indignation at the casual mention of how he disowned his son for wanting a path of his own. I never got to that point with Ammi, but if I were a bit more stubborn, and if she hadn't been lenient enough...it could have been me.

"Erm, yes." He clears his throat. "I feel badly that we didn't tell you, but we certainly didn't expect Sarfaraz to show up to the wedding, either. *That* was a surprise to us all."

No kidding. "If Imtiaz wants him here, then so do I," I say. I rest my arms on the table. "You know... Sarfaraz has been on his own for a long time. And I don't know how you feel, but he's your son. You have to miss him, don't you?"

Mr. Porter pauses in stirring the pot. "You seem very concerned with Sarfaraz."

My face burns. I lean back from the table. "He's become...a friend," I finish, though the word *friend* feels incredibly empty when I'm using it to refer to Sarfaraz. "We started off on the wrong foot on the plane, but I feel like I've gotten to know him well enough. He took care of me while we were trying to get here." Something sweet swirls in my chest. "He could get *really* frustrated with me, but he always stuck by me anyway." When I lift my eyes back to Mr. Porter, he has an undecipherable expression on his face. I give him a pointed look. "You raised a good guy, Dad. I wish you knew him as the man he is now."

Mr. Porter doesn't say anything. He grabs a ladle and pours some chai into two mugs. "You seem to have gotten to know him well in only a few days."

"I wouldn't say a *few* days," I mumble. "But we *were* together the whole time." My heartbeat quickens, and I clarify, "Respectfully, though. We were always together respectfully."

Okay, except for one time, but he doesn't need to know that.

Mr. Porter slides me my mug, and I pick it up with a grateful nod. I inhale the spicy scent of the chai, blow on it, then take a delicate sip. After a few quiet seconds, I lower the mug from my mouth. "Can I ask you something, Dad?"

"Yes."

"Why won't you forgive Sarfaraz for what happened?"

Mr. Porter freezes. "I don't see how it's your business."

"I'm going to be family," I remind him. "It's my business."

He stares at me, but when I don't back down, he lowers his mug back to the table. "You don't have children, Maya. You won't understand."

"I want to try," I press. More like, *I want to know,* but whatever.

Mr. Porter stares down at his cup. "Alright." He raps his knuckles on the counter, thinking for a long moment. When he opens his mouth, he says, "When you do everything you can for your kids, it's disappointing when they don't live up to your expectations."

"Living up to your expectations and being someone they don't want to be are different," I correct. "You can point them in a certain direction all you want, but they're your *kid.* They're not an extension of you. They're their own person."

"I suppose," Mr. Porter huffs. "But it's one thing to want to do what you want, and then it's another to lie about it. I had no idea, and I was completely blindsided. That's not how you treat family, in my opinion. So why should I treat him with respect when he clearly didn't have any for me?"

"Fine, that's true," I relent. "But kicking him out of your family just for wanting his own life is extreme, don't you think? You said that you wanted Mummy to be able to live for herself. Why don't you want the same for your son?"

"I might have made the decision in the heat of the moment," he confesses. "There was so much *disappointment*, I felt, coming from Sarfaraz at the time. He lied to me about what he was studying, he didn't want to take over my company, his marriage ended very messily." He runs his fingers through his graying hairs. "Everything came to a head, and it all exploded. I want my son to be able to live for himself, but it came through deceit, after all I had done for him. Despite the pain, it was still a betrayal."

"But then why didn't you try to reach out? He reached out to you."

"I suppose over time, I had gotten so used to the anger, it was easier to live in it than to admit I was wrong."

I tap my fingers on my cup. "Living in anger may be easy, but isn't living in love more rewarding?"

Mr. Porter sucks in a breath. "I never really...thought of it that way. It's much easier to continue on the way that we've been instead of trying to overcome everything."

"It may be easier, but I think you should at least *try*." As I say the words, I realize I may be acting a tiny bit...hypocritical. I've been holding so much anger at Sarfaraz for not telling me that he knew I was marrying his brother, and I didn't allow myself to consider letting it go. I wanted to stay in my anger because it was easier. Life's too short to stay mad at the people you care about, and Sarfaraz has become one of those people. He might be someone I have to keep at arm's length for a while, at least until my feelings fade, but when I think about it, not having him in my life at all hurts more than having what small amount I can of him. He was still a great friend to me while we traveled. Maybe, someday, we can go back to being the easy stranger-friends we were at the start of this trip.

He clears his throat, staring into his mug. "I admit I may have been *hasty* in the past," he says. "And I do have my share of regrets. But I don't know if he even wants to reconcile now. He said he came because Imtiaz asked him. It doesn't mean he wants to mend our relationship."

"He might surprise you." A smile teases my lips. "He's certainly surprised me, more than once."

Mr. Porter tilts his head to the side. "As long as we're sharing, may I say something?"

"Of course."

"Imtiaz is my dear son, but he can be...all over the place," he admits. "It's the doctor thing. Sometimes he doesn't know where his priorities should lie because he's stretched so thin. Because of that, he can lose focus on what matters. Don't give up on him."

I bite the inside of my cheek. "I won't."

Mr. Porter stares at me above the top of his cup. "Do you know why my first marriage ended?"

When I shake my head, Mr. Porter goes on. "We were very young," he begins. "Fresh out of college. We rushed into things. My parents didn't want the relationship to be haram, and her parents didn't want her to marry a Muslim. She...had a complicated relationship with them, so she would do anything to spite them, including marrying someone they disapproved of. She gave birth to Sarfaraz a year or so later, and that's when we realized we may not have been as ready as we convinced everyone we were." He plays with the handle of his mug, not quite looking at me. "All of our friends were still going out late at night, meeting up whenever and wherever, had enough money to blow on stupid things. But we had a spouse to come home to every night, a mortgage that needed paying, and a baby that seemed to drain us of all our finances."

He takes another sip, longer this time, and I wonder how his tongue isn't burnt. "At some point, we realized we lost who we were in trying to make *us* work. We decided we'd be happier without each other, so we divorced not long after Sarfaraz's first birthday. She hasn't kept much contact with Sarfaraz, and even less with me. And just like that, I wondered how the life I planned for myself went so wrong." He rubs a hand over his forehead. "There I was, barely twenty-six, with a son who relied on me for everything. Yet, I worked tirelessly, studying in law school while still being the best dad I could. And I owe so much of that to Ayesha." He practically glows at the mention of his wife's name. "We met by chance at the masjid. We fell for each other pretty fast, and before I knew it, I was married again, but I knew this time I wasn't making a mistake."

I've been quiet through his whole speech, but now I ask, "How? How did you know?"

"Because I can take one look at Ayesha and know that she understands me in ways no one else does. She's willing to check out my interests. Even though my ego always wants to be right, I'm ready to see from her point of view when we argue. And at the end of the day, no matter what, we come back together, because we see all the good and the bad and pick each other anyway," he replies. "I know you have a good heart, Maya," he says, which makes the guilt sit heavier in my gut. "My divorce was necessary for me to find happiness, but I don't want you or Imtiaz to go through what I did. Remember that as long as you're there for each other, you can make it through anything."

I stay silent, confusion flooding me. Because when I think about it, it hasn't been Imtiaz who has done those things for me, and who I do them for. It's been Sarfaraz.

He steps away from the kitchen, leaving his now-empty mug on the counter. When he looks at me again, kindness reflects back at me. "Make sure you get some sleep," he says. "I'll give some thought on what you've said, as long as you give some thought to what I've said."

With that, he shuffles out of the room.

32

**Maya's Law #32:
Happily-ever-after isn't guaranteed.**

I step into my bedroom, shutting the door behind me. For a second, I stare at my empty bed. I'm already dreading the terrible night's sleep I'm going to get lying there alone.

With a jolt, I realize I want to spend the night with Ammi. It's my last night as a single woman, and I want to spend it in my mom's arms. I know she can be a lot, and sometimes it feels like she's holding me back, but she's my mother, and when we go home, I won't be returning to her house with her.

I grab a fresh set of underwear and shalwar kameez and pad over to the bathroom. I peel my clothes off, kick them out of the way, and then step into the shower stall.

I let the hot water hit my face for a while, then when I open my eyes, I stare down at my mehendi-adorned skin and it hits me—this henna is on my body because I'm getting married tomorrow.

I'm getting married tomorrow. To someone I don't love. To someone I'm not even sure I fully *know*.

I slide down to the floor. The water continues to pelt at me, but I ignore it as I bring my knees to my chest and wrap my arms around my legs. I sit there for a long time. I don't know how long exactly, but eventually the water shifts from hot to cold, and I force myself to stand back up. I furiously scrub my body. When I step out of the shower, I'm sure I'm missing a few hairs, and my skin is red and raw, but that purge is exactly what I needed.

I dry myself off and put on a new kurta and pajamas, scooping up my dirty clothes for the laundry. I'm about to head down the hall to Ammi's room when I happen to look out the window. My face contorts when I recognize a figure walking toward the exit, and my stomach drops when I recognize the figure to be Sarfaraz, pulling his luggage behind him. An Uber sits idling in front of the gate.

Dread overwhelms my senses, filling my lungs and stealing my breath. He can't leave. Not without fixing things between us. Not without hearing what I have to say.

Without thinking, I drop the bundle of clothes and dash down the hall. I nearly trip twice on the stairs, but I remain steady on my feet until I hit the last step. I slip on the floor because my feet are still damp, but I don't let it hinder me as I make it to the front door.

I push the gate open and step through. He's about to round the corner when I call, "Sarfaraz!"

The sound of his name is enough to make him stop and look over his shoulder, confusion on his face. His eyes widen when he recognizes me, and he stops in his tracks. Clutched in his hand is the new phone that one of my uncles got for him because his is currently with a bunch of goons. "Maya?"

I huff, struggling to catch my breath. I open my mouth, but I only manage a faint wheeze. My head spins, and I hold up one finger while dropping my head between my knees.

The sound of his suitcase's wheels screeching against the pavement is the only indication that he's walking back over to me. Once his feet appear under my gaze, I suck in one final breath and push myself back up. Sarfaraz looks from my still-wet hair to my ragged shalwar kameez before stopping at my feet. "You're not wearing shoes."

"Huh?" I blurt. I look down to see that I am, in fact, bare-foot. "Oh." I lift my face back up to him. "I didn't think to put any on. I was so focused on getting to you." I eye his suitcase, and the dread from before creeps its way back to my chest. "What are you doing?" I look over to where a car waits idly. "You're...you're not *leaving*, are you?"

Sarfaraz sighs deeply, and it sounds like it came from the very depths of an old soul. "I'm sorry, Maya."

He reaches for the handle of his suitcase, but I intercept him at the last second, my fingers wrapping around his. I grab the cuff of his jacket. "But you can't leave!" I protest.

Sarfaraz pulls himself out of my grip, and my fingers instantly miss his touch. "I... I can't."

"You can't what?"

He looks away from me. "I can't stay."

Anger bubbles to the surface. I won't make this easy for him. I grab his arm and force him to look at me. "Why not?"

Sarfaraz growls and wrenches himself out of my grasp again. "I can't stay and watch."

I pause for a moment, staring at him. And then it dawns on me what he's really trying to say.

He can't stay and watch me get married.

For some reason, fury blazes my belly instead of sympathy. "So, you're going to leave?" I demand. "You're going to leave your brother on the most important day of his life because you can't deal…" I clamp my mouth shut when his jaw clenches. Even though I feel things for him, and I'm now sure he feels them for me, neither one of us has said anything out loud. It'd be too cruel—speaking words that are supposed to spark hope in your heart when we both know all they can do for us is extinguish that flicker. "If you loved him, you wouldn't abandon him."

I guess Sarfaraz is choosing violence, too, because he steps closer to me, tossing a finger in my face. "Don't talk to me about my brother. I love him. So much, in fact, that I bore the brunt of our father's expectations so that *he* could pursue what he wanted. So much that I'm willing to do whatever makes him happy, including putting my own pride aside and coming to be at his wedding, giving our family a chance to become whole again. So much that I—" He cuts himself off, turning his face away.

So much that he's accepting the pain of letting Imtiaz marry me. Still, I frown at his finger before pushing it away from me. "I *can* talk to you about your brother, and I *will*, because it seems like you don't know anything about him anymore!" I stomp my foot. "You didn't even know the name of his *fiancée*!"

"You're one to talk."

My mouth thins. "What?"

A laugh of disbelief splutters out of his mouth. "You don't know *anything* about him. And you're supposed to *be* his fiancée. You've been engaged for three years yet you still know nothing about him. Do you even like him?"

My blood boils. "Don't you *dare* talk about my feelings for Imtiaz! You don't know anything about them."

"I know that if you had the choice, you wouldn't be going through with this wedding," Sarfaraz tosses back. "You said it yourself, Maya. You only agreed to it because you wanted to get out of your house."

His words burn shame into my skin. "At least I'm going through with it. I'm keeping the promise I made. I'm not *abandoning* him, unlike you."

"And unlike *you*, at least I love him," he snaps. "But you don't even know if you ever will."

"That's because of my curse!" I blink my tears away. "I can't love anyone because I never get the chance to!"

"God, enough with the fucking curse!" Sarfaraz fumes, and I flinch at his rising tone. He notices my body tensing, and he leans away from me. He also drops his tone, but it's still icy as he continues, "You're not cursed, Maya. You're just scared that if you love someone, they're going to leave you. You avoid love because that way, if they do leave, it won't hurt."

His words pour over me like ice water, shocking my senses, making me shiver, blocking out any rational thought other than, *Oh, God, this hurts*. The tears that I've been holding back spill. "That's not true," I say, my words barely a whisper.

Sarfaraz pinches the bridge of his nose, and when he drops his hand, all the anger and tension has left his face. "Maya, you've had a string of bad luck, *especially* in love. Do you really think it's because bad things just *happen* to you? Or is it because you're already so convinced that only bad things can happen to you that you just accept it?" He grabs my arms, giving them a light squeeze. "Look. No one knows better than I do the pain of loving someone who ends up leaving you," he starts, and for the first time since we met, he allows all the raw emotion burning him up to flood his features. Anguish sears his eyes. Agony ripples across his cheeks. His lashes are wet, clumping them together. Pain, whole and unbridled, fills every inch of his face. "But being here the last couple of days, seeing my family again, seeing *your* family… It's made me realize how much I was missing love in my life. I've been wandering around with an emptiness in my soul. I thought I could live without love, that I was *better off* without it, but I was wrong." He uses two fingers to tilt my chin up. "If *I* can admit that love is worth paying the price of pain, then you can, too. Pain is always going to be a part of the package when it comes to love, Maya. You can't miss out on it just because you're scared."

I stare up at him in utter disbelief. If you told me a week ago that The Jerk sitting next to me on a plane would be giving me a speech about how love is worth it, I would have laughed until I choked. But now, looking into his deep brown eyes, eyes that I've found so much comfort in, that light me up whenever I look into them, I can only bury my face into his chest.

Sarfaraz stumbles back, but he quickly regains his composure and holds on to me tightly. He presses his face into my neck, and I feel him shudder against my body. I reach up and cling to his jacket, fisting the material. I expect my breaths to come out in heavy sobs, but to my surprise, my tears are silent.

After what feels like only a minute but forever at the same time, I slowly pull my face away from him. I tilt my head back, and Sarfaraz dips his chin. Our lips are so incredibly close; I would only have to push up to my tiptoes, or he would only have to lower his chin for our mouths to meet. It'd be the easiest thing to move forward, to forget everything that keeps us apart.

Easy in theory, but cruel in practice.

Sarfaraz curls a damp strand of hair behind my ear, and I twist the material of his jacket between my fingers. My heart stutters, and the words spill out before I can stop them. "If you can give me one reason..." I start "...only one, why I shouldn't marry him..." my voice drops "...I won't."

Sarfaraz's chest stills, his fingers freezing over the shell of my ear. He searches my face, though I don't know what he's looking for. He moves his fingers to my chin, runs his thumb along my lower lip. Just when I think he's about to kiss me, he says, "You should marry him. Get your independence and live how you want to."

I drop my chin. I don't see his face as he lets go of me, as I take a step back from his embrace. When I look up, I won't be filled with disappointment. I'll be stronger. I'll be okay.

I tilt my face up and force my chest to cool, my breath to calm, my tears to stop. Sarfaraz's face is undecipherable. His fingers clutch the handle of his suitcase. "Where are you going to go?" I ask. "It's late."

"I'll find some hotel for the night," he responds. "Shouldn't be hard."

"And tomorrow?"

"I'll quietly leave on a flight home."

I grind my teeth. "Okay."

Sarfaraz rubs his fingers together, and at the last second, he extends his hand to me. "Good luck with my brother. I know he's going to make you happy. And I hope that you can accept that happiness someday."

I don't know how many goodbye handshakes I've exchanged with Sarfaraz. Every time I've said goodbye to him, we somehow end up crossing paths again one way or another. But I have a feeling that this time, the goodbye to what we shared will be permanent. The next time we see each other, we'll be in-laws.

Drinking in a steadying breath, I place my hand in his. I picture him pulling me in, wrapping his arms around me, kissing me until I can't think anymore.

But all he does is gently shake twice. Then he lets go. "Well. Khuda hafiz, then."

"Khuda hafiz," I reply, my words as numb as the rest of me.

He grabs his suitcase again, then puts his back to me. He steps past the gate and heads toward the back of the Uber to put his stuff away.

I stand there, staring at his retreating form, wanting to call him back, but I push the urge down. I watch him open the trunk, put his suitcase in, and then walk to the back door. He briefly hesitates, gripping the handle. He looks over at me. "I've been meaning to say something," he starts.

My face brightens. "About what?"

"Your laws," he explains, and that light dims again. "I know you say that you use them to make sense of the world…but that's what you did as a kid. You're an adult now. Maybe… maybe some laws are meant to be broken, if it's going to help you grow."

I blink to keep my tears from falling. "Yeah. Maybe."

"Right." A storm of emotions brews in his eyes, ranging from pain to longing to regret, but he gives one final wave before he slides into the car.

Once his car rounds the corner, once I'm sure he's gone, I head back inside. I grab the dirty clothes that I dropped on the floor in the hallway, then head to my room to put them in the laundry basket. I don't bother turning the light on; I just go inside and dump the clothes in the corner. I head for the door again but stop in my tracks when I notice something on my dresser that wasn't there before.

It's the snow globe I bought Sarfaraz in Switzerland. The one that I snuck into his suitcase and hoped he'd see when he returned home and unpacked. The one that I hoped he'd look at every now and then and remember our impromptu trip. That I hoped would make him remember me.

My heart falls from my chest to my feet. Slowly, I reach out and pick up the globe. The tiny flecks of fake snow immediately swim around in the dome, showering the happy couple inside and providing a romantic background for them.

First, I thought that the little man and woman inside were happy, that the vibrant colors and the breathtaking backdrop provided them with the perfect scenery for a perfect life. Then

I wondered if they were sad. If one of them was cheating on the other, if they were hiding their pain behind artfully hand-painted grins.

Now I know the truth. I don't know what they're feeling. They're putting on the faces of a joyful couple, but no one truly knows what's going on behind the scenes. The smiles so lovingly crafted on their mouths could be faker than the snow in their tiny world, or they could be realer than the glass that encircles them. Their gorgeous backdrop prevents them from living in the real world, but it also protects them from the harsh reality that those of us on the outside have to live in. Maybe they chose each other. Maybe they didn't. But no matter what, this is their reality.

I step back until my spine hits the wall. I cradle the snow globe carefully as I slowly slip down to the floor. I stare at them the whole time. The man and woman living in their perfect bubble. I let out a quiet sob, then press the snow globe to my chest as tears roll down my face.

I look through the window with blurry vision. The moon is bright tonight, round and full. People always reference the moon, the chaand, in their love poems. She's the most beautiful thing you can compare someone to. Taking a stroll in the moonlight is the most romantic thing you can do. Just staring up at her with someone you love is magical enough. But no one talks about how she takes that love and then abandons you, never reciprocating those feelings. You can stare and stare and stare at her, but she'll still disappear, leaving you with only the harsh light of the sun to burn your skin and make you feel incredibly stupid for loving something that you know leaves at the end of each night.

Sarfaraz said my curse wasn't real, and maybe it isn't, but all I know is that right now, my bad luck will always be with me—and getting married won't magically fix it.

33

Maya's Law #33:
The past will always haunt you.

After a while, I wipe my tears away and stand up. I put the snow globe into a drawer. I'm not sure if I ever want to look at it again.

With that done, I leave the room. I didn't notice it earlier, but my wet hair sits heavily against my upper back, seeping through the cloth and sticking to my skin. I shift uncomfortably, squeezing some residual water out. I guess I was so concerned with stopping Sarfaraz that I barely towel-dried my hair.

I stop in front of my mother's room. I tentatively knock on the door. There's no answer, so I twist the doorknob and let myself in. I know I should probably have waited for a proper response from her, but she's barged into my room enough times over the years without knocking that I think I deserve a pass.

Light snores echo around the room as I tiptoe over to the bed. I peer at her face for a second. Even in the darkness, I can make out her soft features: her elegant nose, her delicate cheekbones, her firm chin. The only hints of aging are the few graying hairs on her head, and she'll quickly cover them up with dye once she notices them.

Her breath hitches, and she blinks her eyes open. "Maya?" she croaks, her voice thick with sleep. She begins to push herself up. "What's wrong? Why are you in here?"

"No, no, lie back down," I quickly say. I grab the blanket and pull it back so I can crawl in next to her. I get as close as I can, nestling my head in the crook of her neck. "I didn't... I didn't want to be alone tonight."

"Oh, of course," she croons. She wraps her arms around me and holds me close to her chest. "My baby is getting married tomorrow. I'm going to miss you so, so much."

I drink in the lingering scent of her signature Michael Kors perfume, and for a second, the nostalgia spreads like an ache through my veins, only to be interrupted when she mentions missing me. I swallow back a groan. "I'm not going anywhere, Ammi. It's not like I'm dying."

"No, you're not," she agrees. She gently runs her fingers through my hair. "But things won't be the same. For twenty-eight years, you've always come home to me. And after Hibba got married, I wasn't as sad because I still had you. But you won't be coming home to me from now on."

I tilt my head up. "I'm still my own person. I'll come see you whenever I want. Just because I'll have a husband at home, doesn't mean you're not my family."

"I know that. But relationships are difficult. You can't live how you used to. You're not making decisions for only yourself. You must compromise, and it's not going to be easy." Her fingers pause. "Marriage is the hardest thing in the world."

"Is that what happened with you and Baba? You couldn't reach a compromise?"

"Yes...and no," she admits. "I don't think we were compatible. But what did our parents care of compatibility? His parents thought I was a good girl, and my parents thought it was an excellent rishta. We met only a few times before agreeing. But how can you know someone after such a short while? And know them well enough to make such a huge, life-changing decision?"

My stomach clenches. "What if you have spent time with them?" I whisper. "What if you meet the other person...and for some reason, they know your soul?"

"Oh, Maya. That kind of love is only found in poetry, not real life. All you can do is meet someone and hope it works." She runs her hand along my back. "And it's certainly worked for you, right?"

I'm silent for a moment, then I say, "Right. I guess it's just... with the wedding tomorrow..."

"You're scared?" Ammi tilts her head to the side. "It's okay to be scared. I certainly was. So much was changing for me, and I didn't know what the outcome was going to be. I could only hope that I would end up happy; I had no guarantees."

I gulp. "I'm sorry you didn't end up happy, Ammi."

"Now, who said that?" she asks. "I'm very happy with how my life ended up. I don't have the love of a husband, but I have the love of my two daughters, and that is always going to be enough for me." She wipes at a tiny tear poking out of the corner of my eye. "You and your sister are my whole family."

"You're my family, too." I sniffle. "I've never needed anyone more than you and Baji."

"But it's not about *needing* someone, jaanu," she says, her voice as gentle as a leaf. "The love of your sister and the love of your mother are different from the love you find from a partner."

"You know it's okay not to have that love, right?" I point out, wincing as the words leave my mouth. Here we are, having a sweet moment, and I can't resist the urge to correct my mother's old-school thoughts. "It's okay to want to be alone."

To my surprise, Ammi nods. "It is, if you want." She curls a strand of hair over my ear. "But, Maya, you've never wanted to be alone. And I don't want you to be alone, either." She presses me closer to her. "Listen, beta. Your sister has her own family now. I'm not going to be around forever. Before you were engaged, I worried so much about what was going to happen to you when I was gone, because you so stubbornly refused to let me find a husband for you, or to look for one yourself, even though I would have accepted anyone you brought home as long as you were happy." She smooths my bangs back. "But that's all changing now. You're going to be married. You're going to be happy." She blinks quickly, and her throat bobs. "My baby is grown." She runs her thumb along my cheekbone. "I'm so proud of you, Maya. I know I don't say it often, and I should say it more, but I am. You've been through so much, but you've gotten to such a good point in your life." She taps the spot between my brows. "Things can only get better from now on. And it all starts tomorrow." She kisses my forehead. "So, you should do us both a favor and let us sleep. You don't want to have bags under your eyes for the wedding."

Right now, listening to my mom, who stares at me with equal parts happiness and pain, it hits me. My whole life, I've thought Ammi was overbearing; that she cared too much about what others thought; that she put her own wants before mine. But she never did that. It was always me. I was the one who dictated my life according to what others were going to say about my mom. I was the one who made decisions to ease her burden. I put her wants before mine. She's never expected me to do anything I didn't want to. She defends me to families who try to speak ill of me. She reassures me when I fall into a spiral. She gives me choice. And I couldn't see that because I didn't want to. It's so much easier to give control of your life to someone else because it prevents you from having to make any kind of life-altering decisions of your own, because then you have no one to blame but yourself when it all goes wrong.

All my mom did was try her best with the fate that Allah gave her. Maybe now it's my turn to do the same.

I swallow the growing bulge in my throat. "Right," I say. "I'm sorry I woke you."

"Don't be sorry. I should have come to your room in the first place. I should have known that you'd be worried, even scared. Your life is going to change completely." She kisses my forehead, then rests her chin on my head. "But everything's going to be okay. *You're* going to be okay."

I lift my arm and place it on her stomach, snuggling closer to her. As I will my body to relax, I can only pray that she's right. She *has* to be right.

Because no matter what, I'm getting married tomorrow.

34

Maya's Law #34:
If you think it's too late, it is.

I don't know what non-desi weddings are like—I haven't been to any—but brown weddings, *especially* for the bride, tend to be a happy yet somber occasion. Everyone's thrilled that two people have chosen each other for the rest of their lives and are completing half their deen...until they remember that the girl is leaving her family and her home and everything she's ever known to start a new life.

It's why I can sit in the makeup chair and look absolutely miserable.

My makeup artist, Laiba, frets over the heavy bags under my eyes. "What's happened to your face?"

I stare up at her, a dreary air enveloping me. "I don't sleep well," I deadpan.

Ammi flashes me a disapproving glare from her spot on the bed where she's pulling my jewelry out of a suitcase. "Maya, don't stress yourself," she scolds, as if those words are supposed to make me feel less stressed. She smiles at Laiba. "My poor daughter is riddled with nerves. Please, take good care of her."

Hibba Baji watches the whole exchange with an unconvinced stare. She flashes me a look of concern. When I shake my head, she returns her attention to Iqra, making sure there aren't any lines in her shalwar kameez before sending her off.

Laiba huffs as she switches brushes. "Well, you're lucky I'm one of the best. I can take care of this so you'll look absolutely beautiful on your wedding day."

I can't quite believe it. It's my wedding day.

I expect to feel dread, sadness, maybe even panic, but all I feel is numb. I was numb when I stepped into the shower. I was numb when I dried myself off. I was even numb when I put on my wedding dress. I found it while we were window-shopping, and I fell in love with it instantly. It's technically a two-piece dress. In the classic Pakistani style, the sandy blouse is long-sleeved, and the hem of the kameez stops above my knees. The skirt is heavy and full and trails behind me. Strips of pearly beads intertwine with lace in a zigzag pattern, and small cream and pink flowers scatter along the skirt.

Gold dusts my eyelids, though Laiba blended it, so it fades outward into black. She sweeps black eyeliner across my lash line, at the top and at the bottom. She dabs the barest brush of blush to my cheekbones, making it look natural instead of painted on. The finishing touch is a swipe of red on my lips, making them look big and bold. She does my hair in poofy curls, gathering the top half at the back of my head and pulling it into a side-part.

Laiba leaves once her work is done, so it's me, Ammi, and Hibba Baji in the room. I fiddle with the jewelry Ammi

brings over to the vanity and sets in front of me. I pull on
a pair of red and silver chudiyan. I put on a couple of rings,
too, though I make sure to leave my actual ring finger bare.
My engagement ring might be with a bunch of pricks who
robbed us, but Imtiaz will still need to slide the wedding band
around my finger.

Ammi places another choker around my neck, but this one
is gold, with a large smooth stone in the middle. She drapes
another necklace over my head, gold with silver stones, that
stops right in between my breasts. I slide in the jhumkas myself, because putting on earrings is definitely something I can
do, but I have her place the tikka on my forehead, making sure
it doesn't slide out of place by pinning it to my hair.

Once it's secure, the last thing to put on is the veil. It's the
same sandy color as my dress, but it takes both Ammi and
Hibba Baji to pin it securely to the back of my hair so it's not
in any danger of falling off. When it's done, they both take a
step back to drink me in.

I tentatively stand. I shyly drop my gaze, not used to so
much fanfare or so much attention on me. "How do I look?"

Despite the "you're doing the wrong thing" look in her eyes
earlier, Hibba Baji tears up. "You look beautiful, Maya," she
says. She wraps her arms around me. "I'm so happy for you."

That makes one of us. I smile because Ammi can still see
my face. I pull away from the hug, and when I do, Ammi has
tears slipping down her cheeks. "Meri pyaari beti," she coos.
She steps forward and carefully cups my face, making sure she
doesn't smudge my "hundreds of dollars" makeup look. "This
is your big, big day."

Okay, I might not be 100 percent about this decision, but
at least it's worth it to make my mother happy, and to not
further ruin her reputation in the eyes of our community. "I
know, Ammi."

"You're going to have someone to take care of you," she continues. "My work with you is done."

My happy face drops. I can see Hibba Baji set her jaw, but that doesn't stop the groan that rumbles my chest. "I don't *need* anyone to take care of me, Ammi," I grit. "I can take care of myself." I step back, out of her grip. The warm fluttery feeling I experienced while lying next to her last night slowly seeps out of my body. "I'm not marrying Imtiaz because I need to be taken care of."

"Jee, jee, of course not," Ammi pacifies. She reaches out to adjust my veil. "You're marrying him because you love him."

Love. I know it's not something I've experienced much romantically in my life, so I thought I would be okay with waiting to see if it would happen to me after I got married. In fact, I used to think that marriage wasn't only about love—it's about compatibility, wanting the same things, and being able to make compromises when necessary. It's about mutual respect and knowing the other person. Love is something that's an added bonus. It makes the colors around you brighter, it makes the breeze feel better, and it makes the grass smell sweeter. It doesn't have to be there, but if it is, you're one of the lucky ones. You'll know for sure that the person going through the sunflower field with you won't let go of your hand. And it's not bad if you decide to wait for love to grow; it's ultimately up to you as an individual.

But after everything I've experienced in the last few weeks, I finally see that I don't want to wait for love to grow. Even though people keep telling me that I never know what's going to happen in the future, I think I've always known, deep in my bones and with every beat of my heart, that I can never love Imtiaz in the way that I'm supposed to. In the way people write love poems about. In the way people yearn for when they watch rom-coms. And in the way Imtiaz *deserves* to be loved.

I think about the way he agreed to have the wedding in Pakistan because my family's here. Most of his family and friends couldn't make it because it's expensive to fly to Pakistan, but because he cared more about what I wanted, he agreed to have his wedding here while people *he* wanted were missing. I think about how whenever we were together at home, he'd be happy to do whatever I wanted because he was having fun if *I* was having fun. And I think about the fact that *despite* knowing my intentions to leave for another country for two whole years after getting engaged, he still trusted me enough to let me go because it's what I wanted—and, quite frankly, what I *needed*.

Mr. Porter is right. Imtiaz doesn't deserve the humiliation of me leaving him and he doesn't deserve to marry someone who doesn't love him and doesn't know if she can ever love him in the way he wants.

Guilt ensnares my stomach and holds on with a vice grip. My throat closes up, and something in my chest twists. *Imtiaz doesn't deserve this* repeats over and over in my head until it drowns out every other rational thought. This isn't even about me anymore; this is about me hurting someone who I was… *using*. The word causes the guilt to sit heavier in my gut, but it's what I did. I *used* him without thinking about the consequences. I *used* him so I could escape.

The thoughts swirling around in my head make me move without thinking. I step away from Ammi's grip. "Not even that," I say. "I'm marrying him because I'm *tired* of feeling caged!"

Ammi takes a step back. "Kya? I don't understand."

I loose a strangled breath. "Imtiaz is a great guy," I start, "but I'm not in love with him, and I don't know if I can ever be. I only agreed to get engaged because it got you off my back."

Confusion stretches across Ammi's forehead, but she steels

herself and puts her hands on my arms. "You're just scared. I know we talked about it last night, Maya, but you don't have to be afraid. You're worried that what happened to Baba and me is going to happen to you, but I promise you it won't. You're going to be fine."

"How do I know that?" I push her arms off me, and I continue despite her stunned expression. "How do I know that I won't wake up one day and find my side of the bed *empty*?" I suck in a deep breath and blink away my tears. "I know love can happen after marriage. I've seen it, so I'm hoping that it happens to me. But what if I wake up one day and realize I've been sleeping next to a stranger my whole life? What if I wake up one day and realize that I spent the only life I have being unhappy?" My mind drifts back to my conversation with Sarfaraz last night. "I thought being married was enough. I thought the gamble was worth it." I lift my head. "But I want to be married to someone I *know* I love. I never thought it would happen for me, but that's because I was pushing it away. And I don't want to push it away anymore. I was willing to see if I could fall in love after marrying him but that was before—" I cut myself off.

I think Ammi's shell-shocked, because anger doesn't color her face, nor does sadness. Confusion floods her features. "Before what?"

I stay silent, but Hibba Baji opens her mouth. She's been quiet during the whole exchange, but now she says, "Before she met Sarfaraz."

Ammi's eyes widen to the size of saucers. "You're in love with *Sarfaraz*?"

"No." At both of their unimpressed faces, I wince. "Fine, I don't know if I love him but…but he makes me feel things. Things I thought I never could." I move on before they can ask any more questions. "I don't know how I feel. But what I *do* know is that I want more in my life than to be married because you won't let me have any freedom. I'm an *adult*, Ammi. I don't need to be taken care of, I don't need to please people I don't know, and I *definitely* don't need to be married to be happy." I clench my fists. "You're right. I don't want to be alone. But you can still be alone when you're with someone, and in my opinion, there's nothing worse than that feeling. I need to be with someone who I *know* won't make me feel like that. And I don't want to have to start over two or ten or twenty years from now when I realize that I didn't marry the right person for me in the first place."

I huff, all the steam flushing right out of my system. With my body cooling down, I'm fully registering what I said. I can't believe all that stuff…*poured out of me*. But I can't bring myself to regret saying it. I think the words have always been there, lying dormant, the emotion hiding under my skin until it couldn't be hidden anymore.

Ammi opens and closes her mouth a few times. Her brows move up and down like a caterpillar is crawling on her forehead. It's finally happened—I've stunned a brown mother into silence. "I didn't know you felt like that," she settles on.

"That's because I didn't want you to know. I knew it would be worthless telling you how I feel, because how I feel has never mattered. Every time I want to bring it up, you make a comment about how happy you are that I'm not going to be alone anymore…and then the guilt takes over."

She chokes out a sob as she comes over to me, grabbing my face. "*Of course* what you feel matters, jaanu," she breathes. "Your happiness is all I've ever wanted. I thought I could help make you happy by getting you married, because it would mean you would be in love and safe and secure."

"I don't need—"

"To be married to be secure," Ammi finishes for me. "I

know. But, beta, you need to realize that I grew up in a time where the only way I could get any freedom was to be married. And that didn't work out for me, so I had to struggle *alone*. I'm damn proud of the job I did with you and Hibba, but I know firsthand how *hard* it is to be alone. That's why I needed to know that you two would be taken care of. I know what it's like to grow alone. I have my daughters, yes, but you have your own lives. I don't have anyone to be by my side, and while I don't regret focusing on you two instead of finding someone to marry again, I do feel sadness." She rests a hand on her chest. "This is not a feeling I would wish on my worst enemy, let alone my own dear daughters. I'm not going to be around forever, Maya, and I know that sounds very cliché, but it's an anxiety you'll understand when *you're* a parent. But…" She brushes at a tiny tear that escapes my eye. "But if this isn't what you want…"

I sniffle deeply. "It doesn't matter," I insist. "Our whole family is out there waiting for me to get married. I promised Imtiaz I would marry him, and I don't want to break that promise. I have to do it now."

"No, you don't."

I stiffen, my blood running cold. I turn around, and Imtiaz stands in the doorframe. I have to admit, he looks incredibly handsome in his black sherwani. The light in the room reflects off the gold buttons that line his chest. A mauve-and-gold shawl is draped over his arms. To complete the regal look, a shimmering gold turban sits on top of his head.

When I heard his voice, I expected his eyes to be red, his nose runny, his lips puckered like he's trying to hold back tears. Instead, he has a kind smile on his face. He dips his head at Ammi and Hibba Baji. "Could I have a second alone with Maya?"

My stomach churns as Ammi and Hibba Baji awkwardly

shuffle out of the room. Ammi shuts the door behind them, and then it's just Imtiaz and me. I pull on my fingers. We stand in tense silence, and it feels as thick as the heat outside at the height of the day.

I can't take the quiet anymore. I clear my throat. "I can explain—" I begin.

"I think I kind of always knew," Imtiaz cuts in. I clamp my mouth shut, and at my silence, he continues. "That you didn't love me."

A bulge forms in the back of my throat. "Imtiaz—"

"And I was okay with that," he interrupts, and again, I quiet down. "Truth be told, I don't know if I loved you, either. I mean, when the rishta came to me and we met again, I thought it would be nice to get to know and possibly marry someone I already knew in the past. I thought maybe it was even some kind of fate." He chuckles. "I mean, who would have thought that a girl I knew in university would end up being the first rishta that my parents brought to me? She's pretty, she's smart, and she's ready for a commitment. I knew we were rushing things, but I knew I couldn't let this opportunity pass me by. I thought we could get to know each other and things would work themselves out. And for a while, it *did* feel like that. We got along way better than I thought we would, to be honest.

"But I had my concerns, too," he goes on. "You were always hesitant, but I was okay with you taking your time to open up to me. I thought that once we were married and things settled, it'd be okay." When he looks at me, I expect anger or sadness to cloud his features. Instead, I see something like... acceptance. "Do you love me?"

My breath catches. "I could try." After a beat, I ask, "Do you love me?"

"I could try, too," he admits. "But honestly... I think we're too different. With my work schedule and with how little we actually know each other, I think it'll make things harder for us." Imtiaz clicks his tongue. "I don't think it's fair to base a marriage on a gamble, do you?"

I chew my tongue. "No."

He smirks ruefully. "We shouldn't get married, Maya."

His words hit me like a wave, but instead of despair filling my lungs, it's relief. "Are you sure?"

Imtiaz steps over to me. He grabs my arms and gives them a light squeeze. "Maya, I don't think I was ever ready to get married, either. I knew my work schedule wasn't going to be fair to you, and after spending my entire life buried in textbooks, I wanted some time for myself. I truly didn't think I wanted to settle down yet. But my mom kept insisting it was time for me to find someone, and if I waited too long, then there'd be nobody left for me to choose from." He lifts a shoulder. "You know desi moms."

I make a noise that's a half hiccup, half laugh. "Yeah, I do."

"I thought that because we already knew each other, things would fall into place, but I don't think that's going to happen anymore. So…" He drops his hands. "Let's not get married. And so it's not on *your* conscience, *I'm* the one dumping *you*."

I laugh, the sound light and airy instead of tight like it was before. "Are you sure?"

"Yeah," he starts. "I have a lot of respect for your izzat. Yes, people will talk about you because you were the one dumped, but at least they won't be saying that you were a vixen or something because you broke up with me."

I snort again. He laughs, as well, and for a full minute, the two of us crack up at the absurdity of the situation. After a moment, though, I sober up. I offer Imtiaz an apologetic look. "I'm sorry."

"Don't be," he insists. "This means that we won't be wasting our time being with each other when we should be with people we love instead."

"True," I agree. I fix him with a hopeful look. "Can we still be friends?"

Imtiaz's mouth relaxes. "I'd like that."

"Good," I say. "I'm going to need a friend to help me send back all the wedding gifts. I can't do it on my own."

"Don't worry, I'm not going anywhere," he assures me. Suddenly, Imtiaz's face morphs into panic. "Speaking of which, you need to get to the bus station."

"What?"

"Bhaiyya," he explains, gaining momentum. "He called to wish me luck this morning. He said that he couldn't get a flight out of Karachi, so he's going to take a bus to Islamabad. He's probably on the way to the station right now. I may not be going anywhere, but he's leaving."

My chest twists as I stare at Imtiaz. How did he know? Were we *that* obvious? Or maybe he overheard me talking with Ammi and Hibba Baji; I don't know how much he heard. Either way, my palms grow sweaty. "Imtiaz…"

"Maya, it's okay," he asserts. "I noticed there was some weird tension between you guys that first day, and I thought I was imagining things, until I passed by the door and heard you talking. I *promise*, it's okay. My brother's been through so much, and I love him, and I care about you, so if you two can figure out how to make each other happy, I'm fine with that. Even if you don't love him, I know you like him."

I do. I *do* like him.

"That, plus…" He grabs my wrist and pushes my chudiyan out of the way. نارفراس stares back at me. "I noticed this at the maiyun. I suspected before this, but at this point, I definitely knew something was up."

I grimace. I point to the mehendi. "This wasn't my fault, though. It's a funny story—"

"Which you don't have time to tell." He drops my wrist. "You need to stop him. If you don't, he's going to go back home and spend the rest of his life alone."

"That's assuming he even *wants* to be with me. I asked him once—" I cut myself off as Imtiaz's eyes widen with surprise "—which I'm really sorry about, by the way—but he told me to get married."

"That's just my brother's annoying, righteous self," he dismisses. "Always putting himself last." He grips my arms tighter. "Please, go after him. It may not have worked out between us, but you're still my friend, Maya. I want you to be happy. You *deserve* to be happy. I want my brother to be happy. And if you two are going to be happy with each other, then you should go for it."

I *do* deserve to be happy. Dr. Khan's been right all along; I need to put myself first. "Right." I glance at the clock in the corner of the room, and despair floods my gut. "Damn it, it's already eleven! I won't make it in time!"

"Yes, you will," Imtiaz assures me.

"How? It's Dhuhr right now. The traffic is going to be insane because people are headed to and from the masjids all over the city. No car is going to make it to the bus station."

"Then we'll take my uncle's motorcycle."

I blink. "You can ride a *motorcycle*?"

"Now's not the time," he reminds me. "We need to go."

I stare at him uneasily. "Are we really running out on our wedding so you can take me to your brother?"

"Yeah, but let's be real." He smirks. "This will be *way* more entertaining than our wedding."

35

Maya's Law #35:
Sometimes love isn't enough.
Some laws are made to be broken.

There's no time to change, so I have to leave the house in this giant wedding dress. I pick up my skirt and follow behind Imtiaz, but I stagger to a stop when I realize Ammi and Hibba Baji are still lingering in the hall.

Ammi looks between the two of us. "So? What's happening?"

Imtiaz looks at me, then back to my mother. "We're not getting married, Auntie. I'm sorry. And we need to stop my brother from leaving the country."

Ammi looks to me. Before she can speak, I open my mouth. "Ammi, I need to—"

To my surprise, though, she cuts me off. "Is this what you want?"

Silently, I nod.

"Okay. You go. I'll take care of everything here."

A rush of relief overwhelms me, and I tear up as I throw my arms around my mother. She hugs me back, her grip around me tight. I snuggle into her, like I did when I was a kid. I inhale the familiar scent of her perfume, and in that second, I know even if things don't work out today, I'll be okay.

"This is sweet and all," Hibba Baji interjects, "but you don't have time for this!"

"Oh, right," I say.

We quickly let each other go, and Ammi gives me one last kiss on the forehead. "Go on."

Most of the family have left for the masjid already (I do *not* envy Ammi or Hibba Baji right now, who will have to deal with the immediate fallout of the bride and groom deciding not to get hitched, after all), so we don't run into anyone as we rush through the house. Imtiaz opens the gate for me, and we head for the motorcycle. He gives me a helmet, and I slip it on over my veil, which is too tightly secured to my head for me to take it off. I have to gather my veil and my skirt and hike them both up so I can settle on the back of the motorcycle without risking the cloth getting caught in the engine. Tiny cracks splinter in my heart every time a new layer of dirt dusts along the edge, but I don't have the time for that right now.

Imtiaz kick-starts the engine, I wrap my arms around his torso, and we're flying down the street. My hairspray-soaked curls whip in the breeze, and I spit strands out of my mouth.

He expertly weaves through the traffic. In Pakistan, there's no such thing as a single lane; you go wherever you want. I would even dare to say the traffic is worse than in Toronto or New York; at least in those cities, most of the time, people follow traffic laws.

I catch a few stares from people in the cars next to us. A giggle erupts from my chest.

"What?" Imtiaz shouts over the wind.

I lean forward to say into his ear, "This is the most cliché moment of my life. As someone who has had terrible luck with romance in the past, I can't believe I'm riding on a motorcycle in my wedding dress to stop a guy from leaving for the airport."

He chuckles. "Does it make you feel any better that the guy is your fiancé's brother?"

I'm glad that we're already at a stage where we can joke about it. "Definitely."

Thankfully, because we're on the motorcycle, it doesn't take us long to reach the bus station. Imtiaz gets off first, and he has to help me off because of the layers of skirt. Once I'm secure on the ground, he jerks his head toward the entrance of the station. "Go on, then."

I know I'm crunched for time, but I still take a moment to cup Imtiaz's face and kiss his cheek. I leave a red stain on his skin, but I don't have the time to care. I skim my thumbs over his cheekbones. "Thank you," I say.

"Yeah, well..." He waves me off good-naturedly, and though I still don't know him that well, even I can tell it's masking some hurt. "If you guys don't end up getting married someday, I'm never forgiving you."

I give him a sad nod, which he returns. Then, I pick up my skirts and run toward the station.

I'm glad I fought against Ammi when it came to the shoes, because the heels are just short enough that I can still run in them without the fear of twisting my ankle or toppling over. For some reason, though, there are a *lot* of people in this bus station. I catch numerous strange stares at my attire, my panicked expression, and my running, but I ignore all of it as I

scan the crowds. Imtiaz didn't say *which* bus Sarfaraz was taking, so I have no idea what I'm dealing with. My only hope
is to find his face and pray he hasn't set his mind firmly on
leaving. I'm sweating, my dress is heavy, and I haven't slept
properly, so I'm exhausted—but I'm not giving up.

Finally, I see a very dark, very familiar head. The body is
clad in a red sweater and dark-wash jeans. I'm out of breath
from running, my legs ache, and my lungs feel like they're on
fire, but I gather all the strength I can and shout, "Sarfaraz!"

A few people turn at my outburst, but the only person I
care about turns around with surprise. His eyes widen when
he registers my face, and they somehow widen even more
when he takes in my outfit. I gulp in another lungful of air,
grab my skirt, and stomp over to him. He takes the hint and
starts walking toward me.

When we meet in the middle, we're both silent. Me because I'm struggling to catch my breath, and Sarfaraz because
he can't seem to find any words *to* say. He can only stare at me
in utter shock. After a stunned moment, he speaks. "What are
you doing here?" he asks, his voice numb. "You're supposed
to be at your wedding."

I look down at my outfit, then back up at him. "Well, I
was planning on being there…" I explained, twisting my fingers. "But the mood kinda died when I called off the wedding, so I bailed."

Sarfaraz's jaw drops. "You called it off?" he wonders, a hint
of hope lining his tone.

"Actually, Imtiaz did…" I correct "…when he realized his
bride didn't want to marry him."

His lips pull downward. "Maya, if this has anything to do
with—"

"Watch the ego," I cut him off. "You didn't do this." I
pause, tilting my head to the side. "Well, not technically.

What you did was help me realize that marriage needs to be more than one person constantly giving up. It needs to be about compromise. It's about the messy fights, but it's also about making up and making messes and showing up for each other, every day."

Hope lines his forehead, but his tone is still hesitant as he asks, "What are you saying?"

"I'm saying I don't know if I love you," I start. "It'd be crazy of me to say that after only like, a week." I step closer to him. "But I do know that I can't sleep at night unless you're the one next to me. I know that no one has made me feel so safe or secure since my dad left. I know that when I think of happiness, I think of your laugh, because it's all I need to hear to make me smile. I know you're a terrible travel companion, and a know-it-all, and that you'd rather pull away from love than walk toward it because you've been burned too many times." I step toward him again, and now we're chest to chest. I have to tip my head back to continue staring into his eyes, which are starting to get misty. "I know we drive each other crazy, and that we've hurt each other, and we probably will hurt each other again." My throat tightens, and I drop my voice. "But I know we can count on each other to be there, even when it's hard." I raise a shaky hand and caress his cheek. His stubble is scratchy underneath my fingers, but it sends a thrill through my stomach. Sarfaraz relaxes immediately when I touch him, sending a flare of hope down my spine. "And what I know the most is that when it comes to us, I don't know anything." My heart thumps against my chest, threatening to fall right out. "But if you're willing, I want to find those answers with you."

Now that the words have rushed out of me, I stop, trying to collect myself. Sarfaraz doesn't move. He doesn't pull away from my touch, but he hasn't responded yet, either. My stomach flips, and for a second, I think I've made the wrong decision, that maybe he's too good of a man to want to get with his brother's ex, or that he doesn't like me the same way I like him, but before my thoughts can spiral any further, Sarfaraz gently reaches up. He wraps a stray curl around his finger, and then tucks it behind my ear. I open my mouth, but he swallows my words with a kiss.

Any and all rational thoughts fly right out the window. I grab his face, kissing him back. We're in a public place, but neither one of us cares as he wraps his arms around my lower back and pulls me to his chest. I thread my fingers through his hair, snaking my arms around his neck as we continue to kiss. His beard scratches my face and smudges my lipstick, but I don't even care. In fact, I relish in the tingles that touch my face and run down the rest of my body.

We both have to stop for air. We're panting, our breaths coming rough and ragged, but Sarfaraz breaks into a huge grin as he nudges his nose against mine. "I can't believe you did this." He laughs breathlessly. "I can't believe you ran out on your wedding."

"Technically, *I* was the one who got jilted," I remind him, a giggle rumbling my chest. "But I can't, either. I didn't know I had it in me."

He pulls back. "What about your laws?"

I hum for a second, then grin. "Well, I spoke to my lawyer, and he told me that some laws are meant to be broken."

Sarfaraz smirks. "Sounds like a terrible lawyer."

"I'm definitely paying him too much."

He laughs, and I'm reminded again of why it's my favorite thing: it sounds like a warm loving home. His face drops, and he tightens his grip around my waist. "I'm sorry I didn't fight for you," he whispers. "Last night when we said goodbye, I knew what you were asking. I couldn't bring myself to take away what could have been my brother's happiness, even if it meant sacrificing my own. But…" He toys with the end of one of my curls. "I know that's a sore spot for you."

"It's okay," I tell him. I rest my palm on the spot where his pulse races under my touch. "I needed to fight for you, too. I needed to stop running."

When he beams at me, it's like he's brought light to an incredibly dark cave. "So," he starts, "you've beaten your bad-luck curse."

I click my tongue, gripping his arms and leaning back. I pretend to take in his body. "I don't know," I tease. "You still seem like a real risk."

Sarfaraz flashes me a look that says he's not impressed, so I let go of him and step back. He frowns. "What are you doing?"

I don't respond. Instead, I drop down to one knee. He doesn't even bother to conceal the shock flitting on his face, his jaw going slack. I smirk. "Sarfaraz Porter, will you go out on a date with me, and then take it from there? With no pressure from anyone on what we do and when we do it?"

He shakes his head, but he still laughs. "Yes," he answers. He hauls me to my feet. He sweeps me into his arms and lifts me into the air, spinning me a few times. He sets me back down on my feet, then kisses me again. It's a quick moment, but I remind myself that it's not the last kiss I'll ever receive from him. "Okay, so I definitely missed my bus," he states.

I gaze up at him. "You know, sometimes the wrong bus can take you to the right station."

Sarfaraz leans back. "Isn't it a *train*?"

I can't help the impressed squeal that erupts from my throat. "So, you *were* paying close attention when we watched *Crash Landing on You!*"

He shrugs nonchalantly, but he still grins. "So, now what?"

I grab his wrist and check his watch. "Well, it's past Dhuhr." I look up at him. "We could either hit up my wedding reception where both our families are waiting around and wondering what happened, or we could go grab lunch somewhere."

Sarfaraz pulls his lips back at the mention of our families. He pretends to think on it for a second, then says, "I think we should grab lunch."

I laugh, and for once, the sound isn't strangled, like it had to be pulled from the parts of my soul I was once convinced were dead. "It can be our first official date."

"Showing up to a first date in a wedding dress?" He cocks a brow. "Reeks of desperation, don't you think?"

"What can I say?" I loop my arm through his, resting my head on the spot below his shoulder. "I've decided to be someone who runs *toward* love instead of away from it."

Our fingers interlock. "And who, pray tell, convinced you to be said person?" he wonders, his tone light.

I stare up at him, and when our eyes meet, a sense of calm settles in my belly. "Some guy I sat next to on a plane. He was oddly insightful."

"You'll have to tell me all about him," Sarfaraz comments as we reach the exit.

"Don't worry," I assure him. The doors in front of us open. "We've got plenty of time."

EPILOGUE

I burst through the door, my heels skidding against the hardwood floor. "I'm so sorry I'm late," I apologize. I shrug out of my brown jacket, hang it on the coat rack, then head over to the orange loveseat and drop my purse in front of it. The soft purple hues of the evening sun stream in through the blinds.

Dr. Khan waves me off. "It's no problem. I'm just glad that you showed up to an appointment."

"I'm sorry," I say again. "I had no idea that I was going to end up staying in Pakistan for the whole summer. My aunts and uncles kept convincing me and my mom to stay later, and then when I got back, I was so busy with the new school year and packing up my stuff from the apartment. And *then* when I managed to make an appointment, I had to cancel because Hibba Baji needed a last-minute babysitter."

"Still," Dr. Khan begins. "The end of June to late October is a long time to go without really talking to me. I know we had a couple of phone calls in between, but I want to know *everything*. Last time we talked, you were getting married. And now you're not married." She leans forward. "What *happened*?"

I smirk. "I did what you said. I did something for *me*."

"And what exactly is that?"

"I realized I was getting married for the wrong reasons." I stare at the tips of my black ankle boots. "I didn't love Imtiaz. And while I was willing to see if I could fall in love with him, I realized that the both of us deserved better than taking a chance on something that big."

"So, you're still single, then?" Dr. Khan asks.

My smile grows bigger. "I wouldn't exactly say that, either."

"You're still with Imtiaz, but you're not married to him?"

"No," I clarify. "We're not together anymore. I have a lot of respect for him, but it wouldn't have worked out."

"Okay," she drawls. "Then who are you in a relationship with?" she questions.

The words come out in a rush. "I'm kind of dating his secret older half brother, who was the guy who sat next to me on the plane ride there but who became…so much more than that."

Dr. Khan blinks a few times. Her pen stills against the notebook in her lap. She clicks it so that the tip disappears, then sets both items to the side. "I'm sorry, you're going to have to start from the beginning."

I do. I start with the airport, then move on to Switzerland, and then Pakistan, and finally, the wedding. When I'm finished, Dr. Khan stares at me for a second. "You do not pay me enough to do this job."

I can't help the laugh that bursts from my chest. "Are you allowed to say that as my therapist?"

"Probably not," she acknowledges with a chuckle. "I'm just

having a hard time believing that the Maya Mirza I know would do something like that."

"I know." I suck in a breath. "What I did to Imtiaz wasn't great, but—"

"No, that's not what I meant," she cuts in. "I meant that I'm surprised you took a stand for yourself like that."

"Oh." I grin. "Well, sometimes you meet people who make you brave."

"I need to meet this guy who apparently did in one week what I was trying to do for three months," she teases. She places her elbow on the armrest of her chair. "How are things going with your families? Tensions must be running high."

"It's not exactly…good," I explain. "But it's not terrible, either. My mother is very supportive, and she's quick to shut down anyone who tries to bad-mouth me, though I'm sure people are still doing it. And Imtiaz, obviously, is cool with it. To be honest, he's way happier to be focusing on his career. We talked the other day, and he told me he led his first solo surgery. I'm super proud of him."

"And their father?" she presses. "You mentioned that the two of you had a conversation in Pakistan."

I tilt my head to the side. "That's the one thing that's still sort of strained. But…" My lips curl up at the corner. "They had a sit-down a couple of weeks after they got back from Pakistan. It looks like things might be on the mend for them." I cross my arms over my chest. "It's rocky, and it's not perfect, but if this trip has taught me anything, it's that nothing in life is perfect, no matter how you try to frame the world. But sometimes you find friends in places you would never guess, and sometimes you have great family members, and maybe, *just* maybe, you'll meet an important person in the way you least expected."

She shakes her head in awe. "That all seems like such a wild coincidence."

"But that's the thing, Dr. Khan. Maybe…maybe it *wasn't* a coincidence. Maybe it was fate." At her inviting stare, I keep going. "I mean, my whole life I've lived as if I was cursed with bad luck. No matter what I did, it seemed like bad things kept happening to me. I thought that sitting next to Sarfaraz on the plane was bad luck. I thought that my plane having to make an emergency landing in Switzerland was even *worse* luck. And then when I thought things couldn't get worse, my future brother-in-law ended up being the guy that I kissed earlier that *day*." I tilt my head. "But maybe that wasn't bad stuff. Maybe it was what I needed to wake up and realize that… bad things kept happening to me because I *let* them happen. I wallowed in the terrible things and didn't stop to realize that I had so many good things in my life. It also made me realize that I always assume the worst." I lean back. "Maybe this has always been God's plan for me."

Dr. Khan smirks. "Now where was *this* Maya in our previous sessions?"

I snort. "She was trying to stay small so that nothing around her could change," I say. "She tried to reset her life by pretending to be someone she wasn't, and when it didn't work, she decided to stay the way she'd always been."

"But then—" Dr. Khan starts, crossing one leg over the other "—that never works, does it? Because as humans, we always grow. Things can never stay the same, and that's not a bad thing. We can't be afraid of it."

"No," I agree. "It's not a bad thing. I'm growing, yes, but I'm not going to be afraid of it. I'm going to continue to grow as the person that I am, not someone I'm not."

"Okay." Dr. Khan claps her hands. "Tell me something you've done to help you grow."

"Well, do you remember my coworker Anaïs?" I ask, and at her nod, I continue. "I asked her to dinner when we got back to work. It started out as a meeting to discuss the plans for the new school year, but we kind of talked about everything. I mean, we've been working together for two years now, but we barely knew anything about each other." I tap my fingers on my lap. "I'm starting small, but it's a good place for me. Maybe soon I'll be ready to really talk to some of the other teachers at the school, but for now I'm comfortable with Anaïs."

"Wow," Dr. Khan breathes. She points to me. "*This* is a moment that therapists wait for. To see their patients really start to flourish, no matter how long it takes." She leans forward. "I think this is the start of a beautiful life for you, Maya."

I grin. "I do, too."

She sits up. "Now, tell me about—"

The blaring of the alarm on her phone cuts her off. Dr. Khan practically pouts. "Our session is over already?"

"Well, I did come in late," I remind her. I grab my bag from the floor. "I promise, next time I come, I'll be on time. I have to get going, though—there's something wrong with my car, so Sarfaraz is picking me up."

"Sarfaraz?" Dr. Khan repeats. She peeks over my shoulder. "He's *here*?"

"He is," I confirm. "He told me to call him when I need to be picked up, but I bet you anything he's sitting in the waiting room."

"How do you know?"

My face lights up. "I just do."

I grab my jacket from the coat rack. As I slip it on, I say, "Same time next week?"

"You got it."

I give her a wave, then open the door and step into the waiting room. I shut the door behind me and scan the faces until I find the one I'm looking for. When I do, my smile grows.

Sarfaraz sits off in the corner, as I expected. He balances his iPad on his lap, and his concentration scrunches his forehead as he reads. He looks up when he hears my approaching footsteps, though, and he brightens at the sight of me. "Hey." He checks the time on his phone. "I didn't realize your session would end so soon."

"Us being late cut into my time," I explain. He opens his mouth, but I wave him off. "It's not your fault. It's my car's. But what can you do? I guess I should get the oil checked more often."

I wait for a response from Sarfaraz, but when he stares at me, I tilt my head. "What?"

"Nothing," he says. "I was just waiting for you to blame your curse."

I playfully hit his arm. "Ha ha," I fake laugh. "Joke's on you. I'm not blaming my curse, because I'm *not* cursed." I shrug. "I'm someone with lots of bad luck, but who is working on her attitude toward it."

Sarfaraz grins. "I'm really liking this new calmer Maya." He puts his iPad away in his briefcase. "Maybe she'll let me pick the movie we watch tonight."

"Oh, I wouldn't count on it," I tease.

He mock-sighs, then stands up. His hand automatically finds mine, and my chest swells as our fingers entwine. "Ready to go?"

"Yeah."

We walk out of the building, and an unexpected breeze blasts us in the face. "Brrr," I say, the sound falling from my mouth before I can stop it. "It's *cold* for late October."

"It's definitely weird," he agrees. He brings our joined hands to his mouth and blows some air on them. "We could pick up some soup. It'll warm us up."

"That's a good idea," I say as we head for his car. Autumn has settled nicely, with the leaves changing from vibrant reds to softer oranges and browns. Lots of leaves already cover the ground, and the breeze from earlier cuts through the branches and loosens more of them. They fall gracefully around us, like rain or snow, but even better, because as opposed to the whiteness of snowflakes or the transparency of water, the leaves bring a burst of color to a world that could always use more of it.

Maple leaves also remind me of something else. I grin as I stare at them as they fall around us. Sarfaraz looks to me, curiosity in his eyes. "What's got you so happy?"

"You know all about my number one favorite Korean drama," I start. "But in my second favorite K-drama, *Guardian: The Lonely and Great God*, they had a saying about maple leaves. It was a big motif in the show."

"Which was?"

"The female lead said that if you catch a falling maple leaf, you'll fall in love with the person you're walking with," I answer.

Sarfaraz looks up at the leaves swirling to the ground around us. He reaches up and snatches a perfect one right out of the air; it's bright red, has no rips or breaks, and a long, intact stem. He holds it out to me, a cheeky smirk on his face. "For luck," he teases.

I scoff but snatch the leaf from him anyway, laughter warming my chest. I already know that I'm going to laminate this leaf like Ji Eun-Tak did to the one Kim Shin caught for her in the show. I loop my arm through Sarfaraz's and snuggle close to him.

"For the record," he begins as we reach his car. "I don't need a leaf to tell me to fall in love with you." We stop by the passenger side door, and the look he gives me—pure adoration and amazement—nearly makes my heart stop. He reaches up and cups my chin, his fingers the lightest, softest touch against my cold skin. "I already did that a long time ago."

I smile, and my response comes effortlessly. "I love you, too."

I know perfect moments don't exist, but when he presses his lips to mine, I decide that this one is pretty damn close, and that's good enough for me.

★ ★ ★ ★ ★

ACKNOWLEDGMENTS

I'm going to be honest: when I was younger, I never read acknowledgments pages. For me, a book ended with the last word of the story.

Now I know that's not true. Books begin and end with so many people behind you, and I obsessively read acknowledgments pages to see who helped form the book in my hands. I'm so excited to thank all the people who made my book possible.

To my wonderful agents, Uwe Stender and Annalie Buscarino. You gave me not one but two chances and have been with me every step of the way. With your guidance, my books become the best versions of themselves. You not only support my unhinged behavior, but you're so encouraging of it, and on the days where things feel bleak, I remind myself I'm so lucky because I have the two of you in my corner. I wouldn't want anyone else. Thank you to the rest of the team at Triada US for all the hard work you do!

To my incredible editors, Leah Mol and Mina Asaam. You both plucked my baby from your inboxes and have done nothing but champion her since then. From the first time I spoke on the phone with each of you, I knew your editorial visions would help me take my book and my writing to the next level; I just didn't know you'd take me to a place I couldn't even imagine. You two love Maya and her messiness just as much as I do, and more than that, you both understand her (and me!) on a level that I only dreamed someone would. To Alex Niit and Carina Guevara, and Sam Combes and Carrie May for such beautiful covers! You produced two gorgeous and unique covers that not even my wildest dreams could have come up with. To Nora Rawn for your hard work in helping Maya get across the pond. To Dana Francoeur for your expert eye and strong editorial skills. And to the rest of the teams both at MIRA and Simon & Schuster UK for your tireless work in helping to get my book baby out in the world.

To my parents for everything you do. I know it must have been pretty horrific for you that I spent my childhood playing with doctor toys and then grew up to say I wanted to be a writer, but you've never told me that I couldn't do it, and you've supported me ever since. Thank you to Sabrina and Haaris for being the best siblings a girl could ask for. I'm sorry I skip out on sibling gaming sessions to write, but I think this is an even exchange. To my extended family—my khalas and khalus, mamus and mamis, phuppos and phuppas, chacha and chachis, my grandparents (those still here and those who have returned to Allah) and all my cousins (and cousins-in-law!), both older and younger, for all your excitement for me. Alhamdullilah, I have been blessed with an incredibly supportive family.

To all my friends. Rebecca Borges, you have been my soul

sister since we were four years old. Thank you for always sitting on the other side of the phone while I gushed about books. I've lived more of my life with you than without you, and I hope I never have to experience life without you. And to Lorietta Borges for welcoming a little brown girl into your family all those years ago; you're one of the greatest blessings of my life. To Sam Beck and Areeba Sharafuddin—we're literally so old because we've been out of high school for so long, but I thank God every day that you two were the ones I stayed friends with. Sam, you're one of the most supportive and loyal people I know, and I love our spontaneous "Hey, let's grab a bite to eat" trips. Areeba, you and I are truly the Romeo and Juliet of North Park Secondary School because an International Business and Technology student and a humanities student met in grade nine drama class (which was *our* Capulet party) and everything changed. You're so fun to be around, and every time we talk, I come away happier. You both fill my life with so much joy. To Ariene Dela Cruz and Emily Vultao—you girls were the best part of university, and even though our experience was cut short because of the pandemic, I'll always be so grateful to the two of you for the great times we had. To Wara Hussain, Soumya Saini, Sidra Weqar, Fatma Adam (special shout-out to Sumaiyyah Adam!), and Margaret Sut—I appreciate your support and excitement so much, and I always will!

To all the friends I met through publishing and some of the earliest readers of *Maya's Laws of Love*. To Jessica Lewis, the very first friend I made in the writing world. You truly held my infant hand and introduced me to the community, and for that I'll always be so grateful. To Eunice Kim for being my literal Yoda whomst I would perish without; you're the best fraaaand! To Elora Cook for being so kind. To Xiran Jay Zhao for always lifting me up. To Ananya Devarajan for being the absolute sweetest. To Aamna Qureshi for always being on the same wavelength as me. To Kelly Andrew for always being excited for me. I'm sorry I gaslighted you into thinking that you were actually wrong about the plot twist in this book, but it must have been so satisfying to be right. To Maeeda Khan for being the coolest person I know. To Sidrah Mughal for being one of the earliest supporters of this book. To Ann Liang for making me feel like a fifteen-year-old girl again with your writing; it's something that's so special to me. To S.K. Ali for being the best mentor for me to look up to. To Brittney Arena, for your positivity read and all your hilarious reactions. When I was feeling down about this book, you helped to renew my faith in it. To Aqsa for your encouragement from the beginning. To Carolina Flórez-Cerchiaro for your helpful feedback. To Pooja for all of your wonderful comments.

To the GLS—Rhea Basu, Aliyah Fong, and Zoulfa Katouh. Rhea, my cutest babe, you're one of the funniest people I know, and I can always count on you to make me laugh even when I'm having a terrible day. Aliyah, my literal child, your brain is so big and vast, and I'm so lucky you share it with me. Zoulfa, my unhinged sister, you're so smart and talented, and I can't believe you wanted to be friends with me because I'm just a rat in a trench coat. Thank you for letting me borrow Salama and Kenan and imagine them in a different kind of might-life—a crossover for the ages, truly. I don't know where I'd be without any of you.

To all the authors who took time out of their busy lives to read my book and provide lovely blurbs—I'm still in such awe that people I've read and admired for years have said such wonderful things about my book. You will always have a reader in me!

To BTS: Kim Nam-joon, Kim Seok-jin, Min Yoon-gi, Jung Ho-seok, Park Ji-min, Kim Tae-hyung, and Jeon Jungkook. In the terrible time of 2020, you all gave me a reason to live. Your love and appreciation for ARMY is something that is so special and truly felt across the world. I'm so lucky to live in the same era as you. Min Yoon-gi, I've only seen you in concert so far, but one day I *will* see OT7. Together, we are bulletproof, and I will always purple you.

To Taylor Swift. Thank you for providing the best soundtracks for all my books and for being someone who always fights for herself. Your entire career is proof that with hard work, dedication, and self-belief, anyone can achieve the impossible.

To Hyun Bin and Son Ye-jin for choosing to be in *Crash Landing on You* and giving the world one of the greatest love stories. In this book's timeline, from when I wrote the very first draft in 2021 to its publication in 2024, you went from coworkers to dating to engaged to married and, finally, parents. In every draft as the years went on, I had to update the part at the bridge each time you announced something. Now, I'm not saying that it's because of me, but I am saying thank-you for showing me what swoony, heartwarming love is, both on and off the screen.

To every book blogger, Bookstagrammer, BookToker, bookseller, librarian, and book reviewer who read *Maya* and had such wonderful things to say. And thank you to every reader in general. Whether you preordered this book or are picking it up years from now, thank you for giving me and my book a chance. You're the reason I write, and without you, I'd have no reason to do any of this.

And last but never ever least, thank you to Him, Al-'Aleem, the All-Knowing. Everything that I am, everything that I have, and everything that I will ever be is solely because of You. Thank You for being my biggest source of hope and love on the days when I stumble in the dark. And thank You for Your sign all those years ago. I heard You loud and clear: being a writer is the path You have meant for me to be on. I promise I won't stray again. Alhamdullilah.

MAYA'S LAWS OF LOVE

ALINA KHAWAJA

Reader's Guide

mira

1. Each chapter in this book begins with one of Maya's laws as an epigraph. Do you think these served an effective purpose? Why or why not?

2. Maya has a complicated dynamic with her mother; she obviously loves her very much, but sometimes gets overwhelmed by her. What did you think of this relationship? What are some ways in which Maya is similar or different from her mother? Did their dynamic remind you of any relationships in your own life?

3. *Maya's Laws of Love* is rich with Pakistani and Muslim culture. Have you learned anything about this culture that you didn't know before? Did it challenge any preconceived notions you had? Why do you think such representation in books is so important?

4. Maya acknowledges that she doesn't have many friends and struggles to make and keep them. Have you ever felt that way? Why do you think it can be difficult to make and maintain adult friendships?

5. Maya traveled to South Korea to teach for a couple of years prior to the events of the book. Is there anything you'd move across the world for? Why or why not?

6. Maya and Sarfaraz experience lots of trouble while trying to make it to their final destination. Have you ever been on a trip where it felt like everything went wrong? Was there anything to learn from it? Were there any positive experiences that came out of it?

7. *Crash Landing on You* has a big impact on Maya's life. Is there a piece of media that has greatly affected your life in some way? Why do you think the art we consume can affect us so much?

8. Maya feels a lot of obligation toward certain cultural aspects of her life. Have you ever felt pressured to bend to culture? Why might someone bend or not bend?

9. Maya struggles with independence, as well as figuring out what she wants in life. Has there ever been a moment in your life where you felt like you weren't in control? Did you do anything to change it? And if you didn't, would you make a different choice now?

10. Sarfaraz figures out that he is the brother of Maya's fiancé earlier than she does and keeps it from her. Do you think that was the right choice? Was it justifiable? If they hadn't ended up together in the end, how might this have affected their future family dynamic?

11. Similarly, do you think Maya was right when she decided to marry Imtiaz despite her feelings for Sarfaraz? Was she being selfish or selfless?

12. The book explores a discussion of love versus arranged marriages, which is a topic that is hotly debated in South

Asian cultures. Maya strongly believes that love can happen after marriage, and this is seen with certain characters in the book, like Salama and Kenan. What do you think? Do you believe that love can bloom after marriage? Why or why not?